"Ms. Savoy's grace... ...sense of humor enhances... ...provoking story, and I wanted to learn more about these two wonderful individuals looking for love."

—4 1/2 Stars, Top Pick, *Romantic Times*

"Readers anxious to find new talent in the romance genre should spend some time with Deirdre Savoy's latest creation. . . . ALWAYS is one finely tuned and crafted romance; it vividly illuminates the circuitous path two people will travel to find true love. Deirdre Savoy is an important and promising author on an artistic voyage. Her ALWAYS is one charming and appealing read."

—Emma Wisdom, *The Chattanooga Courier*

"ALWAYS is a major achievement from an author with only two novels in her portfolio. Ms. Savoy already possesses the skill of a veteran writer. With lyrical precision, she pens one of the most powerful stories of the year, and establishes herself as one of Arabesque's best. A book worthy of every one of its five stars!"

—Wayne Jordan, *ROMANCE IN COLOR*
www.romanceincolor.com

"Ms. Savoy has once again taken my breath away with her newest release, ALWAYS. Her writing is exciting and fresh with characters who are refreshing and a joy to read about. ALWAYS shows us the depth of emotion between two people whose love began as puppy love, but turned into a deep and faithful love between two adults. I give two thumbs up to Ms. Savoy for her wonderful new book, ALWAYS."

—Very Highly Recommended, Robin Peek, *Under the Covers*
www.silcom.com/~manatee/utc.html

"ALWAYS is a worthy successor to Deirdre Savoy's debut novel, SPELLBOUND. It is a wonderful second-chance romance about love, family secrets, betrayal, and loyalty. The novel also is a good showcase for the author's incomparable sense of humor."

—4 Hearts, Gwen Osborne, *The Romance Reader*
www.theromancereader.com

"[ALWAYS] depicts the powerful emotions evoked by love in all its guises: the sweet naiveté of puppy love, the randy exploitation of singles 'love,' the breathtaking euphoria of first love, the heartaches of illicit love, and the enduring power of true love. The result is an immensely satisfying romantic read. Author Deirdre Savoy has a talent that bears watching."

—Kathleen Langan, *Painted Rock*
www.paintedrock.com

ONCE AND AGAIN

Clearly, Nathan was angry with Daphne, but he had no right to be. She had every right to be angry with him. How long had he been standing there spying on her? It wouldn't surprise her if he'd been watching them through the peephole in the door.

"I thought you said you weren't going to do that every time I come through the door."

"I said I wouldn't unless I was worried about you, which I was. You never come home this late."

She pushed away from the door. "Well, forgive me for not keeping you abreast of my social calendar."

Daphne took a step in the direction of the stairs, then turned back. She couldn't resist throwing one more bit of fuel on the fire.

"And just so you know, Robert is an excellent kisser."

"You call what he gave you a kiss." Nathan strode toward her, grasped her upper arms and pulled her up against him. His mouth descended on hers, claiming her lips in a fiery kiss designed to conquer. A tremor shivered through her as his tongue invaded her mouth, plundering, insistent, demanding a response from her. Despite herself, she moaned and her hands slid around his back to hold him closer.

ONCE AND AGAIN

Deirdre Savoy

ARABESQUE
BET BOOKS

BET Publications, LLC
www.bet.com
www.arabesquebooks.com

ARABESQUE BOOKS are published by

BET Publications, LLC
c/o BET BOOKS
One BET Plaza
1900 W Place NE
Washington, D.C. 20018-1211

All Kensington Titles, Imprints, and Distributed Lines are available at special quantity discounts for bulk purchases for sales promotions, premiums, fund-raising, and educational or institutional use. Special book excerpts or customized printings can also be created to fit specific needs. For details, write or phone the office of the Kensington special sales manager: Kensington Publishing Corp., 850 Third Avenue, New York, NY 10022, attn: Special Sales Department, Phone: 1-800-221-2647.

First Printing: May 2001
10 9 8 7 6 5 4 3 2

Printed in the United States of America

For my father, Eugene Nelson Savoy, family patriarch, also known as Dad, Pop, Grandpa, Uncle Buster, Uncle Woolly and the Bank of Savoy. Whenever we called on you, you were there, showing us with your patient, gentle guidance what it is to be a man.

All of our lives have been enriched by your presence. We love you, Daddy.

ACKNOWLEDGMENTS

Special thanks to Joi Gordon for allowing me to witness firsthand the good work being done at Dress for Success, NY.

Thanks again to Johnny Rodriguez of Marc Anthony Productions.

Thanks to Petra LaMantia for her inspiration in creating Nathan's grandmother and Joyce Ortiz for correcting my Spanish.

Thanks to Snr. Carlos of Rincon de España for his culinary expertise and wonderful restaurant.

And a very special thank you to all my writer friends, both published and unpublished, who have provided advice, support, good humor, a shoulder to cry on, and some of the best times of my life. You guys are the best!

Prologue

Friday, November 13

Nathan Ward stood at the front of the church, where, in less than fifteen minutes, he would relinquish his freedom. He wore a black suit, which in his mind befitted the occasion. If he could have gotten away with wearing a black arm band to signify the loss of his bachelorhood, he would have done it. As it was, he half-expected someone to get up and object to this marriage, most likely his grandmother. At the moment, she clearly and audibly recited the prayers on the rosary beads clutched in her fingers.

Nathan surveyed the walls of the ornate structure that surrounded him. The church was fashioned in the shape of a cross with a gothic spire rising from its center. Stained glass windows winked back at him, depicting the twelve stations of the cross. Rays from the setting sun washed through the glass, casting a rosy glow. A perfect setting for a wedding. Too bad it had to be his.

The old church he remembered from his youth hadn't been half as lovely. It had burned to the ground while he still attended the grammar school across the street. Supposedly some altar boys had broken into the cabinet housing the sacramental wine, drunk themselves silly, and knocked over one of the lit candles stationed unfortunately close to a set of highly flammable curtains. In truth, it had been a cigarette, hastily discarded when they thought they heard one of the priests approaching.

Nathan hadn't been in a church since. He wouldn't be completely surprised if the heavens did open up, as his sister had portended, and a bolt of lightning fried him to a cinder. The infamous Nathan Ward in church? Unthinkable.

Nathan checked his watch. Eleven more minutes. Eleven more minutes until she walked through that door and ruined both their lives. He could handle it. He was a grownup. He would accept his obligations. If the fates wanted to punish him for one night of mind-blowing, earth-shattering sex, then so be it. He would take Monica as his wife, though he knew she would be as much a failure as a wife as she had been as a mother, a woman, a human being. Monica existed only for Monica. Other people just got in her way.

Well, she'd done one thing right! She'd given him the most beautiful, most precious daughter a man could wish for. Emily was the one thing out of this whole fiasco he didn't regret. For her, he'd stroll through the fires of hell and be a happy man. Emily was the reason he'd agreed to go through with this farce. As much as he dreaded it, he also wanted it to be over.

The priest had suggested he await his bride in the small vestry at the side of the church, but Nathan had declined. He had never been one to kowtow to propriety and tradition. No need to start now. Next to him stood his best friend and best man, Michael Thorne, and Michael's wife, Jenny. Jenny held Nathan's six-month-old daughter in her arms, cooing softly to the baby.

Nathan touched his fingers to his daughter's cheek, brushing back a curl of jet-black hair. She'd gotten absolutely nothing from him. Not his eyes, his hair color, his complexion. It was as if Monica had spit her out completely in her own likeness. If Emily continued to follow in her mother's footsteps, she would be a beautiful woman—on the outside. He would make sure she was beautiful on the inside as well. He bent and placed a soft kiss on his daughter's forehead.

In response, Jenny glared at him, turning in a way that put the baby out of his reach. "We're bonding here," she protested.

"You'd better watch it," he teased Michael. "Next thing you know, she'll be wanting one of her own."

Casting an intense look at his wife, Michael said, "Maybe sooner than you think."

Nathan watched as Michael walked away from him, going to stand next to his wife. With an arm around her waist, he pulled her closer, bending to whisper in her ear. Whatever he said caused Jenny to laugh softly and color to rise in her cheeks. In a telling gesture, Michael's hand came to rest on his wife's abdomen.

A wave of pure envy washed through Nathan, not for himself, but for his daughter. That was what he wished he could offer Emily: two parents who loved her and cared for each other, not two near-strangers who wrangled with each other, each using Emily as leverage against the other.

Nathan turned his attention to the assembled guests. The few that had shown up on Monica's side reminded him of chickens trapped in the wrong henhouse. They looked around, heads bobbing, apparently waiting for someone familiar to appear. To his knowledge, no one from Monica's family had shown up yet.

His gaze slid to the opposite pews that held his family, settling on a young woman seated by herself in the back of the church. The streak of white hair at her temple was a dead giveaway. Her otherwise black hair was braided in a simple style and pulled back from her face.

He remembered that face, those deep-set dark brown

eyes, those soft, full lips and their effect on him. She didn't seem to have aged at all in the fifteen years since he'd last seen her. Daphne.

What was she doing here? He'd invited all of Michael's family to the wedding. She was the last one he would have expected to show up. Maybe it was simple morbid curiosity—the same reason people gather around a burning building. They might be horrified, repulsed, but at the same time, they can't look away. Maybe she expected him to back out at the last moment. She of all people knew how much he valued his freedom.

And, as usual, she was ignoring him. He followed her line of vision to a portion of stained-glass window that he knew didn't interest her at all. She'd pulled that tactic often enough for him to know she was aware of him watching her, aware of every move he made. He smiled, shoving his hands into his trouser pockets. After all these years, some things hadn't changed.

Another image superimposed itself on his consciousness: Daphne as she'd been at fourteen, a tall, slender nymph with cinnamon skin and deep brown eyes. Even then she'd had that streak of gray running through her shoulder-length black hair.

Some of the kids from school had been planning to go up to Rye, New York, for the fireworks display on the Fourth of July. The girls had decided to go shopping for bathing suits and couldn't dissuade the guys from tagging along.

Daphne had stood off to the side as the other girls picked out the tiniest bikinis to try on. He'd known she was too modest to ever wear anything that skimpy. Besides, she'd been the only girl in the group with any bustline to speak of. It had been obvious, at least to him, that she'd been self-conscious about it.

She'd been ignoring him, but at one point, he caught her eye. He gestured with his chin toward a more modest swimsuit, silently urging her to try it on. He'd figured that without a suit, she'd find some lame excuse to avoid the trip, to avoid him. She'd rolled her eyes in response and turned her back to him.

They'd had to pass through the children's department on the way out of the store. Nathan walked behind her, paying more attention to how well her shorts clung to her backside than to what she was doing. Suddenly she turned around to face him.

"Oh, look, Nathan," she'd said, and he'd realized she held something in her hand. "I've found the perfect bathing suit for you." She'd held up a hideous, ruffled, hot pink and lime green little girl's bathing suit and pressed it against his chest. "What do you think?"

"Man, that's cold," one of the other guys had said, while the girls had tried in vain to hide their giggles behind their hands.

She'd smiled up at him, a smile of triumph. As she turned to walk away, he grabbed her wrist. "Why do you hate me so much?"

She'd narrowed her eyes, pulling her arm as far away from him as he allowed. "I don't hate you, Nathan," she'd answered. "I just dislike you intensely."

She'd shaken off his grasp, tossed the bathing suit in a pile with some others, and walked away.

Nathan, unfazed, had watched her departure with a smile on his face. It hadn't been the first time he'd been the brunt of one of her jokes. She'd said it because she knew she could get away with it. She knew he liked her. Everyone knew it. There was no other reason for him to have insinuated himself into her circle of friends. He was a grade ahead and three years older than she. He knew she hated the way his interest in her caused speculation about her. She'd been determined to make him pay any way possible.

That was Daphne. Her and that sister of hers. The neighborhood used to call them "The Thorne Girls," as if it were a disease in need of a cure. Haughty, aloof, untouchable, they carried themselves as if they were better than everyone else. To Nathan's mind, they were. Daphne, especially. Smart, sexy, funny, with a strong sense of the sardonic. She'd had a gleam in her eye that said she didn't have to take anything from anybody if she didn't want to.

He didn't know why that day, that time was one of his fondest memories of her. Maybe because it was the first time he realized she wasn't as indifferent to him as she pretended to be. Maybe because on that day he'd decided that nothing, *nothing,* was going to stop him from getting through that wall of ice she'd built around herself.

And nothing had.

"Excuse me, Nathan."

Nathan tore his gaze away from her, realizing the priest stood at his side, a troubled expression on his face. "What is it, Father?"

"This came for you." The priest held out a folded sheet of note paper. "I'm sorry." The priest patted his arm before moving away.

So much for privacy, Nathan mused, noting the number of eyes focused on him. He turned his back to the guests and unfolded the paper. He recognized Monica's handwriting immediately. He read the three words over and over, to make sure his mind wasn't playing tricks on him. *I'm not coming.* She'd signed it with a single initial, *M.*

Nathan sat on the red-carpeted stairs leading up to the altar, threw back his head, and laughed. *I'm not coming.* The three most welcome words he'd ever seen. Never in a million years would he have expected Monica to renege on their deal. He laughed until tears ran from his eyes and his ribs began to hurt.

"Virgen Sancta," he heard his grandmother say. "You're

in God's house," she scolded him in Spanish. "Get up off the floor."

Nathan had a feeling God would approve, even if his grandmother didn't. Fate had smiled on him once again, saving him from a situation he knew would have been a disaster. "Thank you, thank you, thank you," he whispered to the ceiling and whatever lay beyond. He'd been saved, and he vowed in that instant to start behaving like the responsible adult he was supposed to be. He would get his act together, settle down. Lord knew, he needed to. When his next birthday rolled around, he'd be thirty-nine years old.

Nathan wiped his eyes, looking out at the sea of faces staring at him with concern. They all probably thought he'd lost his mind, when in truth he'd finally come to his senses. Nathan focused on his best friend, Michael, who came to stand next to him.

"Well? What does the note say?" Michael extended a hand to him. Nathan took it, rising to his feet.

In a voice that carried to the back of the church, Nathan said, "She's not coming."

Nathan grinned as his grandmother clasped her hands and looked heavenward in gratitude.

Michael started to laugh, clapping Nathan on the back. Michael alone knew the real reason he'd agreed to this marriage. "You have got to be the luckiest man in America."

"Don't I know it."

Nathan endured the offerings of condolence from his family, the pats on the back, the sympathetic looks on the faces that gathered around him. His attention was focused elsewhere, on the back of the church, where Monica's guests were making a hasty, disgruntled exit. Daphne was gone.

Immediately, he felt a sense of sadness that nothing else that day had been able to inspire. Well, what had he expected her to do? Offer to kiss it and make it better? That was definitely not Daphne's style. What did he want from her, then?

He knew only that he'd never forgotten her, that today wasn't the first day he'd searched a crowd hoping to see her face. Over the years, he'd imagined seeing her so many times that he wondered if her appearance today had been only one more mirage to trick him.

And every time he thought of her, a feeling of incompleteness, a lack of closure accompanied the memory. All those years ago, she'd shut him out, never explaining why her feelings for him had changed. Not even Michael knew, or would tell him. Maybe that's why she'd come. She'd felt it, too.

It's not over, Daphne Thorne, Nathan vowed, looking toward the back of the church. Maybe he was crazy for needing to make sense of a romance that had been dead for more than fifteen years. But Daphne had been here, and, in the cosmic scheme of things, there had to be some reason for that.

"So what do we do now?" Michael asked.

Nathan shrugged. Surely, Monica had some new scheme up her sleeve. He'd worry about Monica and her machinations later. He'd arranged for a small reception at a restaurant in the city. No use letting it go to waste. He put one arm around his sister, the other around his grandmother, leading them down the center aisle of the church. "I think we've got some celebrating to do."

One

One month later

Victoria Davenport was dead. There was no getting around that. Daphne Thorne stood at the gravesite, shivering in the frigid December air. Thick, ominous clouds promised snow, but as of yet, hadn't produced any. She clutched a single flower in her gloved hand. Soon it would be her turn to lay a rose on the ornate silver casket that housed her friend's remains.

Friend. How inadequate that word seemed. Victoria had been so much more than that. Although they were separated by race, age, and class, Victoria had been her mentor, her business partner, and the most generous woman Daphne had ever known. Outwardly, Daphne presented a controlled, businesslike front. Inwardly, she felt bowed by the loss. It was as if someone had ripped out a big chunk of her life. It was as if she'd lost her mother all over again.

She glanced around at her fellow mourners. There must have been twenty cars in the procession to the cemetery. Dressed in fur and cashmere, silk and jewels, they looked more ready for an elegant cocktail party than a funeral. Who were all these people? Business associates, she assumed, or members of New York society into which Victoria had been born. People who came due to obligation, not caring. It saddened Daphne further to realize most of these people looked more impatient than circumspect. She counted very few faces that, like hers, mirrored the grief they felt.

The casket was laid out on a bower to be interred later in the family mausoleum. Daphne stepped forward, placing her rose on the mound of others. "Good-bye, Victoria," she whispered. "Sleep well."

For the first time since she'd heard about Victoria's death, Daphne felt the salty sting of tears in her eyes. It seemed so final now, so real, so irrevocable. She stepped away, swiping at her eyes with her fingers. Not looking where she went, she bumped into another mourner.

"I'm sorry." Daphne looked up into the cold, gray eyes of Victoria's twenty-nine-year-old stepson.

"Anytime."

Daphne pursed her lips, noting the expression on his face: half suggestive leer, half shark-toothed grin. Today of all days, why couldn't he behave himself? How had Victoria raised such a son? In truth, she hadn't. Bradley Davenport was definitely his father's child.

"Excuse me," Daphne said, her voice as glacial as the weather. She walked away from him and, like the others, headed back to her car. She shivered as she slid into her seat, over the frigid upholstery, and behind the still colder steering wheel. Even when the car's heater kicked in, she continued to shiver. The cold went deeper than the goose bumps that had risen on her arms. It went down to her soul.

Pulling up in front of her house, she found her usual parking place occupied by a sleek black sports car, one of those manly cars that announced its owner's gender a mile away. Who did she know who would drive such a car and have the audacity to park right in her spot?

It was probably a complete stranger, but all the same, an image of Nathan formed in her mind. Nathan as she'd seen him a month before. He'd inherited his olive coloring and hazel eyes from his Hispanic grandmother, his straight aquiline nose and square jaw from his father, and his ego from every monarch that had ever walked the planet. He was six feet, two inches of gorgeous male animal.

And at one time, he had been hers.

Daphne sighed. She didn't want to think about Nathan. She'd spent the last fifteen years trying to forget him. The day he'd walked out of her life, she vowed never to think of him again. But how did you forget a man whose face stared back at you from billboards, whose voice crooned to you from the radio, whose biggest hit proved to be a song he'd written for you? You didn't, but life went on just the same.

Over the years, she'd convinced herself she was completely indifferent to him, that time had cleansed her of feelings for him, both good and bad. When she'd seen him last month, she knew she'd been lying to herself. One glance at him, and all the memories, all the emotions, came flooding back to her.

She'd looked away from him when she noticed him turning her way. He would have seen it all there on her face. She couldn't have borne that, especially knowing he was set to marry another woman. It might be a flaw in her character, but she had too much pride for that.

She found a parking spot around the corner on Second Avenue. Pulling her collar up against the wind, she walked slowly back toward her town house. Her body ached, and her eyes burned. It was barely noon, but the sky was dark enough for it to be midnight. The only thing she could think about was dragging herself up the stairs into her nice warm apartment and putting herself in a hot, hot, fragrant bath.

That was what she needed. A soothing bath, a glass of wine. Something to take the edge off, dull the pain, obliterate the bone-deep cold that claimed her. She started unbuttoning her coat as she walked up the stairs, past the empty first-floor apartment.

Reaching into her pocket, she pulled out her keys. The lock turned easily, as it always did. Yet a feeling of unease gripped her. Something was wrong, off kilter. Without turning on the light, she groped for the baseball bat she kept by the door. Her fingers connected with—nothing. Only air where the bat should be.

Suddenly one of the living-room lamps flickered on and a man rose from her sofa, turning to face her. He slung the bat over his shoulder. "Is this what you're looking for?"

Daphne straightened, taking in the familiar hazel eyes, the sardonic grin, the tall, rangy body clad in jeans, a black turtleneck, and a leather jacket. She let out the breath she'd been holding, willing herself to relax. Her shoulders drooped. "Nathan."

"In the flesh."

All the glorious flesh. Though it had been fifteen years since she'd seen him, all of him, she still remembered. She shivered again, but this time a flood of heat, not cold, caused the reaction.

She pushed those thoughts from her mind. If she knew anything, it was that Nathan had no intention of seducing her. What did he want, then? What made him think he could barge into her apartment uninvited? Well, hadn't she invited him back into her life by showing up at his wedding that wasn't? A foolish mistake.

She still couldn't fathom why she'd felt compelled to go. It had been more than simple curiosity. She *had* to know if he'd go through with it. At least she hadn't made a complete fool of herself. When all the commotion began, she'd slipped out of the church and driven home.

"What do you want, Nathan?"

In answer, he dropped the bat onto the sofa cushions and walked toward her.

She watched him warily, every synapse of her body on alert. *What did he intend to do?* She had half a mind to scream at him not to come near her, like some hysterical woman. She didn't trust him. He wouldn't do anything to hurt her physically. She knew that. But emotionally, he'd always been able to tie her in knots.

Only a few inches separated them when he stopped his advance. She inhaled, and the scent of his citrus-based cologne reached her nostrils. It reminded her of lush, tropical fruit and a memory better left unexplored. His arms came around her through her open coat, settling on her waist. Gently, he pulled her closer, until her face was pressed against his chest. "I heard about your friend. I'm sorry."

For a moment she stood there, melting into his embrace, letting the heat of his body warm her. She'd forgotten how good it felt to be held by him, by anyone. It had been a long time since anyone had offered her simple comfort. Those feelings were so intoxicating and yet so dangerous. She pushed away from him.

"You went to all this trouble to offer your condolences? You didn't have to break into my house for that." She stepped away from him, shrugging out of her coat and tossing it onto the back of her sofa. "How did you get in here, anyway? I know I didn't leave my door unlocked."

"I knew you weren't here, so I let myself in."

He held out a set of keys, the ones she'd given to her brother, Michael. No way would Michael have given Nathan the keys to her apartment. Narrowing her eyes, she snatched the keys from his hand. "You lifted these from Michael's house, didn't you?"

"I prefer to think of it as having borrowed them for a time."

"You can think of it any way you want to. What it really is, is larceny." What it really was, was typical Nathan, thinking he could do whatever he wanted and get away with it. "Look, Nathan, I'm tired, I'm hungry, and I'm in no mood for guests. I'm sure you can let yourself out." She started to walk around him, going toward the stairs and the haven of her room above.

"Don't you want to know why I'm here?"

She turned to face him, cocking her head to one side. Defensively, she crossed her arms in front of her. "Not particularly." *Liar,* a voice in her head accused. "But I don't suppose you're going to leave until you tell me, are you?"

Nathan shook his head. "Nope."

Daphne exhaled heavily, touching her fingertips to her temple. All her day needed was a bit of Nathan's high drama. She straightened, dropping her hands to her sides. "Okay, Nathan. Spit it out. What do you want?"

"I want to rent the downstairs apartment from you."

She blinked and shook her head, completely shocked. "You've got to be kidding. Why would you want to do that?"

He sat on the top of the sofa, facing her. "I don't suppose I have to remind you my fiancée neglected to show up to our wedding."

"That was quite obvious."

"Well, she's disappeared. Nobody, not even her father, knows where she is. Until she resurfaces, I'm raising my daughter alone."

Poor baby, Daphne thought. Her mother missing and irresponsible, unrepentant Nathan for her father. How would she fare in his care?

Stop it, she told herself. She was being unfair to him. She'd seen him with his daughter and seen the love he felt for her. Nathan would be a good father, but at the moment she didn't want to give him any quarter.

"What does that have to do with me?"

"I want to lie low for a while, until I figure out what I'm going to do."

She snorted. "I wasn't aware that East Eighty-first Street was the end of the earth."

"It isn't. But it *is* quiet. No one would know Emily and I were here."

"Sounds like hiding out to me."

"If that's what you want to call it."

Daphne studied his face. His expression was unreadable. This wasn't the glib, extroverted Nathan she knew. Then again, his fiancée's jilting him must have wounded him to some degree, his pride if nothing else. She didn't imagine he was used to being refused.

"Why don't you stay with your grandmother? I'm sure she'd welcome you."

"Sure she would. But being a man, in her eyes, makes me incompetent to take care of any baby, even my own. I'd be lucky if I got to put my daughter to bed at night. I want to raise her my own way."

Despite herself, Daphne smiled, picturing Nathan's diminutive grandmother waving him away from the baby's crib with the wooden spoon she used to carry. He would be lucky to see his child if his grandmother decided against it.

"Come on, Dee," Nathan pressed. "It's only a temporary arrangement. Until I get back on my feet." He took hold of her hand, stroking her palm with his thumb. "I would think after all we've been through together, we could at least be friends."

She bit her lower lip, her eyes riveted to the sight of her hand wrapped in his. It was such a simple touch, and yet so stirring. A tingling warmth began in the pit of her stomach, radiating outward through her body.

"How much rent are you going to charge me?"

She looked up at him, seeing a familiar smile on his face—the little half smile that used to make her forgive him for anything. Every time except the last one. It wouldn't work now, either. She snatched her hand away from his.

"How much rent would I charge you?" She grabbed the first amount that popped into her head. "Ten thousand dollars a month."

Nathan shrugged. "If that's what it takes."

"You're crazy."

"You already knew that. Look Daphne—"

"No, you look. There's nothing to talk about. The apartment is already rented. The new tenant is moving in at the end of the month."

"I see." Nathan rose, his hazel eyes raking over her. She knew he didn't believe her, but stopped short of accusing her of lying. "I'm sorry I wasted your time, then."

He went to the door, flung it open, and stepped into the hall. The door closed behind him on its own steam. "Good-bye to you, too," Daphne said to thin air.

Then she rushed to the big window in her living room that overlooked the street. *What was that all about?* she wondered. Nathan could buy and sell her town house ten times over without making a dent in his bank account. The idea of him renting the little downstairs apartment strained credulity. He could afford to live anywhere he wanted.

Watching the street below, she saw Nathan climb into the black car out front and drive away. What did he want from her? She hadn't gotten an answer from him, not one that satisfied her. He'd said he hoped they could be friends. He would think there was a possibility of that. He'd been the one to walk away—literally. He'd left town, leaving her to explain to all the curious friends and relatives what had happened. She'd told them all to mind their own business. What could she have told them? She hadn't known herself.

She was glad she'd lied to him. There was no tenant moving in at the end of the month, and no prospect of one. She hadn't even finished remodeling the kitchen after her last tenant caused a grease fire that consumed every appliance and most of the cabinetry. It would probably be another month before the apartment was livable. And if she knew Nathan, his interest wouldn't last that long. He'd find someone or something else to catch his fancy. Now that she'd thwarted his plans, whatever they really were, she'd probably never hear from him again.

So why did she feel so disappointed?

Daphne arrived at the offices of Sullivan and O'Shea at exactly ten o'clock the following morning. Everything about the law firm bespoke old money, from the Park Avenue location to the ankle-deep gray carpeting, to the cherry wood furniture buffed to a high gloss. The place was deathly quiet, though Daphne knew that hundreds of people worked on the three floors the firm occupied here in the midtown office and even more were employed at the Bond Street headquarters downtown.

The meeting was to take place in the conference room on the twentieth floor. As she walked the short distance from the reception area to the conference room, a feeling of unease shivered through her. Why would anyone bother with an official reading of a will anymore? Why not just fax everyone a copy of anything they needed to know? The idea of sitting around listening to the last wishes of someone who was now beyond the pale of caring what actually happened to their possessions struck her as slightly macabre.

"Welcome, welcome," a male voice boomed, as she crossed the threshold into the conference room. Jonathan Craig rushed toward her, his hand outstretched. Jonathan had been one of Victoria's lawyers for as long as Daphne had known her.

"Hello, Jonathan." She shook his hand, then leaned forward, knowing the greeting he expected was her kiss on his cheek. "How are you?"

Jonathan sighed. "I'll be better after this is over with Since we're all here, why don't we begin?"

Jonathan stepped aside. Only then did Daphne realize that Bradley Davenport sat in one of the chairs at the massive conference table. He stood and inclined his head toward her. "Daphne."

"Brad." She noted the cool, contemptuous stare he gave her as he retook his seat. He leaned back in his chair, draping one leg indolently atop the other. He was obviously not pleased with the proceedings, not pleased to have her there. Did he see her as some sort of rival for his stepmother's estate? Daphne held no expectation that Victoria had left her anything. She didn't want anything. Victoria had given Daphne the only gift worth giving while she had been alive: her friendship.

Daphne allowed Jonathan to lead her to a seat and settle her into it. She sat directly across from Bradley. Jonathan took the seat between them. While Jonathan readied the papers before him, Daphne glanced at Brad. Outwardly, he was a handsome man. He wore his black hair short and fashionably styled. He had a firm jaw, straight patrician nose and full, sensuous lips. The kind of body women would swoon over, especially when he was decked out in thousand-dollar Armani suits as he was now. Bradley Davenport should have been a lady killer.

But then you looked into his eyes: cold, steel-gray eyes that always sent a shiver through her. If the eyes were the windows to the soul, something in Bradley Davenport had been dead an awfully long time.

"I'll spare you all the legalese," Jonathan said finally. "And the minor bequests, which are numerous. Victoria was a very generous woman."

"Can we get on with this?"

Bradley's irritated tone cut through Daphne. They were here to find out what Victoria had given them, *given* being the operative word. In her mind, Bradley hadn't earned one drop of Victoria's largesse. At the very least he could be civil.

"Of course." Jonathan's voice was as smooth as glass, but as he turned to her, Daphne noted the color rising in his cheeks. "Daphne, Victoria has bequeathed to you her entire personal wardrobe, with the stipulation that you keep it for yourself and not donate it to the business, some jewelry, several pieces of artwork, as well as other lesser items."

But not one word as to how Victoria planned to dispose of her half of the business? When they'd set up their partnership agreement, it had stated that if either of them should die, the deceased partner could bequeath her share of the business to her own heirs. That had been six years ago, before Daphne had met Bradley.

The way Victoria had talked about him, Daphne thought he was a young child, who might grow up to want to participate in the business. In reality, Bradley was only five years her junior.

After meeting him, Daphne knew there was no way she could work with him on a daily basis, nor could she imagine him wanting to waste his time on any venture that wouldn't substantially increase his profit.

Daphne had meant to speak to Victoria about revising the agreement so that the partnership would dissolve upon either of their deaths. The surviving partner would have to compensate the other's heirs financially, but would retain complete control.

But Victoria would have wanted some explanation for Daphne's change of heart. How could she tell her best friend that she found her child, albeit a stepchild, objectionable? Daphne hadn't found a way. Thinking she had all the time in the world, she hadn't pressed the issue.

Victoria had been a young woman, only fifty-three. But age hadn't mattered, when her plane fell from the sky, crashing only a few hundred yards from the ski resort that had been her destination.

Besides, Victoria had known that Daphne and Brad didn't get along, though Daphne had kept the depth of her dislike to herself. Victoria must have realized that a partnership between the two of them was untenable.

". . . the remainder of her estate she has bequeathed to you, Bradley," she heard Jonathan Craig say, "including her partnership in Women's Work."

"What?" Daphne rose to her feet. With one swipe of a pen, Victoria had made her equal partners with Bradley. From the smirk on his face, she knew that was exactly what he had hoped for. Why? Why should he care what happened to the company? He was a successful stockbroker. He certainly couldn't want for money, not the paltry sum she and Victoria had been making from the company.

"Looks like we're in business together."

Bradley rose and extended a hand to her, which she ignored. She turned instead toward Jonathan, feeling his hand on her shoulder.

"Victoria also asked me to give you this." Jonathan extended an envelope toward her. She recognized Victoria's stationery. She took the envelope from Jonathan's grasp, inadvertently crushing the letter inside.

"If there's anything I can do . . ."

She accepted the older man's embrace, shutting her eyes tightly to forestall the tears that welled in her eyes. She shook her head. What could anyone do now? She could only hope that Bradley intended to be a silent partner, as Victoria had become the last couple of years, allowing her to run the business as she saw fit. Fat chance of that happening.

Victoria, why did you do this to me? her mind screamed. *Why did you do this to them?* She thought of the women she worked with. Many of them were indigent, homeless, escaping abusive relationships. Bradley Davenport didn't need to be around any woman, let alone women like those who might be easy prey for him. She was whole, competent, nobody's patsy, and still he made her flesh crawl. What had Victoria gotten her into?

Daphne stepped back, looking into the warm blue eyes of Jonathan Craig. "Thank you."

"I'll leave you two alone now." He patted her arm. "Read the letter."

When Jonathan left, closing the door behind him, Daphne reached for her coat. She had to get out of there. She'd deal with the repercussions of Victoria's will later. Victoria had betrayed her. Bile rose in her throat, choking her, making her want to retch. She stuffed her arms in her sleeves, picked up her handbag, and turned to leave.

"The first thing we do is get ourselves another lawyer."

Daphne spun around to face him. She didn't understand his animosity toward Jonathan, but knew it existed. "We?" She folded her arms in front of her. "*We* are not going to do anything of the sort. Jonathan was your mother's attorney, not mine."

"My stepmother's."

"Whatever." Bradley always made sure to stress that distinction, and she wouldn't bother to argue the point now. "I'm going home."

She moved toward the door, but Brad moved faster, blocking her exit.

"Aren't you going to offer to buy me out?"

In all honesty, she hadn't thought of that. Still, she didn't trust Bradley to be on the level, or keep his word once he gave it. "What's your asking price?"

He didn't miss a beat. "One hundred thousand dollars."

"I don't have that kind of money." At least not on hand. He knew she didn't. That undoubtedly was why he had named the figure with such glee. He was playing some game, and she didn't know what it was.

"I'll let the deal stand for sixty days. After that the price goes up." He stepped aside, pulling the door open. "See you in the office on Monday morning, *partner.*"

She wanted to smack that smug look off his face. Smack him and go on smacking until all her anger and disillusionment abated. That might take forever. "Put it in writing," she barked, pushing past him.

She stalked down the hallway, going to the elevator bank, then into a thankfully empty car. Who knew if what he offered her was ethical or even legal? Knowing Bradley and the confidence with which he'd stated that outrageous figure, he knew full well that his suggestion was not only legal but to his best advantage.

She'd call her lawyer first thing Monday morning, but Daphne knew what she'd say. Something just short of "I told you so." She'd advised Daphne against putting such an open-ended clause in the partnership agreement. But Daphne had trusted Victoria implicitly. She supposed she only got what she deserved for putting her faith so completely in another person.

But, any way she sliced it, she'd have to give him something if she wanted to get rid of him.

One hundred thousand dollars. At one time she'd made more than that in a year. As a senior marketing manager for Grey Pharmaceuticals, she'd been able to afford anything her heart desired. She'd hated it though. Being black and female was a recipe for disappointment in corporate America, or it had been in her case. Her superiors had hired her, probably to fill some affirmative action quota, but she'd known from the beginning that they'd had little faith in her. Despite her successes, despite doing everything right, she had known the only direction for her to go was not up, but out.

When they'd ignored her concerns about using an African-American sports figure to promote taking an aspirin a day to prevent heart attacks, she'd had enough. Black men were less likely to be under a doctor's care and more likely to suffer from uncontrolled blood pressure, a combination that left them more susceptible to hemorrhagic strokes if they were to follow that regimen. She hadn't necessarily wanted them to change the ad; a stronger caution for black men to see a doctor before deciding to self-medicate would have sufficed. But even that proved too much of a concession for them to make for her.

She'd quit after that, foregoing any severance package she was entitled to had she allowed them to fire her. She didn't bother looking for another job in her field. She'd found she no longer had the stomach for it. She'd registered at Columbia University the following semester, gaining a social work degree a year and a half later.

No one had understood her decision to abandon such a lucrative career for one that paid so little and offered so much heartache. No one but Victoria, who she met at a charity event. Despite their differences, they'd felt an immediate bond. They'd started Women's Work two years later.

Daphne exited the elevator when it stopped, walking out into the mocking New York sunshine. She'd taken a cab that morning, knowing there would be nowhere to park on Park Avenue. She decided to take the subway home. Its dark, dank interior better suited her mood.

One hundred thousand dollars. She supposed she could ask her younger brother for the money. But that would be admitting defeat, admitting they were right about the fool-hardiness of opening a business that barely kept food on her table. Quite a comedown from her childhood, when she'd always been known as the perfect daughter, never making a mistake, always the one to land on her feet. If they'd only known how much she'd kept from them, not wanting to tarnish her image.

She'd always survived on her own, and she would continue to do so. There had to be another way. Of course, she wouldn't need the full amount. She could bankrupt her savings, see what she could eke out of her investments. She might not really need that much.

Who was she kidding? However much she needed was beyond her means at this point. She'd sunk all her savings into her town house, figuring she'd live on the income from the apartment. She didn't even have a tenant at the moment. She wouldn't have food on the table if she didn't take care of that.

She did have one option as far as her apartment went, but that was insane. She'd be asking for trouble. Well, what did she have now if not trouble?

Once inside her apartment, she went directly to the phone. She had to do it now, before she thought about it too much, before she talked herself out of it. She dialed his number, tapping her foot nervously as she waited through one, two, three rings. At last he picked up.

"Hello?" a familiar masculine voice said into the phone.

"Hello, Nathan?" she said. "How soon do you want to move in?"

Two

Daphne watched from her front window as the movers on the sidewalk below unloaded box after box from the back of the truck. What had she gotten herself into, letting Nathan Ward move in? She'd seen him early that morning when he'd rung her bell looking for the keys. She'd had the urge to tell him she'd changed her mind, that it was foolishness for the two of them to live together like this. She couldn't do that, though. Not without risking all she'd worked so hard to achieve.

She saw him then, coming out to direct the men. The movers carried in a large object wrapped in the padded blankets universal to all movers. Nathan hefted a box from the truck. Even from her vantage point she could see the pull of his muscles as he walked toward the house. Her gaze traveled to his face. She hadn't realized he was watching her, but when their eyes met, he winked at her.

Immediately, she turned and sat on the window seat, clasping her hands in front of her. It would be all right. Nathan wanted to stay here only temporarily. How long could that be? One month? Two? She could endure that. Especially since she would be out at work all day. The only time she could possibly run into him were evenings and weekends. She knew she could at least find somewhere else to be on weekends.

The only problem was the kitchen. Nathan hadn't balked when she'd told him about its unfinished state. He'd said he had a portable fridge he could use until better accommodations were ready. But he would have to cook sometime. He'd have to warm the baby's bottles. Until she got the kitchen fixed, they'd share the one up in her apartment. A back staircase connected the two apartments. She would have to remember to unlock the door so that he could come up without disturbing her.

That would be a neat trick, for Nathan not to disturb her. His presence alone disturbed her. Or rather, her reaction to his presence. After all this time, after all she'd been through because of him, how could she still be so moved by him on a physical level? Why didn't anger or resentment rise to the forefront when she thought about him?

She didn't want to hate him; she wished that instead she felt absolutely nothing one way or the other. But that was impossible as long as all her thoughts centered around his touch, his smile, the way he'd made her feel loved, cared for, special. That was before he'd gotten what he wanted and left town, leaving her to face the worst crisis of her life alone.

He would never know. If it killed her, she would never let on how deeply he affected her. She could handle it.

If she knew anything, she knew how to keep a secret.

Fifteen minutes later, Daphne was dressed and on her way out the door to meet her niece, Alyssa, for a day of last-minute Christmas shopping. She had barely enough time to make it to Grand Central Station to meet Alyssa's train from White Plains. Daphne shrugged into her coat as she let herself out of the apartment and headed down the stairs.

The outside door was ajar, as three burly movers continued to bring in Nathan's belongings. The object they carried was large and long, obscured by padding. The inside door to Nathan's apartment was also open. She waited for the movers to squeeze past, then took a brief, curious glance into his apartment. Though not as spacious as the two upstairs floors the apartment was still large by New York standards. It opened into a hallway that led to the two bedrooms at the back. The living room lay to the right, where the movers unveiled the object they'd just carried in: a purple leather sofa. Good lord! Only Nathan could get away with having a purple leather sofa in his living room.

She didn't see him, though. Time to get going while the getting was good. She was nearly out the front door when she heard him call her name. She turned back to see him coming from the small enclosed kitchen on the left. He wiped his hands on a blue dish towel, which he slung over his shoulder as he walked toward her. He wore a pair of faded, skin-tight jeans and a white T-shirt that stretched across his chest in an appealing way. She swallowed. Hard.

He pulled an overstuffed white envelope from his back pocket and extended it toward her. "I forgot to give this to you earlier."

Puzzled, she took the envelope from him, sliding the flap open. Her eyes bulged as she counted all the crisp one hundred dollar bills. Thirty thousand dollars. "What's all this?"

"Standard moving-in requirements. First month's rent, last month's rent and security deposit." Leaning against the door frame, he smiled down at her. "I hope you don't mind cash."

She didn't mind cash at all. She minded the pang of guilt she felt for taking so much money from him. Her last tenant hadn't paid an eighth of what she'd asked from him. She'd only stated that figure because he'd made her angry. She extended the envelope toward him. "Look, Nathan, you don't have to—"

He straightened, pushing the envelope back toward her.

"Yes, I do. I agreed to ten thousand a month, and that's
what you're going to get. If you think that's too much, I
don't care. Donate it to charity if you want to. But I am
not taking it back."

He walked away from her, into his apartment, and closed
the door behind him.

Daphne gritted her teeth, sick of men, sick of their ultimatums and their money. She didn't have time to argue
with him now. She stuffed the envelope into her purse,
pulled the door closed behind her, and stomped off down
the street in the direction of Grand Central Station.

Amused, Nathan watched her departure from his cur-
tainless living-room window. Again, he pondered the question that had been plaguing him since she'd called to ask
him to move in: What had happened to make her change
her mind?

The Daphne he knew didn't operate on whims. Nor was
she pleased to have him there. When she'd opened the door
to him that morning, she looked more ready to boot him
down the stairs than welcome him to her home.

Was she in some sort of trouble for which she needed
money? That seemed the only reasonable explanation to
him. Though it defied common sense, it rankled him that
she wouldn't have come directly to him for what she
needed. Despite their past, she had to know that he would
help her in any way he could.

Laughing at himself, he shook his head. Who was he
to complain about the lack of directness in her motives?
He hadn't come clean with her, either. Despite his impul-
sive vow in church, he'd made no move to see her. She
didn't need him in her life, him and all the attendant problems he would bring. But he'd spent every night since then
sleepless and alone, thinking about her.

He'd finally given in to his need to see her, to close a
chapter of his life that seemed perennially open. Then he'd

seen her vacant apartment, and knew that the solution to both his problems lay with Daphne.

She hadn't given him the release he'd wanted from the past, however. Seeing her up close, holding her, he'd felt a rush of memories surge through him. Sweet memories of the only person, male or female, who'd ever loved him, not because of familial obligations or because he paid her salary or because he made his living seeking adoration, but simply because she chose to. It ate at him, like a wound that never healed, that he did not know why she'd withdrawn from him.

Turning, he flopped onto the window seat, feeling the crunch of the other envelope he carried in his back pocket. He pulled Monica's letter from his pocket, wondering why he felt compelled to carry it with him.

He still didn't know exactly where she was. She hadn't bothered with a return address. The only reference to where she'd run off to was the Parisian postmark on the envelope. He slid the single sheaf of pink paper from its envelope and read it for perhaps the twentieth time since he'd received it four days earlier. The handwriting hadn't changed; the letters formed the same cryptic words; the message filled him with the same rage that had risen in him the first time he'd read it.

Damn her! What kind of bizarre game was she playing? She had to be lying, laying another trap for him to fall into headfirst. What other motive could she have for telling him this? Nathan exhaled, willing the anger he felt to abate. It wouldn't do him any good to speculate. Monica's mind was as slippery as a sheet of ice—and just as dangerous. Ironically, at one point he'd thought they might be able to work out their differences and get along. That idea had lasted until the day Emily was born and Monica reverted to form.

And now she'd run off to God knew where. He supposed

he could find her, if that were his goal. Track her down and
confront her about the contents of her letter. But he had
Emily, and that was all that mattered to him. She might be
too young to understand her mother's duplicity, but he'd be
damned if he would allow her to be harmed by it.

He knew Daphne had to be more than curious about his
motives for moving into her town house. She'd already
guessed part of it, with her comment about him hiding
out. As of yet, she hadn't pressed the issue, but he had
no idea what lie he'd give her if she did.

And he would have to lie. He couldn't risk that she
would throw him out. That had nothing to do with Emily,
and everything to do with her. For as sure as he knew rain
fell down instead of up, he knew what he wanted wasn't
closure, but an opening, another chance to make things
right with her. And he couldn't tell her that. Not yet. She'd
have him and his things on the street so fast, they'd be
wind burned.

No, for the time being, Daphne would have to remain
in the dark.

It was nearly ten o'clock that night when Daphne
tramped through the front door of her town house. Alyssa
had dragged her from store to store, until "shop till you
drop" became more of an actuality than a slogan. After
that, they'd had a late dinner, lingering over the chocolate
chip cheesecake they'd ordered for dessert. They'd so lost
track of time that they'd had to sprint through the train
station to get Alyssa to the right platform on time.

Now Daphne, too tired to move at a normal rate of
speed, leaned her back against the open door to shut it.
She closed her eyes momentarily, visualizing her nice
warm bed, fluffy pillows, and an alarm that would not
wake her until ten o'clock the following morning.

She opened her eyes, and looked directly into Nathan Ward's handsome face. Startled, she drew in a quick breath, her hand flying to her chest. Annoyed at herself for letting him fluster her, annoyed at him for being there in the first place, she said, "What are you doing out here?"

"Waiting for you."

"Are you going to do this every time I come through the door?"

"Only when I'm worried about you."

She pushed off the door, letting her bags drop to the floor beside her. "Why on earth would you worry about me?" She slipped out of her coat and hung it on the coat rack.

"It occurred to me after you left that I shouldn't have given you that much money to carry around in your purse."

He shouldn't have given her that much money, period. She crossed her arms in front of her, raising one eyebrow in silent challenge. "Afraid I might lose your precious money?"

"No, hoping you didn't get mugged. People walk differently, act differently when they have money on them. Unsavory types usually pick up on these things. And, it's your money."

She said nothing to that, too tired to argue the point further. She walked to where she'd left her packages. "Good night, Nathan." She bent to pick up her bags, intent on heading up to her apartment. Nathan was quicker than she and had the bags in his hands before she could reach them.

"I'll take these up for you," Nathan said. "In a minute. While you're down here, why don't you take a look at what I've done to the place?"

At that moment she couldn't care if he'd painted every wall in the house the same purple as his sofa. "Some other time." She reached for her bags.

Nathan stepped away from her, drawing the bags out of

her reach. "Come on, Dee. It won't take long. And I have something for you."

Hands on hips, she glared at him. What could he possibly have that would interest her? Mentally, she erased that thought. He had plenty that interested her. That was the problem. Still, refusing his invitation might make him curious as to the real reason she declined. "Five minutes."

"That's all it will take." She looked at him skeptically as he took her hand, leading her inside his apartment. Whatever his motives were, she was too tired to fight him over them. He stopped at the first archway on the right, leaning her shopping bags against the wall.

"This, as you know, is the living room."

She glanced around the room, which was decorated in black and white, the sofa providing the only dash of color. A black-and-white rug covered the polished hardwood floors; curtains with a simpler design hung at the windows. Paintings hung on the walls and a floor-to-ceiling bookcase stood against the far wall, complete with books and other knickknacks. It looked as if he'd been living here for years.

"You did all this by yourself?" she asked, looking around.

"Mmm-hmm. My mama didn't raise any slouches." With a hand on her elbow, he led her past the kitchen. "That must have been some fire you had in there."

"Not really." She surveyed the room. The spaces where the refrigerator and stove had occupied were vacant, the walls where the cabinets had been, burned black. It looked a lot worse than it had actually been.

"The fire was out within minutes," she said. "Thanks to quick thinking and a handy fire extinguisher. The worst part was all the soot, which got everywhere, even in my apartment, and the powder from the extinguisher, which I still can't get rid of."

She stopped, pressing her lips together to keep from saying anything further. Her tongue had run away with her, babbling out a stream of nonsense no one other than a firebug would care about.

They stood at the threshold of Nathan's bedroom. She'd had to repaint everything after the fire, and for this room the painter had talked her into a midnight blue. Afterward, in the daylight, it had seemed much too dark a color for the room. But now, at night, it spoke to her of mystery and exoticism. Nathan turned up the dimmer on the light— not all the way, only enough to erase most of the shadows—and the impression deepened.

A king-size bed with a metallic-black frame and dark blue bedding took up the far wall. The same black metal was evident in the other pieces of furniture. It completely suited the room, suited him. Despite the hard angles and planes, it struck her as a place of seduction. She tried to swallow, but suddenly her mouth was devoid of moisture. Who did Nathan plan on entertaining in this room?

"What do you think?"

She glanced up at Nathan, who stood beside her. His hazel eyes were friendly, crinkling at the corners, his smile innocuous. A completely ordinary question. Since she didn't have any ordinary answers, she took another tack. "Where's your daughter?"

"At my grandmother's. I'm picking her up tomorrow."

"I see." She moved toward the adjacent room, away from his. "Is this her room?" Of course it had to be. There were only two bedrooms in the apartment. His answer was a soft chuckle as he passed her, going to flick on the light in the smaller room.

"It's beautiful," she said, her voice barely above a whisper. She stepped into the room, stopping at the antique white crib, decorated with a white organza coverlet. She touched her fingers to the soft fabric, letting her fingers stray over the plush stuffed bunny at the foot of the bed.

Then an old-fashioned hobby horse in the corner of the room caught her attention, drawing her to it. "I haven't seen one of these since I was a child."

She looked at Nathan, who leaned against the doorjamb, watching her with an amused smile on his face. "You're not going to tell me I'm too extravagant, are you? I've already heard it from every woman in my family."

"Not me." He'd filled the room with every toy imaginable, including a Pooh bear so enormous it would more likely frighten a child than comfort her. She picked up a pink mitt that lay on the ornate white dresser. "But a baseball glove?"

"I don't intend to be one of those dads who thinks all his daughter should do is sit around and look pretty."

"That's not what I meant. Nathan, she's only six months old."

"Then I'll be ready when the time comes."

But she wouldn't need it for years, and he wouldn't be here that long. It occurred to her that all his furnishings suggested permanence, not the decorating scheme of someone who planned to stay only a short while. It occurred to her to ask him exactly how long he intended to stay, when he straightened, wiping his palms on the front of his jeans.

"As I figure it, you owe me two more minutes on this two-cent tour. Come back into the living room for a minute."

He walked away, leaving her in the bedroom. She knew she should get out of there, not only out of the room, but out of his apartment. He treated her too casually, as if they were old friends, with nothing standing between them. But he'd said he had something for her, and for the life of her she couldn't help but be curious about what it was. That was dangerous. Cats weren't the only things killed by curiosity.

She turned out the light, closing the door behind her. Whether she wanted Nathan's surprise or not, there was only one way out of the apartment, since she'd forgotten to unlock the back stairwell—the way Nathan had gone. She had no choice but to follow.

Nathan paused at the living-room doorway, watching Daphne examine one of the pictures that hung on the far wall. It didn't surprise him that she'd been drawn to that sketch, a charcoal portrait of a dark-skinned girl with a bow in her hair, and a hint of sauciness in her pose. He'd bought it because it had reminded him of her, of what she must have looked like as a young girl before he'd known her.

Knowing she didn't suspect his presence, he let his gaze rove freely over her. She'd never worn clothes designed to show off her slender figure, but the baggy pants and oversized sweater she had on now could serve no other purpose than to conceal it. He wondered if she were still self-conscious about her breasts, as she had been when she was younger. Her stance, with her arms folded across her chest, suggested that was true.

What did she hope to accomplish with that gesture? Certainly not to discourage his attention. Seeing her standing there like that fueled the same yearning in him that it always had, the urge to push her hands away and explore that which she sought to keep hidden.

Mentally, he shook himself. He didn't want to scare her off, but to make her relax around him. She never would if she read his intentions in his eyes. He schooled his features into a benign expression and stepped farther into the room.

"If you like that one, I can get you a print of it."

Startled, Daphne turned toward Nathan, dropping her hands to her sides. "Excuse me?"

"The sketch," he said, nodding toward it. "If you like it, the artist sells prints of his work. That's the original."

She said nothing, her mind occupied with the sight of him walking toward her. He really was the most handsome man she'd ever seen, with his tawny complexion, beautiful eyes, and proud carriage. He stopped in front of her, extending a bottle toward her that he held by the neck with one hand. In the other hand he carried two crystal champagne flutes. Until that moment, she hadn't realized he'd been carrying anything.

"This is for you," he said.

"Champagne?" She took the cold, slick bottle from him. It had obviously been chilled on ice that had begun to melt. "What for?"

"Well, for us." He set the glasses on a side table next to her. "I thought we ought to toast our new living arrangement."

"That isn't necessary."

"I know, but I really do appreciate your helping me out."

That's all he wanted? To toast her for helping him? For one crazy instant, she'd thought Nathan planned on implementing Seduction Scenario number one. She would never have allowed such a thing to happen, but it wouldn't have hurt her ego any to know he suffered from some of the same longings that she did. He dashed her hopes completely by adding, "I meant it when I said I hoped we could be friends."

Feeling suddenly churlish, she crossed her arms in front of her, leaning on one hip. "What exactly would this friendship entail?"

"All the regular stuff. No high-wire acts or jumping through flaming hoops."

Despite herself, she laughed. "I'm serious. If you want

to be my friend, what are you offering? I've learned that with you it's best to know all the details up front."

If her barb stung him, he didn't show it. "I don't know." He took the bottle from her, beginning to untwist the metal cage that housed the cork. "We could look out for one another. If you needed something, you'd allow me to help you with it, and I could do the same for you. We could have a civil conversation from time to time."

So he *had* noticed the shift in her mood. Unsure whether that pleased her or not, she looked down at her feet. "That doesn't sound too unreasonable."

The cork slid from the bottle with a loud pop. The bubbling liquid flowed over the lip of the bottle. Daphne quickly got one of the glasses to catch it. "I must be losing my touch," Nathan said, laughing.

Nathan grinned down at her as she replaced one glass with the other. With his thumb, he swiped away a drop of the champagne that had splattered her cheek, then he licked the moisture from his thumb.

She watched him raptly, heat rising in the cheek he'd grazed. No, there wasn't a thing wrong with Nathan's touch. She took a step back from him. "What shall we toast to?"

Nathan set down the bottle and took one of the champagne flutes from her. He raised it in salute to her. "To new beginnings."

"To new beginnings," she echoed. She sipped from her glass, wondering exactly what they'd begun today. She doubted that all Nathan wanted from her was her friendship, though she couldn't imagine what else he might want. She didn't have anything else.

He refilled his glass, adding a few drops to hers. "In the spirit of our newly declared friendship, can I ask you what made you change your mind? About letting me move in here, I mean."

She shook her head. "No."

Nathan snorted. "Same old blunt Daphne. I've missed that, you know."

"Why?"

"You have to realize that most of the people around me are so damn obsequious. If I say the sky is green they start discussing which shade. It's refreshing to have someone willing to say the sky is blue, and that's that."

Deciding to turn the tables on him, she said, "Do you mind if I ask you a question?"

"No, go ahead."

"Why did you want to move in here?"

Clearly, he hadn't been expecting that question. His throat worked, but no sound came out. "It's complicated," he said finally.

His answer was a lot less direct than her simple "no" had been, but the message was the same: Keep out! He didn't want to discuss his motives any more than she did hers. So much for his claim of wanting a friendship between them. No relationship could survive without honesty, and between them there wasn't any. At any rate, she'd wasted enough time with Nathan for one evening.

"It's getting late." She set her wineglass on the table. "Thanks for the champagne."

She started toward the door, disconcerted when Nathan followed her. How far did he intend to go? She stopped once she'd crossed the threshold to his apartment, and turned to face him, intending to bid him good night. The words died in her throat when she looked up at his face. His expression hadn't exactly changed, but in his eyes she saw an intensity that hadn't been there before.

He'd always been able to make her tremble at his touch. Nothing about that had changed. When he cupped the side of her face in his palm, she couldn't help the tremor that shivered through her. His head slowly lowered toward hers.

For a moment, she simply stood there, dumbstruck. He could not be intending to kiss her. Either he was crazy or he thought she was. She'd made the mistake of getting involved with him once. Twice was out of the question.

She took a step back from him, brushing his hand away from her face. "Don't even think I'm interested." She saw the look of surprise on his face, the way his mouth opened, to protest his innocence, she presumed. "Don't, Nathan, just don't. Whatever it is you're about to say, I doubt I'd believe it anyway."

Turning, she stalked up the stairs to her apartment. "Damn you, Nathan Ward," she muttered, as she struggled with her key in the lock. Once inside, she got the key to the back stairwell and unlocked it. For good measure, she closed and locked the double doors that led to the kitchen. Nathan could have free reign of the kitchen without having access to the rest of her apartment, to her.

It occurred to her that she was doing in a physical way what she could not manage on an emotional one—shutting him out. She didn't care. Since she'd been foolish enough to let Nathan move in, the least she could do was try to minimize the damage. She readied herself for bed, confident she wouldn't have to see Nathan again unless *she* chose to.

It wasn't until the next morning that she remembered she'd left her shopping bags in his apartment.

Three

"¿Mijito, me estas escuchando?"

Hearing the exasperation in his grandmother's voice, Nathan's ears pricked up. No, he hadn't been listening. He'd phased out soon after she'd begun her little *lectura* on proper infant care. He answered automatically, without thinking. *"Si, Abuela."*

"Now, I know you're not paying attention if you're speaking to me in Spanish."

Nathan focused on his grandmother seated in the rocker across the room from him. Little Emily was in her arms, finally asleep after a long bout of crankiness. He felt a nip on his hand and looked down at his lap. Gigi, his grandmother's spitz collie, looked up at him, her pink tongue bobbing in her mouth. Another feminine complaint of neglect. He scratched the fur between her ears. "Not you too, girl," he whispered.

"Nathan, stop playing with the dog and listen."

He gave the dog one last pat and pushed her from his lap. She groused at him, settling on his feet and gnawing on his left shoe. "I'm sorry. What were you saying?"

His grandmother gave him a harassed look. "What is it, Nathan? What has you so preoccupied that you can't pay attention for five minutes?"

He suppressed the urge to tell her she'd been going on

for considerably more than five minutes. Nor did he want
to discuss his current situation with his grandmother. He
hadn't even told her that he'd moved into Daphne's apartment. It was better that she not know—easier, at least.
Then she couldn't call him hourly expecting a report on
Emily's well-being.

"It's nothing." He stood, stepping over the dog at his
feet. "I'd better get going."

"But the baby's sleeping. Can't you wait until she wakes
up?"

He shook his head. "It's better if she sleeps on the ride."
Nathan bent to take his daughter from his grandmother's
arms. "Shh, sweetheart," Nathan crooned, when the baby
began to fret. He lifted her to his shoulder. "Daddy's here."
She immediately quieted. Nathan smiled, feeling a surge
of satisfaction. At least one person trusted him to take care
of her, even if she was too young to know better.

Crossing to the changing table in the corner of the room,
he laid Emily down and gently put on her snowsuit. He
wrapped her in a blanket his grandmother had crocheted
for one of the family babies years ago. Picking up the
baby, he followed his grandmother downstairs and toward
the front door.

Predictably, his sister and his cousin materialized from
whatever hidey hole they'd disappeared to during his grandmother's lecture. Each of them kissed the sleeping Emily
good-bye, looking up at him as if he were taking her off to
the nearest baby seller instead of his own home. He supposed he should be grateful that his daughter had so many
people who loved her and were willing to look after her, but
his family's lack of faith in his ability bothered him.

Nathan bent to kiss his grandmother's cheek. "Good-
bye, *Abuela,* thanks for everything."

She patted his back, as she'd always done. As if he were
a child. "You know, you are both welcome to stay here."

"I know." He hefted the bag with Emily's things over his shoulder. "I'll call if I need anything."

Without looking back, he headed through the front door, out into the late-afternoon sunshine. He strapped Emily into her car seat; then, straightening, he looked down the street in the direction of Daphne's father's house. Two blocks down, but a world away. He knew she was there, that she spent most Sundays looking after her father. He also knew from Daphne's brother, Michael, that Jasper Thorne did not need his daughter's ministrations. He suffered through them anyway, simply to please her. Daphne, it seemed, needed to be needed.

For the first time in his life, he understood that feeling. In any other family in America the eldest male could expect some sort of deference, a little respect. Not in his. Not only did he come from a household where even the dog who nipped at his feet was female, the women made no pretense of claiming him the head of the family as a salve to his male ego.

No, the women in his family were definitely in charge. They didn't need him—not his time, his guidance, or his concern. About the only thing they required from him was his money, which he gave without qualm. He knew if he agreed to it, they would absorb Emily into their midst and raise her without seeking one word of input from him.

In many ways, he had no one but himself to blame for that. He'd lived the last ten years of his life doing exactly as he pleased, without regard for anyone else's feelings or concerns. He knew the universal refrain they chanted as he went about disgracing the family name or merely disappointing them. They'd shrug and say, "That's just how Nathan is." If they had no faith in him, he'd earned every bit of their distrust.

It had been different when his mother was alive. She'd been the only one to hold him accountable for what he did, to demand something from him. His mother and Daphne. Nathan laughed to himself, remembering a time when he'd upset her and she'd refused to speak to him for days. He'd gone to her house to beg her forgiveness one more time. She'd opened her bedroom window and tossed down an old pair of her father's shoes with a note that read, *Keep walking*.

She hadn't needed him, either, but she'd wanted him. With Daphne that had been enough.

But she didn't want him anymore. Her closed-door message hadn't been lost on him. That was his own fault, too. He'd moved too fast. Last night, as he'd followed her to the door, intending to bring her bags upstairs as he'd promised, she'd turned, surprising him. He'd gotten caught up in watching Daphne's rear view. In his face she must have seen the unguarded expression of the desire she inspired in him. He hadn't thought; he'd merely done what he wanted to do. Or tried to. In typical Daphne fashion, she'd put him in his place, but good.

With a wicked grin, he slid behind the wheel of his car. Daphne could shut him out of her apartment if she wanted to. Her bags were still in his. If she thought he was above ransoming them, she was mistaken. With Christmas only a few days away, she'd have to get them sooner or later. Hopefully sooner.

Daphne arrived at her office in a foul mood at ten o'clock Monday morning, having just come from her lawyer's office and hearing the news she'd expected. Her lawyer's advice amounted to: pay the man and get him out of your hair. Since there was no provision in their agreement for one partner to sell to the other, all bets were off. Brad could ask for any amount he wanted, which left her to decide whether to accept his offer.

Her lawyer's only suggestion had been to try to get him to lower his asking price, an idea Daphne found distasteful. She would not bargain with the devil, not even a human one.

She greeted Sherry, the new receptionist, with as warm a smile as she could muster. Unused to sharing her troubles with anyone, Daphne refused to start now. "Hi, Sherry. How was your weekend?"

"Fine, boss, but there's a man in your office that says he's your new partner. I've been trying to reach you on your cell phone since he got here."

Daphne swore, a word that made Sherry's eyes widen. Despite his threat to do just this, she hadn't really expected him to show up. "How long has he been here?"

"He was in the hallway since before I got in. When I opened the door, he stormed right into your office, and, well, he was too big for me to stop him."

Daphne smiled for the first time that day. Sherry was five feet, two inches tall and slim enough that she still shopped for her clothes in the girls' department. "I'll take care of it."

Daphne stalked down the hallway, gripping the handle of her briefcase as if it were the hilt of a sword. She saw the curious glances from the two women who served as employment counselors as she passed their desks, but she didn't acknowledge them in any way. There were only two offices at the end of the corridor, her tiny one and the even smaller one that Victoria had used when she came to the building. Daphne swung through the open doorway of her office. Bradley was seated in her chair, his feet propped up on her desk, looking through her appointment book as if it were his to do with as he wished.

"What do you think you're doing?" she demanded.

Bradley straightened, placing his feet on the floor. A derisive smile graced his lips, and his eyes were as cold as ever. "Morning, partner. Just going over our schedule. Looks like we have a busy day."

"We? I'd think you'd be taking a step down in the world to worry about who's cleaning the Findley house this week." She dropped her briefcase onto the chair by the door. "Don't you have some little old ladies' savings accounts to squander?"

"Not at the moment." He grinned, surely the most evil expression Daphne had ever seen. "I thought I'd take this office. The other one is much too small."

She knew he had no intention of setting up shop there. He simply wanted to bait her, to anger her. She wouldn't give him that satisfaction. She leaned against the door frame, affecting an indolent pose.

"Suit yourself," she said in a voice as syrupy as sugar. "But I must warn you. Despite the contents of your mother's will, which only you and I were privy to, no one else here knows you from Adam. If you'd ever bothered to visit Victoria here, that might be a different story. . . ."

She shrugged, letting her words trail off. "But as we speak, my secretary is on the phone with building security. I would, of course, have to tell them who you are, but they tend to be a bit overzealous in performing their duties. By the time all that got straightened out, you'd be in police custody. Wouldn't that make an interesting item for the *Times'* society page?"

By the scowl that came over his face, she knew he hadn't missed her insinuation—that she would keep her mouth shut until that's exactly what happened. It would not do for him, a respected member of the financial world, to be arrested for trespassing, even if he were later cleared of it.

"You wouldn't dare."

A hint of a wicked smile curved the corners of her mouth. "Want to try me?"

His glacial gray eyes fastened on her, sending a chill

through her, but she stood her ground. This was her place, and she wouldn't let anyone come into it and push her around.

He surged to his feet. "This isn't over," he muttered as he walked past, deliberately bumping into her as he made his exit. She said nothing, merely watched him until he'd left not only her office but the outer office as well.

Exhaling heavily, she shut the door behind her. She couldn't help the broad grin that broke out across her face. It had been a bluff, and fool that he was, Bradley Davenport had fallen for it. Building security consisted of a pair of frail old men who couldn't catch one cold between the two of them. Thank goodness he'd believed her ruse. She might never have gotten rid of him otherwise.

Taking her seat, she steepled her fingers and rested her chin on top of them. She would have to plan how to deal with Bradley until she could get together the money she needed. He obviously wanted to stir up trouble, though she couldn't fathom why he'd bother. She'd gotten rid of him easily today. Next time, she might not be so lucky.

The lights were out in Nathan's apartment when she arrived home late that night. She wondered if that meant he was sleeping or if he were still out. She decided it didn't matter, as long as she didn't have to see him. She'd put in a hard day's work and she felt tired and disheartened. Although she still had her savings, it would be another month before she could get her hands on any money from her retirement plan. She might get a few thousand dollars from selling the few shares of stock she owned. Aside from that, she had no other resources and not even half the money she needed.

She thought of the "rent" Nathan had paid her. That didn't count. No matter what he said about it belonging to her, she couldn't keep it. She'd gone to the bank at noon, intending to put the bulk of it in an account in Emily's name. The bank refused her, since she had no documentation that such a person existed. She'd deposited a reasonable amount in her savings account, and opened a separate account in her own name into which she put the balance. She'd have to find a way to give it back to him later.

Dressed in an old, comfortable blue terry-cloth robe, her braids tied up in a ponytail, she headed downstairs to the kitchen. After the day she'd had, she'd kill for a cup of hot chocolate, her comfort food of choice. She wanted it the way her mother had made it, from milk simmered to just the right temperature, not one of those horrible instant packages and water. She paused a moment at the wooden double doors, listening for any sound coming from the other side. Nothing. She unlocked the doors and slid one open enough for her to pass through.

"Couldn't sleep either?"

Daphne started, drawing back. Nathan stood at the center island, leaning against the counter. He had a mug in his hand, which she assumed held coffee. A copy of the newspaper was spread out before him.

She should have known better than to assume Nathan wasn't there simply because she hadn't heard him. Not only that, she was trapped now. He'd seen her. She couldn't leave without some sort of explanation. Forget the hot chocolate. She'd grab something quick and eat it in her room.

As nonchalantly as possible, she walked to the refrigerator. He seemed to be acting as if the previous night had never happened. She would, too. "What are you doing up here? I mean, what about Emily?"

He held up what looked like a blue-and-white walkie-talkie. "Have baby monitor, will travel."

Silently, she cursed whoever had invented those things. She peered into the refrigerator, finding absolutely nothing appetizing on the shelves. She sighed, straightening. Maybe she should go to bed, after all.

"Hungry?" She hadn't heard Nathan come up behind her. Suddenly his hands were at her shoulders and she felt his breath fan her cheek. "Why don't you let me fix you something?"

His fingers kneaded her shoulders, gently, impersonally. She wanted to step away from his tender embrace and at the same time wanted his hands all over her. She was trapped in a different way this time. She had nowhere to move. She looked up at him over her shoulder. "Why? Planning to put something in it?"

He laughed. "No. You look beat, that's all."

"Thanks a lot."

"The truth hurts." She allowed him to steer her over to where he'd stood. He pulled over the step stool that sat in the corner. "Here, sit down and tell me about your day."

She arranged herself on the stool. "There's not much to tell." Not much she intended to tell him.

"Why do I get the feeling you're holding out on me?"

"I'm not holding out on you. I'm sure you're not interested in the boring details."

"Let me be the judge of that."

He gathered several ingredients from the refrigerator and laid them out on the counter next to her. "What are you making?"

"My specialty. Omelette à la Nathan."

"Still haven't learned how to cook a decent meal?"

"Can't boil water with a blow torch. But don't try changing the subject. We were talking about your day."

She sighed. "I got a new client today." She picked up a sliver of green pepper that he'd cut and popped it into her mouth.

"What do you do?"

"Try to keep my head above water, mostly. We specialize in helping women get jobs or develop marketable skills."

"Are you nonprofit?"

"No, but a lot of the agencies we work with are. It's only because of our impeccable reputation that we get the clients that we do. We've been very fortunate that way."

"Do you miss her—your partner, I mean?"

Her gaze flew to his. Nathan was too perceptive sometimes. She'd kept saying "we" when there was now only her, or there would be once she got rid of Bradley. Despite Victoria's having saddled her with her stepson, Daphne missed her very much. She couldn't count the number of times she'd picked up the phone to call her in the last few days, how many times she'd looked up from her desk, thinking she'd heard Victoria's voice.

She hadn't realized a tear had slipped down her cheek until Nathan brushed it away with his thumb. "Don't get weepy on me now," he said, his smile sympathetic.

"It's the onions."

He cast her a look that said he didn't believe her. He gathered the ingredients he'd chopped, including the onions, and carried them over to the stove on the cutting board. While he faced away from her, she swiped at her eyes with the back of her hand.

"There's something I have to ask you."

His serious tone commanded all of her attention. "What?"

"Exactly how old is that robe? Looks like it should have been retired to moth heaven years ago."

"It's comfortable," she protested, fingering the collar. "I'm not trying to impress anybody."

"Good thing."

She knew what he was trying to do: divert her attention from the subject that had upset her. It wasn't his fault that her emotions ran so close to the surface these days. He didn't help things any, but he wasn't the cause. Since they'd about exhausted the topic of her robe, she decided to change the subject.

"How does Emily like her new room?"

"I don't think she's noticed. All she does is eat, sleep and poop, like every other six-month-old."

Despite his words, she suspected he had an uncommon pride in his daughter. She wondered if he'd heard from Emily's mother, but decided against asking. She didn't really want to know about this woman Nathan had planned to marry or know what his feelings were for her. It was none of her business, anyway.

"Here you go." Nathan slid a plate in front of her, placing a napkin and utensils next to it. Daphne inhaled breathing in the spicy scent of the eggs. That and another aroma—hot chocolate. He set down a mug of it in front of her, and a mug of coffee for himself. He leaned against the counter next to her. "Well?"

She cut into the omelette with her fork, knowing he was watching her. "You sure there's no arsenic?"

"Not a drop."

She speared a piece with her fork and brought it to her mouth. "Delicious," she said. "What did you put in it?"

"That, my dear, is a Ward family secret." She lifted another forkful to her mouth, but before it could get there, Nathan grabbed her wrist, redirecting her hand toward his own mouth. "Not bad."

"If you do say so yourself."

He grinned. "Modesty has never been my strong suit." He picked up the knife beside her plate and began spreading grape jam on the toast he'd made for her. He handed it to her. Automatically, she took a bite from it.

Nathan said nothing more, allowing her to eat in silence. But he was too close, too familiar for her to be truly comfortable with him. Long before she'd satisfied her hunger, she pushed her plate away from her, downed the last of her hot chocolate, and stood.

"Is that all you plan to eat?"

"I guess I wasn't as hungry as I looked." She carried her plate to the garbage can in the corner, scraped its contents into the trash, and rinsed her plate in the sink. She'd load the dishwasher in the morning before she went to work. Only a couple of dishes occupied the sink anyway.

Turning back to Nathan, she said, "Thanks again for the omelette. Good night." She turned to head in the direction of the double doors.

She heard Nathan's voice call to her. "Don't tell me you're going to be true to your namesake and run off."

She spun around to see him leaning against the counter, an amused smile on his lips. He'd always teased her about being named for the nymph from Greek mythology who a god desired, but whose advances she shunned.

"I suppose, then, that you are casting yourself in the role of Apollo? The god of music, I'll give you, but reason and moderation? You don't know the meaning of either word."

With every word she'd spoken he'd taken another step toward her. He now stood a hair's width away from her, looming over her, crowding her, disconcerting her. He said nothing, merely raised an eyebrow in silent challenge.

She took a step away from him, her back hitting the doors. "And besides, Daphne was neither shy, as some people claim, nor cold-hearted. She ran from Apollo because she wanted to be one of Artemis's virgin huntresses, a position, as you well know, I am no longer qualified to hold."

"I remember. I was wondering if you remembered."

The look in his eyes was all at once so intense, she felt heat rise in her body and pool low in her belly. She remembered that long-ago night, when she'd come to him, needing him, when for once he hadn't turned her away. How could she forget that first time, and all the times thereafter, when they were etched in her brain as if by fire?

"Vaguely."

"And here I thought a woman was supposed to learn something from her first love."

"In my case, it was not to have another one."

Realizing what she'd said, she bit her lip. Seeing the look on Nathan's face, one of questioning disbelief, she bit harder, almost to the point of drawing blood. *Stupid, stupid, stupid!* She'd intended to wound him with her comment, not make herself more vulnerable in his eyes. If she knew Nathan, he'd assume that he'd ruined her for other men. Even if that were true, that was definitely not the impression she wished to leave him with.

"Don't look like that, Nathan. I didn't mean there hasn't been anyone else in my life. But love? That I can do without. Now, if you'll excuse me, I'm tired, and I'm going to bed."

She turned to part the doors and make good her escape, but Nathan's hand reached around her, holding the doors shut.

She whirled to face him. The sarcastic remark on the tip of her tongue died on her lips when she looked up into his eyes.

"Is it all bad? When you think of me, of us, is it all a bad memory?"

For the second time in the last few days, she'd seen a vulnerability in him, and it alarmed her. She wasn't callous enough to ignore anyone who hurt. Especially not him.

"No." She had to look away from him. Most of it was so good that allowing the memories to wash over her was like being bathed in scalding water. It stripped her of her defenses, and she would need every one of them to deal with him.

She pushed away from the door, straightening her spine. "Good night, Nathan."

He extended his hand toward her. Automatically she placed her hand in his. He raised it to his lips and kissed her palm. "Thank you," he said.

She snatched her hand away, wiping her palm on her robe, wiping away his kiss. "Good night," she repeated, then turned and vaulted up the stairs to her bedroom, slamming the door behind her.

Amused, Nathan watched her go. No, Daphne wasn't cold at all. He could feel the fire in her, hot enough to singe. This time, instead of a wall of ice, she'd erected an entire labyrinth, a maze of barbs and nettles to sting his ego and deflate his pride. But he'd gotten to her, if only a little bit.

He went downstairs, gathered her shopping bags, and deposited them inside her apartment, just on the other side of the kitchen door. He didn't want to play games with her, and his plan to hold her packages hostage would be doing just that. Truth was, he wanted her, plain and simple.

Common sense told him that he should leave her alone, not so much for his sake, but for hers. He wasn't in the position to offer her anything but heartache. But he also knew he wouldn't do that. No sense in lying to himself and thinking he would.

Focusing on the stairs that led to Daphne's bedroom above, Nathan smiled a wicked little grin.

"You'd better get your rest while you can, sweet Daphne. The chase has just begun."

Four

For as long as Daphne could remember, Christmas at the Thorne family home had been a festive occasion. The holiday had been Daphne's mother's favorite, a time when only death excused anybody from participating, that death being their own. Camille Thorne had been a generous woman, opening her house to her neighbors Christmas week, making sure all she knew had some semblance of a holiday dinner. Daphne had recognized this same spirit of generosity in Victoria, and it had forged an instant bond between them.

Daphne sat at her place at the dining-room table missing both women. She tried to appear as though she were savoring the meal, but she did little more than push her food around on her plate. Usually, she managed to put on a nice face for the holiday season, but whatever genuine Christmas spirit she might have enjoyed seemed to have fled this year.

She'd like to blame that on Bradley, with his threats and ultimatums. But she knew that wasn't true. It was Nathan living in her apartment that had her disconcerted. She didn't understand him at all. She'd thought for sure he'd try some juvenile trick, like holding her packages hostage until she did something he wanted. But when she'd come downstairs two mornings ago, she'd practically tripped over them. Not only that, he'd left her a note telling her he'd be at his grandmother's house for a few days. Not behavior typical of the Nathan she knew.

Maybe he did mean what he'd said about wanting them to be friends. One friend might inform another about his whereabouts and no one would think twice about it. Maybe he was trying to earn back her trust. But somehow she couldn't bring herself to believe that. She couldn't allow herself to believe that. She still had no more idea of why he'd wanted to move into her apartment than she did the day he'd arrived. The last thing she needed was to get sucked into whatever drama Nathan had embroiled himself in.

Daphne's ears pricked up, hearing Nathan's name on her brother's lips.

". . . his grandmother called me three days ago asking me if I'd heard from him. He disappeared with the baby a week ago, and half the furniture in his apartment is missing."

"It's not funny, Michael," Jenny protested. "I'm worried about him."

"No, it's not funny, just typical. But you'd think the guy would show up for Christmas dinner."

"Look who's talking," her sister Elise interjected. "Until Jenny came along, we couldn't drag you out here, either." Elise dabbed at her mouth with her napkin. "Besides, who wants to ruin everyone's dinner with talk of Nathan Ward, of all people."

Daphne felt her sister's eyes on her, but kept her gaze focused on her plate and her barely touched food. She could just imagine Elise's reaction to finding out that Nathan occupied her downstairs apartment. That was why she hadn't told her. Elise had never cared much for Nathan, and after Nathan and Daphne had gone their separate ways, Elise had seemed to like him even less.

Still, she didn't see any reason for Jenny to be concerned without cause. Not when she knew for a fact that both Nathan and his daughter were a scant two blocks away. Yet she couldn't help being disappointed in Nathan's behavior. So much for him attempting to join the ranks of the grown-up people of the world.

"I'm sure Nathan's grandmother has heard from him by now."

"Don't tell me *you're* actually defending him now. How can you possibly know that?" Elise asked.

Daphne leaned back in her chair, crossed her arms in front of her, and leveled her gaze on her sister. "Because he's been living in my downstairs apartment for the past week and a half."

"What?" Elise exploded. "He's been where?"

Daphne closed her eyes and silently prayed for strength as the table erupted around her. Why hadn't she kept her big mouth shut? Usually she treated her sister's well-intentioned meddling with more aplomb, humor even. Usually, she had enough sense to keep her own affairs to herself.

She opened her eyes to find several other pairs staring back at her. She glanced from Michael's scowl to Jenny's speculative stare to her father's paternal frown. Only Elise's husband Garrett and her two-year-old son seemed unperturbed by Daphne's revelation. Daphne's niece, Alyssa, gazed back at her with wide-eyed admiration. Daphne knew Alyssa thought her to be as old and as dried up as dust, a spinster without interest in men. If nothing else, having Nathan Ward come back into her life gave the lie to that notion.

"Aunt Daphne's living with a guy? Cool!"

"Alyssa, please," Elise groaned. Turning to Daphne, she said, "Do you see what you've started?"

Standing, Daphne focused her gaze on her sister. Where had she been—where had any of them been—when she had actually needed them? She saw no need to explain herself now.

Daphne picked up her plate. "Excuse me. I seem to have lost my appetite." She stalked off toward the kitchen, stormed through the swinging door, and slammed her plate down on the counter with such force that the silverware clattered.

Groaning, she placed her hand over her brow and shook her head. Funny, half the time they treated her as if she were some iron Amazon, the family automaton who looked after their father, organized the family gatherings, and had single-handedly cooked the meal she couldn't manage to eat. That Daphne never needed anyone, possessed no tender feelings for them to bruise. But let her do something that smacked of fallibility, of not following some straight and narrow path of correctness, and they treated her as some sort of lost child, unable to function without their guidance. A perfect Daphne they could handle; a flawed one they could not.

To some extent, she could blame no one but herself. The only people she'd ever let see past her metal facade, her mother and Victoria, were both gone. No, there had been one other, but the less she thought about Nathan, the better.

"Daphne?"

She whirled around, unaware that Elise had followed her into the kitchen. Gone was the combative look on Elise's face, replaced with a look of sympathy.

"Yes."

"I didn't mean to come down on you out there, but what could you have been thinking letting that man live with you? Hasn't he caused you enough trouble?"

"He's not living with me. He's renting my apartment. That's all."

"Oh, really. Nathan Ward, a man with more money than

God, somehow needs to rent that little apartment of yours? Tell me that makes sense. If you ask me, he wants something. And it doesn't take a brain surgeon to figure out what that is."

"I didn't ask you." Daphne turned her back on her sister, busying herself loading the dishwasher. Elise had voiced every one of Daphne's own suspicions, and having them laid bare disturbed her. "I may be your younger sister, but I do have some sense."

"If you're looking for someone, I know plenty of men more suitable than Nathan Ward."

"For goodness' sake, Elise. I am not looking for a man."

"Why not? You're thirty-five years old and not getting any younger. Can you honestly say you'd consider your life complete if you never married, never had children?"

Daphne exhaled a heavy breath. No, she wouldn't consider her life complete. And yes, her biological clock was more like a ticking time bomb than a simple alarm. But that had nothing to do with whether Nathan lived in her apartment or not.

Hands on hips, Daphne faced her sister. "If I'm ever feeling particularly desperate, I promise I'll head over to Sperm 'R' Us and pick up a pint to go."

Elise pursed her lips, an expression that signaled she thought Daphne was being particularly perverse. "I'm going back in to dinner."

Daphne watched her sister walk away, then closed her eyes and sighed. She hadn't meant to hurt her sister's feelings, but Daphne could imagine the sort of man Elise would pick for her. Some staid, solid saint of a man who would kill her with boredom in less than a week. No, thank you.

Then again, she'd had exciting. Being with Nathan was like riding a loop-de-loop without a safety harness. And what had that gotten her? A truckload of grief and a broken heart. She could do without that, too.

But the fact of it was that she didn't have all that much time for debate. True, women were having healthy babies later and later in life these days, but that wasn't Daphne's goal. If she was going to have a child, she wanted it to be born before she was old enough to be its grandmother.

Exiting the kitchen, Daphne went to find her sister. Elise had gone upstairs to change her two-year-old son, who'd gotten more of his meal on his clothes than in his mouth. Daphne paused in the doorway to the bedroom they had shared as children.

"All right, Elise. You win. If you've got someone in mind, have him call me."

Daphne didn't wait for a response. She went down to clear the dinner dishes and spend the rest of the day wondering if she hadn't made things worse instead of better.

Nathan arrived home a little before ten o'clock, depressed, exhausted and as cranky as Emily when her bottle wasn't ready on time. The past few days had been as trying as any he'd known. Though his grandmother had protested, he'd decided that three days in the bosom of his family had been enough.

Nathan removed Emily's snowsuit and put her in her crib. The baby fretted a little but quickly subsided, sucking her tiny fingers in her sleep. "Why did I expect it to be any different?" he asked the sleeping child. Despite showing up with a well-cared-for Emily, who didn't have so much as a spot of diaper rash on her little bottom, his grandmother had read him the riot act, chapter and verse. How could he have been so irresponsible as to not let anyone know where he was? How could he have worried them all like that?

He hadn't intended to worry anyone. In truth, he wasn't used to having anyone checking up on his whereabouts.

Then again, it was Emily's well-being that had concerned his grandmother, not his own. To think he'd actually hoped to prove in some small way that he was capable of taking care of his daughter on his own. He was a grown man; he could do as he wished. But his family's approval, especially that of his grandmother, mattered to him.

Unfortunately, no one else saw things his way. Well, he hadn't earned his reputation as the proverbial black sheep of the family in a day. It didn't look like he'd lose it that quickly, either.

Nathan switched off the light, went into the kitchen, and got a beer from the mini-refrigerator. Popping open the top, he sat on the sofa and propped his feet on the coffee table. He'd come home, hoping Daphne would be there. Just seeing her would have been enough. He missed her. His thoughts had turned to her so often, his mind might as well have been set on instant replay. But her car wasn't parked outside, and he hadn't seen a single light glowing in her windows from the outside of the house. If she was there, she had to be asleep, which was just as bad.

He placed his beer on the table and picked up the package lying next to him on the sofa. It still bore the Federal Express wrapping it had come in when it had been delivered to his grandmother's house two days ago. Scanning the return address, his own apartment on Central Park West, he'd immediately known who'd sent it. How clever! Even if he had refused delivery, the package would have come to him anyway.

He tore off the outer wrappings to reveal a simple, overstuffed white gift box that could have come from any store in America. Inside lay an assortment of exquisite baby clothes. Tiny dresses and booties and an entire layette set that looked handmade.

Nathan picked up the card that had slipped in among

he garments and slid it from the envelope. *Tell Emily Merry Christmas for me. M.*

M. He was beginning to hate the sight of that single script letter. Had Monica forgotten that M also stood for mother, which was what Emily needed, not a truckload of clothing, no matter how expensive? No, Monica was all about Monica. To be involved with her, you needed to be another *M* word: masochistic. He pushed the box onto the sofa beside him. Emily was better off without Monica.

Nathan got to his feet, strode to his bedroom, and retrieved another wrapped box. The present he'd bought for Daphne. He wondered what she'd think of the gift. She'd probably throw it back in his face, but he didn't care. He hiked up the back staircase and entered Daphne's living room via the kitchen. He set the box on her coffee table, leaving on one of the lamps so that she wouldn't come in to a completely dark apartment. Then he returned to his apartment, took a quick shower, and went to bed.

When Daphne pulled up in front of her town house a little after midnight, she immediately noticed the light burning in her living-room window. She'd turned off all the lamps before she'd left. Someone had been in her apartment.

It could have been Nathan, but his apartment was dark, and his car wasn't outside, so she had to assume the light being on was someone else's handiwork.

Once she got inside her apartment, she kicked off her shoes and shrugged out of her coat, leaving it in a heap on the floor. So far, nothing looked out of place, but that didn't mean anything. Hearing what sounded like a chair scraping against the floor, she grasped her baseball bat in her hand and crept toward the kitchen.

She didn't see him until she'd stepped through the double

doors. He sat at the kitchen table, his back partially to her, wearing nothing but a pair of faded jeans. His head was bent toward the baby in his arms as he sung a Spanish lullaby to her.

For a moment, she stood transfixed by the scene before her. Nathan and his child. Her throat constricted and tears pooled in her eyes. She hadn't expected to see him like that. Nor could she have predicted the flood of emotions that would well up in her at the sight. She started to back out of the room. The bat slid from her fingers, clattering against the floor.

Nathan swiveled around in his chair to face her. "Daphne?" She noticed his gaze travel from her face to the bat on the floor and back again. "What's the matter?"

And suddenly she noticed him only as a man. Her gaze roved over his bare chest only partially concealed by the baby's small form. The tears in her eyes receded and she swallowed in a dry throat.

As if reading her thoughts, an amused smile turned up the corners of his mouth and a knowing look came into his eyes. She snapped her mouth closed and bent to retrieve the bat, more than a little tempted to slug him with it.

"I heard a noise. I didn't know you were home."

He gestured in a way that seemed to indicate his attire. "I didn't know you were home, either."

"Then I'll leave you alone to put the baby to sleep."

"Don't go. This is your house, remember? I'm the boarder here."

She continued her retreat. "I don't want to wake her."

"You won't. She didn't bat an eyelash when the bat hit the floor."

Nathan stood. "Come to think of it, you two haven't met, have you?" He walked toward her, stopping only a few inches away from her. "Daphne Alexandra Thorne, may I present Emily Elizabeth Ward, or 'Her Highness,' as I've started to call her."

Daphne looked down at the infant in the crook of Nathan's arm. She looked more like a tiny perfect doll than an actual child. Only the rapid rise and fall of her chest gave evidence of her animateness.

Daphne drew in a long, ragged breath of her own. Though Emily didn't resemble Nathan in the least, she was one of the most beautiful babies Daphne had ever seen. Automatically, her hand lifted to touch the child, but she immediately withdrew it, clasping the bat in both hands.

"She's lovely, Nathan."

"Thank you."

His simple answer, rather than some flip retort, surprised her. She glanced up at him, finding him watching her with an odd expression on his face.

"What?" she asked, curious as to why he looked at her that way.

He shook his head. "I'd better go. Good night, Daphne."

He leaned toward her, cupping her chin in the palm of his free hand. She watched his head lower toward hers, riveted, anticipating what he would do. Just the slightest frisson of disappointment skidded through her when he turned her face to kiss her cheek. Her cheek, but so close to her mouth that her lips parted automatically and her breath drew inward in a gasp.

Slowly, he pulled away from her, his gaze fastened with hers, a sardonic smile on his lips. He ran a finger down the slope of her nose. "Merry Christmas, Daphne. I hope you don't mind. I left you a little present on your coffee table."

She didn't know what to say to that. Did she mind him invading her space or did she mind him buying her a present? Or did she mind the way he'd stirred her senses with a simple touch of his lips?

He didn't wait for a response, anyway. She watched him walk away from her, start down the stairs, and close the door behind him. She touched her fingertips to the spot where he'd kissed her. Still warm, still moist, still tingling.

Daphne spun around wrapping her arms around her waist. Why, why, why couldn't she be immune to him? And worse yet, he knew she was not. He'd seen the interest in her eyes. Hell, it had been more than interest. She'd shown him flat-out desire, and he'd eaten it up as if it were a gourmet meal.

Even now, even though she knew better, she couldn't wait to see what Nathan had bought her. She turned out the kitchen light, padded into her living room, and sat on the sofa. She tore at the package's silver paper to reveal a Saks Fifth Avenue box.

She gasped as she removed the lid. Inside lay the most exquisite silk robe in a brilliant royal blue. Gingerly, she ran her hand over the soft material. She'd never been one to indulge herself in luxury, but she knew a quality garment when she saw one. The robe had cost a thousand dollars if it had cost a dime. She picked it up, laying it out on the sofa beside her.

Beneath the blue robe lay three others: an emerald green, a crimson and a jet black. When she'd laid out all the robes, she picked up the card that lay at the bottom of the empty box. *I didn't know what color you'd like. Nathan.*

She dropped the card into the box, and covered her face with her hands. This was Nathan's idea of a "little" present. What would something "big" be? A hotel?

Of course, she could never accept such an extravagant gift from him. Such a personal gift. But as sure as she knew she'd have to return it, she loathed the idea. Those robes were the nicest things she'd ever owned.

Gathering them to her chest, she lay down on the sofa.

Tomorrow would be soon enough to return them. With the robes covering her like a blanket, Daphne fell asleep.

The worst thing about living downstairs from Daphne, Nathan decided, was hearing every sound she made, every footfall. He'd awakened to the sound of her walking around in the kitchen, making breakfast, he assumed. Barely a half-hour ago, he'd heard her leaving the house, feeling a note of disappointment that she hadn't said anything one way or another about his gift. He acknowledged that part of the reason for giving it to her had been that she'd have to come to him, if only to say thank you.

The doorbell rang, ending Nathan's opportunity for musing. Since the outside bell hadn't been rung, he assumed it must be Daphne returning. Without bothering to check the peephole, he pulled open the door. Michael stood on the other side, leaning against the doorjamb. A Louisville slugger rested against his right shoulder. Nathan's name was spelled out along the head of the bat in big black letters.

Nathan would have laughed if it weren't for the murderous expression on Michael's face. A lifetime ago, a fourteen-year-old Michael had warned him that if he didn't treat Daphne right, he had a baseball bat with Nathan's name on it. He supposed Michael thought it was time to make good on the threat.

Nathan crossed his arms over his chest. "To what do I owe the honor of this visit?" he drawled.

"I find you living in my sister's house, and you have to ask me that question? First Monica, then my wife, now my sister? Is there any woman I know you consider off-limits?"

In his more rational moments, Michael actually credited Nathan with helping bring him and Jenny together, so he obviously wasn't in the mood for reason now. Neither was Nathan, really. Granted, the incident with Monica never should have happened. The flesh had been willing, and the mind hadn't put up too much of a protest. Besides, she'd told him that she'd ended things with Michael, a statement not entirely true.

His relationship with Daphne had nothing to do with Michael; it had in fact predated the friendship between himself and Michael that had started when Nathan started recording for Michael's label three years ago.

"I'd think twice before giving Elise a whirl. That walking skyscraper she married might actually hurt me."

"And I won't? You've got about five seconds to begin that explanation of what you're doing here. And don't bother to tell me whatever sob story you used on Daphne to get her to let you move in here."

"You know, Daphne has a bat just like that one. Is it some sort of Thorne family tradition?"

"The same bat, but my swing is better. You're wasting time."

Nathan groaned. He supposed he did owe Michael some sort of explanation, both as his friend and as Daphne's brother. He knew concern for his sister motivated Michael's presence there. Considering his own track record, Nathan couldn't fault Michael for that. "Close the door, would you? Let's do this sitting down."

Nathan led the way into the living room, sat on the sofa, and propped his feet on the coffee table. He waited to speak until Michael claimed the chair across from him, laying the bat across his lap.

"Do you honestly think I'm trying to take advantage of Daphne?"

Michael sighed. "Truthfully, no. It's you that's got me concerned. You disappear, you don't tell anyone where you're going. Then I find out from my sister that you're here. And she probably wouldn't have said anything if Jenny hadn't been worried about you. What is with you lately?"

Shrugging, Nathan huffed out a breath. "Mike, I'm thirty-eight years old. I'm tired of the life. I couldn't care less if I ever see the inside of another recording studio, couldn't care if I make another tour date. The joys of having some teenyboppers swooning over every utterance out of my mouth has worn a bit thin.

"All I want to do is raise my daughter and take some time to enjoy all that nice money you've helped me make."

"I can understand that, but why here? And why would Daphne let you move in? I didn't know the two of you were even speaking to each other."

Nathan had no intention of answering either question. "Let's just say that each of us has our reasons for our current living arrangement."

Michael shook his head. "Not good enough."

"If you want to know Daphne's motives, ask her." Though Nathan suspected Michael would get the same answer to that question as he'd gotten: Mind your own business. "As for me, all I know is that there is still something between us. I want to find out what it is."

"In Daphne's case, I would have sworn it was called hate."

Nathan shook his head. "She might want to hate me, but she doesn't."

Nathan held his gaze steady as Michael seemed to scrutinize him for a moment. "Good God, you're serious," Michael finally said.

"Of course I'm serious. I'm not that much of a glutton for punishment that I would risk taking her on again if I weren't."

Michael snorted. "If you last more than a month before she tosses you out on your rump, I'll tattoo your name on my butt." When his laughter subsided, Michael added, "Do you honestly think you have a chance with her?"

He remembered the look in Daphne's eyes the night before when she'd walked in on him in the kitchen. She'd wanted him, of that he had no doubt. But wanting on a physical level and on an emotional one were two different things. And he wanted Daphne to feel both. One wasn't any good without the other.

Yet a slow, sure smile spread across his face. There had never been anything he'd wanted in his life that hadn't come to him sooner or later. Whether that was due to persistence or being in the right place at the right time or plain old good luck, he didn't know or care. The fates had been kind to him and he doubted they would abandon him now.

The sound of a baby's cry saved him from having to give an answer to Michael's question.

Nathan stood. "It appears Her Highness is awake. Now's your chance to witness firsthand the joys of dirty diapers and baby drool."

Nathan started down the hallway with Michael following him. Arriving at the baby's room, Nathan switched on the light and crossed to the crib where Emily lay on her back, wailing away. He picked her up and snuggled her against his chest.

"Hi, sweetheart. Did you have a good nap?" Emily's answer was a bloodcurdling yell right in his ear. He grinned at Michael. "It appears someone woke up on the wrong side of the crib."

"She sure has a pair of lungs on her. If she can sing as well as she yells, she's got herself a recording contract one of these days."

Nathan brought Emily over to the changing table and laid her down. "Did you hear that, sweetheart? Uncle Mike is going to make you a star." He continued to coo at his daughter while he changed her diaper and put a new bib on her. She rewarded him with a big sloppy baby grin that made his heart turn over. He picked her up, settled her against his shoulder and turned to Michael.

Michael shook his head, *tsk*ing at him. "You are getting so disgustingly domestic. You're scaring me. You know that, don't you?"

"You're just jealous. How are things going with you and Jenny?"

Michael sighed. "No luck yet. It wouldn't be so bad if Jenny weren't convinced that she can't conceive. None of the women in her family were particularly fertile, and she's had some problems of her own. But we've only been trying for four months. I wish I could get her to relax about it."

If he knew Michael and Jenny, it upset Michael more not to be able to give Jenny what she wanted than it upset Jenny not to get it. But he also knew any show of sympathy was unlikely to be welcomed.

"How do you know it's her? Maybe it's you."

"It is definitely *not* me."

Nathan almost laughed at the indignation he heard in Michael's voice. "Yeah, well, if you do manage to get her pregnant before the month is up, I'll tattoo *your* name on *my* butt."

"I wonder how Daphne will feel about being with a man who has her brother's name tattooed on his posterior."

"Does this mean I have your blessing?"

Michael shrugged. "If you're going to try to win Daphne back, you're going to need somebody's."

Five

She'd put it off as long as she dared. When she got home from work, Daphne folded the robes and put them back where they belonged. Gripping the Saks Fifth Avenue box, she headed down the stairs to Nathan's apartment. She knocked on his door, part of her hoping he wouldn't be home. The kitchen lacked any evidence that he'd been up there before she got home, and his car wasn't out front. Then again, someone had started parking an ancient brown Volvo where Nathan usually parked. If it weren't for the lights burning in his windows, she would have sworn he wasn't home.

She didn't have to wait long before he answered. Nathan swung open the door. A smile crinkled the corners of his eyes, until his gaze traveled lower to the box she carried. "I see you found the present I left you. Coming to say thank you?"

She didn't miss the sarcasm in his voice or the cool expression that came into his hazel eyes. "I can't accept this," she said simply. She extended the box to him, but he made no move to take it from her.

"What's the matter? Were they the wrong size?"

Daphne bit her lip. No, they were the right size. She'd tried on every one of them, and they'd felt like pure heaven against her bare skin. But that wasn't the point.

"Nathan, you know I could never accept something so expensive from you."

"Why not? I can afford it. I've spent more on my cleaning lady."

She cocked her head to one side. Even if he had, she doubted he'd lavished her with such an intimate gift. "I still can't accept it."

"Because it came from me?"

"Yes."

Nathan sighed audibly. "Look, Daphne, I admit I went overboard. I just wanted to give you something you could use. You really helped me out by letting me move in, and you have to admit that robe of yours is the pits."

Finally he took the box she extended toward him. "How about we compromise. You keep one and I'll take the others back?"

Despite herself, she weakened. Besides, she knew she'd simply be churlish to refuse. He'd just admitted that there was nothing personal about his choice of gift. He'd meant to be practical. But Nathan's idea of practicality and the rest of the world's didn't jibe.

"All right."

"Then come on in. I'll help you pick which color." He winked at her before turning to lead the way into the apartment.

Daphne opened her mouth to protest, but Nathan had already disappeared into the living room, taking the box with him. If he'd left it up to her, she'd have chosen whichever one was on top and been done with it. Leave it to Nathan to complicate the simplest decisions.

Sighing, she followed him, leaving the door ajar. She wouldn't be staying that long. But when she got to the archway leading into the other room, she drew up short. Nathan stood in the middle of the living room, a baby blanket tossed over one arm. In his other hand he held what looked like a miniature swing set from which several Sesame Street characters hung. At his feet lay an assortment of stuffed animals and other toys.

She pressed her lips together to suppress a grin. The incongruity of the mucho macho Mr. Ward surrounded by baby toys pricked her sense of the ironic.

She affected a blank look when he glanced at her over his shoulder. She suspected he sensed the humor in her anyway. "I didn't realize what a mess it was in here." He dumped the contents of his arms onto one end of the sofa. "I don't know how women do it."

"Do what?"

"Work, raise a family. Sleep." He motioned for her to sit in the chair across from the sofa. "It seems like every time I lay my head down somewhere, she wakes up."

Daphne made her way to the chair, careful not to step on anything. "What about your career? I mean, haven't you thought of hiring someone to care for Emily when you have to work?"

Nathan bent and scooped up a handful of toys. "For the time being, I haven't got much of a career to speak of. I have a few obligations I couldn't get out of, but for the most part, I'm free to give Emily all my time."

That surprised her. She would have sworn his career meant everything to him. She remembered how driven he'd been as a young man, just starting out. He'd once camped out on the doorstep of a producer he was trying to interest in his band, until the man caved in and listened to the tape. Maybe he'd finally found something that mattered to him more than his music: his daughter.

"Would you like something to drink? I've got soft drinks and a bottle of wine in the fridge."

"No, thanks. I really need to get going."

"If you don't mind, I'm going to have something. I'll be right back."

"Take your time." With any luck, she'd have her robe and herself out the door before he got back. As Nathan exited the room, she sat forward in her chair and reached for the box, which was resting in front of her on the coffee table. Removing the lid, she noticed the emerald green robe lay on top. That wouldn't have been her first choice, but it would do. She lifted it from the box and shook it out.

"Not that one," she heard Nathan say as he reentered the room. He carried a glass of red wine. He sipped from it as he strode toward her. "I'd pick either the red or the black."

He sat, setting the glass down on the table. He pulled the red robe from the box. "Why don't you try it on so you can decide?"

"That isn't necessary."

"Indulge me. If I have to go to the trouble of taking three back, the least you can do is make sure you keep the right one."

She stood, huffing out a breath. "Fine." She snatched the robe from his fingers and pulled it on over her cream-colored blouse and knee-length brown skirt and tied the sash. She spread her arms wide. "How does that look?"

Nathan shook his head. "The black."

Quickly she exchanged robes, not bothering to tie the sash. "There. I'll take the black one."

Nathan grinned. "Good choice."

She couldn't help the answering smile that formed on her lips. He really was incorrigible. And she was being ungrateful. "Thank you, Nathan. It's beautiful."

"No more so than its owner."

Daphne huffed out a breath. "If you're going to start that, I'm leaving."

He flashed her a grin. "I'm not allowed to pay you a compliment?"

"No." Not when he handed them out as freely as chocolate at Hershey Park.

"Then this is going to be a strange sort of friendship we're having."

"And that's what you want? My friendship?"

"That's what I said. Why don't you believe me?"

Because the Nathan she knew was as straightforward as a boomerang. Every time she thought she had a handle on him, he'd turn her assumptions back on her. "I'd better go."

She paused at the archway leading into the hall. One question had been bothering her since the conversation on Christmas day. "Can I ask you something?"

"Sure."

"Why didn't you tell your grandmother you were here? You had to know she'd be worried about you."

"You mean about Emily. My grandmother was worried about Emily. I'd hoped to prove to her that I was capable of taking care of my daughter without her interference."

"And that's important to you."

"It's the most important thing to me right now."

"Why?"

He shrugged. "I don't think you would understand."

"Try me."

He shook his head. "Some other time, maybe. Good night, Daphne."

This was a first, him dismissing her. "Good night," she echoed, feeling unaccountably deflated that he chose not to confide in her.

When she got upstairs, she got ready for bed and checked her answering machine. She played back the lone message, from a man introducing himself as Robert Delaney, the date Elise had set up for her. His well-modulated voice suggested a steady nature.

She dialed the number he'd supplied and waited for him

to pick up. She agreed to getting together for dinner the following evening. When he offered to pick her up, she demurred, remembering Nathan downstairs. She suggested they meet at the restaurant, settled on a time, and hung up.

Daphne surveyed the interior of the posh restaurant on Manhattan's Upper East side, as the mâitre d' escorted her to the table where Robert Delaney waited. She hadn't been able to get out of her office on time, hadn't been able to catch a cab right away, and was presently twenty minutes late for their date.

Now she knew why she'd never heard of this place before. First, she disliked French food, with its heavy sauces and rich desserts. Second, she avoided places that smacked of elitism, as this restaurant certainly did. Despite the size of the establishment, the room was exceptionally quiet, the kind of uptight atmosphere where you'd expect someone's face to crack in half if they actually smiled. Outright laughter would send the patrons into a tizzy. The sooner she got herself out of this place, the better.

Her date stood as she drew closer to the table. His face was handsome enough, she supposed, letting her gaze travel over him. One word came to her mind to describe him: thick. He had a burgeoning pot belly topped off by a barrel chest and a massive neck. She estimated him to be in his early forties. He was a friend of Elise's husband, Garrett, from his days as a college football player. After an injury had sidelined him, he, like Garrett, had dedicated himself to getting into med school. Unlike Garrett, he had already let himself go.

This is what Elise thought would turn her on? No, this is what Elise thought she should marry. The two weren't necessarily one and the same. She schooled her features into a pleasant expression and extended her hand for him to shake.

"Hello, Mr. Delaney. I'm sorry to be late. I got detained at the office."

He enclosed her hand in his, but merely held it. "Please call me Robert, and I suspected as much. You working ladies are always so busy."

You working ladies? Daphne mulled over that statement as she allowed him to seat her. How Neanderthal could you get?

"I hope you don't mind, I ordered dinner for both of us already."

She did mind, but she kept her annoyance to herself. She spread her napkin over her cream-colored suede skirt. "It depends on what you ordered."

She supposed the creaky sound that issued from him was a chuckle. "Your sister told me you had a sense of humor."

"What else did she tell you?"

"Only good things, I assure you."

The appearance of the waiter forestalled any response on Daphne's part. She ordered a glass of chardonnay, while Robert asked for a martini. Daphne raised her eyebrows at that. Did anyone besides James Bond actually drink those things? Daphne sighed. This was going to be a long, long evening.

When the meal ended, Daphne declined Robert's offer of dessert and coffee. She just wanted to get out of there. He'd proved as pompous and self-absorbed as she'd first imagined him. If she had to hear one more story about some celebrity on whose face or butt or breasts he'd performed magical feats of plastic surgery, she'd probably throw up.

And worse yet, she found herself comparing the man who sat across from her with the man who lived down-

tairs from her. A couple of times she'd caught herself
thinking, even Nathan wouldn't say something that egotis-
ical. And truthfully, she never would have been able to
spend an evening in Nathan's company and feel not the
lightest stirring of sexual chemistry. Nathan was a whole
chemistry set by himself.

She supposed she ought to feel relieved to spend time
with a man she had no chance of losing her head over,
but she didn't. Now, what did that say about her?

Daphne removed the napkin from her lap and laid it on
the table. "I have an early day tomorrow."

"I understand. Let me take care of the check, and I'll
take you home."

"That isn't necessary. I'll take a cab."

Sighing, Robert sank back in his chair. "I've really
blown it, haven't I?"

Daphne bit her lip to keep from saying a resounding
yes. "Look, Robert, I think you're a nice guy. But we don't
seem to have anything in common."

"Can I be honest with you about something?"

"Go ahead."

"I know you probably think I'm a pompous windbag,
but I'm not usually like this. I don't really date all that
much. I don't have the time. But when Garrett showed me
your picture, I thought, here is a lady I'd really like to
know better. And knowing Elise, I thought, well . . . If
I'm guilty of anything, it's trying to impress you."

"My sister might be impressed with a place like this,
but I'm not. I prefer a restaurant where the other diners
don't give you dirty looks if you talk above a whisper."

"Truthfully, I've never eaten here before. It is a little
stiff, isn't it?"

She grinned. "A little."

"You know, there's a great place down by NYU that
serves chocolate cake topped with fresh whipped cream

that you could die for, and you have to scream over the college kids to be heard."

"Sounds like my kind of place."

Three hours later, Daphne glanced up at her town house as Robert pulled the car to a halt out front. As far as she could tell, not a light burned anywhere inside. She breathed a sigh of relief. Nathan must already be asleep. She'd be grateful to skip a confrontation with him right now.

Daphne pushed open her car door and allowed Robert to hand her out of the car. After he'd relaxed around her, he'd shown her a side of himself that she liked much better. When he told her that he donated much of his time to a foundation that financed surgery for children born with facial deformities, she'd found in him a kindred altruistic spirit. Maybe Elise's taste in men wasn't as off as she'd thought.

She smiled as she rose to her feet beside him. "Thanks for a lovely evening."

"It's not quite over yet. I'll walk you up."

With a hand on her waist, he led her across the street and up the stairs. When they reached the top of the stairs, he took her keys from her, opened the door and held it for her to precede him. Daphne flipped on the light that illuminated the entranceway and the stairs leading up to her apartment.

"I really do have an early day tomorrow," Daphne began.

"I understand." He took one of her hands in his. "I hope you'll let me call you again."

If he'd asked her that earlier in the evening, she'd have said no. But now, it didn't seem like such a bad idea. "I'd like that."

"Would I be pressing my luck if I told you I wanted to kiss you good night?"

Motivated more by curiosity than by desire, she said, "No, you wouldn't be pressing your luck."

Daphne closed her eyes as he leaned toward her and pressed his mouth gently to hers. His lips were warm and moist, pleasant, but not stirring. No sweeping desire spread through her at his touch. No wild pulses pounded in her veins. When he drew away, she opened her eyes and gazed at him.

"That was nice."

"Yes," she agreed. Nice. Unassuming. *Boring.*

"Well, I'd better go."

She opened the door and let him out. She watched him climb into his car, rev the engine and drive away. Sighing, she closed the door and turned to head up the stairs. Seeing Nathan standing by his open doorway, his shoulder leaning against the frame, caused her to back up into the front door.

Clearly, he was angry with her, but he had no reason to be. However, she had every right to be angry with him. How long had he been standing there spying on her? It wouldn't surprise her if he'd watched them through the peephole in the door.

"I thought you said you weren't going to do that every time I come through the door."

"I said I wouldn't unless I was worried about you, which I was. You never come home this late."

She pushed away from the door. "Well, forgive me for not keeping you abreast of my social calendar. I had a date."

"Is that who that guy was? I thought he was here to inspect the carpet."

"What is that supposed to mean?"

"With all that groveling, I'm sure he got a few carpet

fibers up his nose. 'Do I dare to kiss you good night?'
Nathan mimicked in a high-pitched nasal voice. "Please
Is that the kind of man who appeals to you these days?

"You mean a man who asks instead of taking what h
wants? Yes, that appeals to me *very* much."

She took a step in the direction of the stairs, then turne
back. She couldn't resist throwing one more bit of fuel o
the fire.

"And just so you know, Robert is an excellent kisser.'

"You call what he gave you a kiss?" Nathan strode to
ward her, grasped her upper arms and pulled her up agains
him. His mouth descended on hers, claiming her lips in
fiery kiss designed to conquer. A tremor shivered throug
her as his tongue invaded her mouth, plundering, insisten
demanding a response from her. Despite herself, sh
moaned and her hands slid around his back to hold hir
closer.

Hearing his answering groan, a sense of feminine satis
faction rippled through her. He wasn't any more immun
to her than she was to him. One of his hands rose to cradl
her head in his palm. The other lowered to the small o
her back, joining their bodies as closely as their clothin,
allowed. Even through the layers of wool and suede, sh
clearly felt the outline of his erection against her belly
She couldn't help herself; she arched against him, strivin,
to get closer.

Even as she surrendered to him, he pushed her away
Slowly, she opened her eyes and gazed up at him. His eye
had darkened to a rich olive color. A hint of a smile playe
at the corners of his mouth. For a moment she thought h
would kiss her again. Part of her wanted him to kiss he
again.

Instead, he straightened and ran his thumb down he
cheek. "Now that, Daphne Thorne, is a kiss." Without an

other word, he sauntered back into his apartment and closed the door.

Shaky, trembling, her breathing ragged, Daphne leaned against the wall, staring after him. She ran her tongue along the seam of her lips, and tasted him all over again.

For once she had to agree with him. That had definitely been one heck of a kiss.

Six

Sitting on Daphne's living-room sofa two nights later, Nathan gripped the handle of the baseball bat she usually kept by the door. Although she hadn't locked the kitchen doors on him after that first time, Nathan doubted Daphne looked forward to finding him ensconced in her apartment, either. And after the way he'd kissed her the other night, he didn't plan on taking any chances with her temper.

But he did intend on seeing her. Tonight. In the past couple of days, she'd developed some sort of radar where he was concerned, disappearing the moment he came around. If he heard her in the kitchen, she'd left the room by the time he made it up the stairs. If he heard her at the door, she slipped past him before he had the time to confront her. She was avoiding him, and he planned to put an end to it.

He'd been out of line with that kiss. Seeing her with that escapee from a Milquetoast factory she'd brought home had filled him with such jealousy, he'd barely been able to control himself. But he wasn't sorry. Not after the way she'd melted in his arms. She had so much passion inside her, too much to ever be satisfied with a man who couldn't equal her in that regard.

Maybe that's why she was avoiding him. She'd wanted that kiss as much as he had. Otherwise he'd have ended up with a groin full of knee or some other equally pleasant punishment for touching her. Maybe she avoided him because she refused to acknowledge that in that moment she'd wanted him as much as he'd wanted her.

Hearing the key turn in the lock, Nathan dropped the bat to the floor and stood. He hadn't turned on a light, not wanting to alert Daphne to the fact that someone was in her living room. As the door opened, light from the hallway washed into the room. He saw the look of alarm come over Daphne's face when she first saw him, followed by an expression of relief, then burgeoning annoyance.

"What are you doing in here?" She dropped her purse and briefcase by the door and shut it behind her.

"I wanted to talk to you, and since you've been avoiding me—"

"I haven't been avoiding you. I've been busy." She shrugged out of her coat and hung it on the coatrack by the door.

"With your new *friend?*" He couldn't keep some of the bitterness he felt from seeping into his voice.

"Not that it's any of your business, but yes. I enjoy his company." Nathan followed her as she turned and headed toward the kitchen. She stopped at the refrigerator, got out a bottle of water, and took a swig. She turned to face him. "Is there something you wanted?"

"To apologize. I was out of line the other night."

"The other night?" She shrugged. "I've already forgotten about it."

Like hell she had. Color stole into her cheeks, belying that notion. "All the same, I'm sorry. I saw you two together and, well, you can't blame me for feeling a little possessive. After all, I was your first."

"My, how territorial of you, Nathan. If you're planning on marking your scent all over my furniture, please restrain yourself. The cleaning bill would be astronomical."

"I meant that I can't help feeling protective of you. I still care about you. I don't want to see you get hurt."

She shook her head and stepped away from him in a telling gesture. What did she seek to deny? That he cared about her or that he had a right to?

"I'm a big girl, Nathan. I can take care of myself." She recapped the water bottle and returned it to the refrigerator. "Is there anything else?"

"Spend tomorrow night with me?" She hadn't really been looking at him before, but now she focused a speculative glare on him, probably trying to gauge if he was serious or not. "I already have some champagne," he continued. "We could order in some dinner. Just two old friends ringing in the new year."

She didn't say anything for a long time. "I'm sorry. I've already made a date for the evening."

"I see." Trying to keep the disappointment he felt from showing on his face, from creeping into his voice, he turned away from her. "Well, then, good night, Daphne. Have a good time."

Daphne stood staring after Nathan as he disappeared down the stairs, not knowing what to make of him. He had been the one to hurt her, so why did she feel like she'd betrayed him somehow by making plans with another man? She didn't owe Nathan anything, not even an explanation of her actions.

But truthfully, she didn't look forward to the evening with Robert with much relish. He was a nice man, one she felt completely comfortable with but felt no real spark of attraction for. Nathan, on the other hand, attracted her like a paper clip to a magnet. She'd lied to him about forgetting the kiss they'd shared. Truthfully, the knowledge that she could still respond to him in such a physical way shocked her down to her toes.

And if she hadn't been mistaken, Nathan had been as

affected as she. That surprised her even more. She didn't harbor any illusions that he'd spent the past fifteen years pining away for her. With his looks and notoriety, he could have any woman he wanted. If you believed the tabloids, he'd already had just about every woman in North America worth having.

So what was he doing slumming with her? And why did knowing that she could still move him sexually after all these years give her such a rush?

Daphne sighed. Maybe she was simply like countless other women, blinded from what was good for them by the excitement of a man who would only bring them heart-ache.

Too tired to puzzle out her own motives, Daphne turned out the kitchen light and headed toward the stairs. She hadn't taken the time to see if she had anything in her closet suitable to wear the following night.

Probably not. Usually when she attended a formal function she borrowed something from Victoria. Both women wore about the same size and were about the same height, even though Daphne was a bit bustier and Victoria a little wider in the hips. She'd go over to Victoria's apartment tomorrow and see if her closet contained anything she could wear.

The following afternoon, Daphne let herself into Victoria's apartment on Central Park West. Standing in the foyer, she scanned the room. She hadn't expected the assault of memories that overtook her. All the times she and Victoria had stayed up talking, laughing, planning what they would do. Would she ever stop feeling the loss of the friend that had meant so much to her?

Daphne headed straight for the bedroom, unable to stand the memories. She needed to get out of there as quickly as possible. Victoria's closet spanned the entire length of one wall. Daphne folded back the mirrored doors and surveyed the apparel in front of her: dresses, shirts, skirts, evening gowns, shoes. Victoria had joked that clothing was her one financial vice. She'd loved shopping, although Daphne guessed she'd worn only a small fraction of the articles hanging there. Many still had the store tags still hanging from them.

Daphne unzipped one of the garment bags housing a black satin evening gown with a fitted bodice and a slim, floor-length skirt. Holding it up in front of her, she gauged how she would look in the gown. The simple cut of the garment was deceptively revealing. Thankfully, the gown came with a matching shrug that would allow her a little more modesty.

"The red one would look better on you."

Daphne spun around to see Bradley standing in the doorway to the room. He wore a casual sweater and slacks. In his hand he held a tumbler of what looked like Scotch. His lips were curled in what could only be described as a sneer.

Good lord, just what she needed. More venom from Victoria's stepson. Something about the way he watched her made the hairs on the back of her neck stand up.

"Or how about the lavender?" he continued. With his free hand, he gestured toward another dress housed in an identical clear garment bag. Inside lay a beautiful sleeveless gown, which Daphne knew was a designer original.

"One thing I'll say about Victoria. She always did know how to dress."

And one thing she knew was that Bradley was no fashion consultant. "What are you doing here?"

He raised the glass to his lips, downing the last of the liquid. "This was my mother's apartment."

"Don't you mean your stepmother's?"

"Yeah, that, too." He straightened, crossed to Victoria's

dresser, and placed the glass on the unprotected wood surface. When he turned to face Daphne, a feral smile graced his lips.

"That was some cute trick you pulled with the building security the other day. I bet that pair downstairs were two of the original Keystone Kops."

"That's why it pays to be observant."

"Oh, I notice everything about you. Hot date tonight?"

"Why would you care?"

He gazed pointedly at her breasts. "I can think of two big reasons."

Fighting the urge to slap his smug face, she grabbed the garment bag that contained the matching jacket to the black dress from the closet and slung it over her arm. "I'll stick with what I have."

"Suit yourself."

He took a step toward her and Daphne felt alarm ring through every synapse of her body. Instinctively, she backed away from him, effectively cornering herself with the closet on one side, the bed on the other, and the wall behind her. She doubted Bradley would try to harm her physically. Intimidation, not violence, was his game.

He proved her right when he leaned toward her, close enough for her to smell the alcohol on his breath. "If you need any help dressing—or undressing—be sure to let me know."

"Go to hell, Bradley."

She brushed past him, out of the room and to the front door. Daphne gritted her teeth, hearing Bradley's laughter echoing behind her.

Stepping into the elevator car, she leaned against the rear wall and sighed. She would have to redouble her efforts in coming up with the money she needed, even if that meant mortgaging the town house she'd worked so hard to keep free and clear. The sooner she got Bradley out of her life, the better.

Hours later, Daphne had put her encounter with Bradley out of her mind. She stood at the center island of the kitchen, skimming over the daily newspaper as she sipped from a glass of orange juice. She'd dressed in the black satin sheath, pinned her braids into an upswept style and donned the diamond earrings and pendant she'd splurged on in her other life as an up-and-coming young executive.

Hearing a high-pitched whistle, she raised her head and looked in the direction of the back staircase. Nathan emerged from the floor below.

"You look fabulous, sweetheart."

Daphne couldn't contain the blush that spread across her cheeks at his words. She ducked her head and turned her face away from him.

He came to stand across the counter from her. "Oh, I'm sorry. I forgot. I'm not supposed to compliment you. You look . . . um . . . adequate. Is that better?"

No, that wasn't better at all. His chauvinistic way of complimenting her had reached some totally feminine place inside her. But she couldn't tell him that, so she said nothing. Her gaze roved over him. He wore a pair of casual black slacks and a cream-colored T-shirt. Not exactly evening wear for a night on the town.

She really shouldn't care what his plans were, but after he'd asked her to share the evening with him, she couldn't help being curious about what he intended to do instead.

"What are you going to do tonight?"

"Emily and I will be here. She's got a bit of a cold, and I don't want to take her out."

He'd be here alone on New Year's Eve? She bit her lip. She didn't appreciate what he'd done to her—put her in the rare and uncomfortable position of feeling sorry for him. No one should have to welcome in the new year alone.

"Nathan, um . . . I . . . Are you sure you'll be all right?"

"I'm a big boy. I can take care of myself, too."

"I know. I—" Before she could say any more, the door-bell sounded.

"That must be your *friend.*"

"I-I'd better go." She picked up her jacket and slid it on.

"Good night." Biting her lip, Daphne picked up her evening bag, slung the strap over her shoulder, and headed for the stairs.

When Daphne opened the door to Robert, a slow, appreciative smile spread across his face. "All I can say is, wow!"

She grinned, hearing what sounded like awe in his voice. "You like?"

He moved toward her, cupping her face in the palms of his hands. "You look stunning."

For once, a frisson of excitement stirred inside her. She knew he intended to kiss her. Perhaps a real kiss this time, not one of his usual chaste offerings. A kiss by which she could gauge her attraction to him. She let her eyes drift closed in anticipation.

"So, where are you two kids headed tonight?"

Hearing Nathan's voice, Daphne froze. She was going to have to put a bell on either the door or the man to keep him from surprising her every time she turned around. She glanced up at Robert, who eyed her speculatively. She supposed he had every right to question her relationship to Nathan. Damn Nathan and his sense of perfect timing.

As for Nathan, his indolent pose by his doorway didn't fool her. He must have flown down the back stairs to make it to the door that quickly. Undoubtedly, he'd listened to every word they'd said.

She motioned in Nathan's direction. "Robert, this is Nathan. He rents the downstairs apartment from me. Nathan this is Robert Delaney."

Daphne looked from one man to the other, as each made only the barest acknowledgement of the other.

She felt Robert's hand come to rest on her waist. A possessive gesture if ever there was one. "We'd better get going," Robert said.

Daphne groaned inwardly. A rose was a rose was a rose and a man was a man was a man. Even an innocuous one like Robert turned into a primitive with the right provocation.

But he had nothing to worry about from Nathan. Despite the kiss they'd shared the other night, Daphne doubted Nathan harbored any feelings of jealousy as he claimed. If anything, it wounded his ego to see her with a man he considered his inferior. He'd have to get over it.

Yet, Robert was right about one thing: It was best they got going.

She retrieved her coat from the coatrack and allowed Robert to help her on with it. Poised at the door, she said, "Good night, Nathan."

"Have a good time."

Again she felt a pang of guilt at leaving him alone. She couldn't do anything about it, so she nodded and allowed Robert to lead her from the building.

Seven

When she opened the front door two hours later, well before midnight, Daphne wasn't surprised to see Nathan standing in his open doorway, waiting for her. She leaned against the closed door, waiting for him to say something. Waiting for him to gloat about her doomed evening. Instead he offered her a sympathetic smile that pulled at her heartstrings.

"What happened?"

"Robert's a doctor. He got called in on an emergency."

"He didn't bring you home?"

She almost smiled, hearing the indignation in his voice, knowing that such a thing was taboo in Nathan's eyes. If you took a woman out, you brought her home, period.

"I volunteered to take a cab back."

Nathan raised his eyebrows in a gesture that said what he thought about that situation. Not much. But no one said he had to like what she did.

She pushed away from the door and shrugged out of her coat, hanging it and her purse on the rack by the door. When she turned around, she noted a spark of desire in Nathan's eyes as they scanned her figure. Immediately, an answering emotion stirred inside her. Knowing he wanted her was a powerful aphrodisiac, one she lacked the power to ignore.

She licked her suddenly dry lips. "I'd better go get changed."

"Or you could spend the rest of the evening with me. I still have that bottle of champagne. . . ."

She wondered if this was how the fly felt when the spider beckoned her into his lair. If she used the sense God gave her, she'd go lock herself in her bedroom, out of harm's way. But despite everything that made sense, she wanted to be with him.

"I'd like that."

He held out his hand to her and she didn't hesitate. She walked to him and placed her hand in his grasp.

Nathan led her inside and closed the door. "Are you hungry?"

She shook her head. She'd eaten very little, but she wasn't in the mood for food. She didn't know what she wanted, except that she didn't want to be alone.

"Then make yourself at home. I'll get the champagne."

Daphne headed for the living room, surprised to find it devoid of all the clutter that had been there the other night. In fact, the entire room looked like it could pass a white-glove inspection. Feeling restless, she roamed around the room. She walked over to the window and looked out. She didn't understand the mood that claimed her.

Behind her she heard Nathan enter. She turned to see him carrying a tray laden with two filled champagne flutes and an open bottle of Cristal. He set the tray down on the side table. Then, picking up the two glasses, he walked toward her.

She forced a smile to her face as she accepted one of the glasses from him. "What happened to all the toys?"

"The troops were here earlier today."

She sampled a dainty sip from her glass. "The troops?"

"My grandmother, sister, and a couple of my cousins. Now that they know where I am, they decided to pay me a visit. I'm sure they wanted to see for themselves that I wasn't keeping Emily in some sort of hovel."

"And were they satisfied with your accommodations?"

"The apartment they approve of, except for the kitchen. It's my housekeeping skills they find completely lacking."

"I can't imagine why."

"What is that supposed to mean?"

"Face it, Nathan. You're not the most domesticated man I've ever met."

"And here your brother was complaining I was becoming too domesticated for his taste."

"My brother thinks that any man who can pick his own socks up off the floor is a pantywaist."

Nathan laughed. "I'm not that bad. I do know how to use a hamper."

Daphne smiled as a memory washed over her. "Do you remember that apartment you used to have on Avenue A? The one you shared with, what was his name, Steve?"

"You mean Stanley."

"That's right, Stanley. Not only was the neighborhood downright dangerous, the elevator never worked, and if it weren't for some woman, usually me, coming over and cleaning up, you guys would have lived in absolute neglect."

Nathan took a sip from his glass, watching her with a renewed intensity in his eyes. "Somehow, that's not my most memorable recollection of the place."

Biting her lip, she turned away from him, toward the window. Somehow, that wasn't her most memorable recollection either. Yet she didn't want to wallow in memories of the past. Dealing with the present gave her enough to contend with, a present that left her feeling melancholy and oddly off-kilter. She gulped down the rest of her drink, then placed the glass on the windowsill.

A moment later, she felt Nathan come up behind her, cupping her shoulders in his palms. "Are you all right?"

For once she could be honest with him. "I don't know." She didn't protest as his arms slid around her waist, drawing her back against him. She needed ballast in the emotional storm that buffeted her. Nathan was as good an anchor as any.

"Do you know what I was doing last year at this time? I was in a hotel room in L.A., supposedly hosting a party for some bigwigs on the coast. But I spent the night hiding in my bedroom, wishing midnight would finally come and maybe I could get rid of all those people. They didn't know me, didn't want to know me. They were interested in Nathan Ward the superstar, and I simply didn't feel like being 'on' that night. That was about the worst I've ever felt in my whole life."

Daphne closed her eyes and pressed her lips together. How did he always seem to know what was inside her and find a way to make her feel better? It was uncanny, as if he could read her mind, as if he knew her so well that she didn't have to use words for him to understand.

With those few simple words he'd given a name to her malaise. Plain, old-fashioned loneliness. Victoria had been her one true friend, her rock. Victoria had also been her crutch, her blinder from the knowledge that, outside of work, she really hadn't made any sort of life for herself. She didn't have so much as a cat to come home to. If it weren't for Nathan, she'd be alone right now, living out her misery in solitude.

And she remembered another time, the first time he'd done that for her. She'd been standing at her mother's grave site, wishing she were anywhere but there, listening to the minister drone on and on about ashes and dust and the benefits of heavenly reward.

Tears welled up in her eyes, and she strove to hold them

back. Her mother wouldn't have wanted her to weep. Tears, her mother had believed, were for those who hadn't led a good life, and Camille Thorne had definitely lived a good life.

Suddenly, Daphne had felt someone take her hand. Startled, she'd looked up to find Nathan standing next to her. Her first impulse had been to pull away from him. In all the time she'd known him, he'd never taken any liberties with her, never so much as taken her hand if she hadn't touched him first. But he'd squeezed her hand in a way that had brought two words to her mind: *I'm here.*

For two years he'd been her shadow, annoying her, popping up whenever she turned around. For the first time, she'd welcomed his presence and the simple reassurance he'd offered. Turning her attention back to the minister, she'd laced her fingers with his and smiled a secret smile of acceptance.

Like most of the other mourners, he'd followed her family back to the house. He'd driven that puke-green monstrosity he'd called a car, which operated only in forward gear, and then only sometimes.

He hadn't attempted to talk to her, but every now and again she'd seen him standing off to the side, watching her. She didn't understand him. After all the unkind things she'd said to him, after all the tricks she'd played on him in an effort to discourage his interest in her, why had he come? And why did his silent, patient concern for her seem to soften something inside her?

It had been early evening before most of the guests had started to leave. She stood under the archway to the living room assessing the damage. Most of the food had been consumed. No one had spilled anything major or trampled anything noxious into the carpet. Not bad considering the number of people who'd been in and out all day.

A pair of hands settled on her shoulders, giving her

muscles a gentle squeeze. She didn't need to look to know those hands belonged to Nathan.

"I'd better be going, too."

She hadn't seen him for the last hour or so and had been disappointed to think he'd left without saying good-bye to her. Her mood immediately lifted and she turned to face him.

"I'll walk you out."

She could tell her offer surprised him. He could find the front door as well as anyone else. But he said nothing when she linked her arm with his. Together they walked to the curb where he'd parked his car. Rather than get inside, he sat on the hood, his legs braced apart, his arms crossed in front of him, as if he was waiting for something.

Daphne swallowed. Could he sense in her what she wanted? Having reached the advanced age of sixteen without so much as a decent kiss from a boy, she was hardly in a position to gauge what guys thought or didn't think, knew or didn't know. Worse yet, she knew he knew about her lack of experience. She wouldn't be surprised if he'd made sure no one else had approached her.

His history was a different story altogether. If she listened to neighborhood gossip, he'd already deflowered half the girls within a three-block radius. One of the main reasons she'd always avoided him was on the off chance that any of those rumors were actually true.

But he'd touched something inside her today, something that made her question whether she'd been wrong about him. Either way, they couldn't stand there forever. She had to say something.

She blurted out the first words that came to her mind. "When are you going to get a decent car?"

"When I get a decent recording contract." He ran a hand across her forehead, ruffling her bangs. "Is that what you wanted to talk to me about? My car?"

She shook her head. What she wanted was entirely too foolish to voice out loud. "I-I wanted to thank you for coming."

He ran his hand down her arm. "How are you holding up?"

"I'm fine." She'd given him the same answer she'd given everyone else who'd asked her that question. Somehow, she'd held herself together all day, playing hostess, enduring the countless stories of her mother told by well-meaning friends and relatives. She hadn't shed one tear. But now, with his probing gaze on her, she couldn't seem to hold it together any longer. Tears pooled in her eyes, threatening to spill down her cheeks.

"I miss her so much, Nathan. I don't know what to do."

Nathan's arms closed around her, gathering her against him. She went to him willingly, laying her cheek against his chest. She poured out to him all the words, all the sorrow she hadn't shared with anyone else. She'd had no one else to share with. Her father was nearly prostrate with grief himself. Her brother, Michael, was so angry, no one could reach him. And her sister, Elise, had her boyfriend, Garrett, to console her. Daphne had borne her own grief all alone.

When her tears subsided, he handed her his handkerchief. "Are you okay?"

She nodded, dabbing at her eyes. "Thank you."

"Anytime, sweetheart."

Hearing the endearment on his lips brought her back to her reason for being with him in the first place. Seizing her courage, she leaned forward, braced her hands on his shoulders and pressed her mouth to his. She pulled away almost immediately, but that brief contact left her trembling and slightly breathless. She opened her eyes and gazed up at him. He regarded her with hooded, darkened eyes that bore an expression she didn't understand.

"Is that what you've been waiting for all this time?" she whispered.

He smiled. "It's a start."

He ruffled her bangs again, set her away from him, and without another word, got into his car and drove away.

She lingered at the curb, watching him, wondering what new discoveries the coming days would bring.

Now, in the present, she wondered if she would have done things differently, knowing what she'd set in motion that night. Immediately she knew she wouldn't have changed anything. She had been wrong about him in so many ways. Perhaps she'd misjudged him again, assuming he had some ulterior motive for moving in to her apartment. All she knew was that she'd never felt so safe, so protected as she did now in Nathan's arms.

The sound of horns honking mixed with shouts of Happy New Year outside the window snapped her out of her reverie. She turned to face him. "It must be midnight."

"Happy New Year, Daphne." She watched as Nathan's head descended toward hers. She didn't deny how much she wanted his kiss, how much she wanted to feel connected to him. She welcomed the warmth of his mouth on hers, the heat of his body that seeped into her soul. She fused her body to his, as one kiss turned to many. Sweet-sipping kisses that grew longer and more intense until he finally took her mouth in a breathtaking kiss that rocked her to her very core.

She clung to him, wrapping her arms around his neck to hold him close. Despite herself, she wanted him, all of him. She wanted the ecstasy that only he had been able to give her.

Abruptly, he pulled away from her, looking at her with an expression she didn't understand. She stood there a moment, dazed, wondering about the sudden change in him.

Then he released her, actually pushed her away from him and turned his back to her.

Stunned, she concentrated on dragging air into her lungs. By the movement of his shoulders and rib cage, she could tell he, too, was concentrating on getting his breathing back to normal. He'd been as affected as she, so why had he pushed her away?

"Nathan?"

"Go upstairs, Daphne."

"What?"

"I said, go upstairs."

"Why?"

"Because right now my self-control isn't what it ought to be."

She pressed her lips together, fighting a wave of disappointment she had no right to feel. She had no right to expect he would be as moved by their kiss as she had been.

"I'm here and you're horny. Is that it?"

He snapped around to face her. He took a step toward her so that only a scant few inches separated them. "Don't you think I remember exactly how good it was between us?" As he spoke he traced the swell of her breast above the square neckline of her gown with his index finger.

Daphne closed her eyes and bit her lip. Memories of other times, other places, flooded through her, heating her blood, making her ache. His hand slid down to capture her breast. His thumb stroked a lazy pattern over her nipple. "Don't you think I remember exactly where to touch you to get you to stay with me?"

She pressed her lips together to stifle the moan that rose in her throat. She guessed that if he knew how much he affected her, he would pull away from her. But she couldn't muffle the sound completely. He did exactly as she'd expected, dropping his hand to his side.

She opened her eyes and gazed at him. His eyes were

hooded, and a wistful smile tilted up one corner of his sensuous mouth.

"For a change, I'm trying to do the right thing." He briefly cupped one palm around her shoulder, in a gesture of conciliation. "I don't think your *friend* would appreciate it if we let things go any further."

Daphne lowered her head, feeling heat steal into her cheeks. She hadn't given Robert a single thought since she'd stepped over the threshold of Nathan's apartment. "No, I don't suppose he would."

With a hand under her chin, he tilted her face up to his. "Now, go home, before I change my mind."

Without a word, she pulled away from him and headed toward the door. Tears sprang into her eyes, unwanted and unbidden. She wasn't sure why. Maybe it was because she was on the verge of making another disastrous mistake, and it had been Nathan, *Nathan*, who'd had sense enough to pull away.

Although she knew he was watching her, she couldn't bear to look at him. She'd made enough of a fool of herself that evening without crying in front of him.

With as much dignity as she could muster, she opened the front door, stepped into the hall, and ran all the way up the stairs to her apartment.

Nathan watched her go, a mixture of emotions playing inside him. Half of him wished he'd never been so stupid as to let her get anywhere near that door. But as much as he wanted her, he refused to settle for her coming to him on any terms. He might be as egotistical as she claimed, but when he made love to her, he wanted her with him because she wanted him, not because she was lonely or out of sorts, or, worst of all, because some other man had disappointed her.

"Ah, Daphne." He sighed, closing the door she'd left

open during her hasty departure. "What am I going to do with you?"

He spent a restless night, dreaming of the possibilities.

The next morning, Daphne woke to the sound of the telephone ringing. She reached for the receiver and brought it to her ear. "Hello?"

"So, how did it go last night?"

Daphne groaned, hearing her sister's cheerful voice on the other end of the line. That, and the fact that her sister's question brought to mind her time spent with Nathan, not Robert. She brushed her braids out of her eyes and looked at the clock. It was barely after seven in the morning.

"Do you have any idea what time it is?"

"Time for you to 'fess up. How are things going with Robert? You know what they say, the person you start the new year with is the person you'll end up with."

"Well, then it won't be with Robert. He got called in on an emergency and had to send me home."

"Oh, no. I'm so sorry, Daphne. You were all alone on New Year's Eve?"

Daphne debated whether to tell Elise about being with Nathan. In the end, the truth won out. "Not exactly. Nathan and I had a glass of champagne."

The change in her sister's voice was immediate. "Nathan. I swear that man is nothing but trouble."

"He didn't do anything, Elise." In fact, he'd saved them both from making a terrible mistake. But Elise didn't have to know that. "He was a perfect gentleman."

"I'll bet. So, when are you going to see Robert again?"

"I don't know. We didn't make any plans."

Daphne sighed. She didn't want to leave her sister with the false impression that she expected any great romance to blossom between the two of them. "Look Elise. I like Robert a lot. He's a really sweet man."

"But—"

"But I can't see anything serious developing between us."

"And this is on the basis of what? A few dates? If you remember, I couldn't stand Garrett when we met, and we've been married for more than fifteen years."

True, but even from the beginning, their animosity had camouflaged a powerful attraction. That wasn't the case with her and Robert.

"I'm sorry, Elise. I know he's a good friend of Garrett's—"

"He's a good man."

"But not for me."

"This is because of *him,* isn't it?"

Daphne wished she could say that Nathan had nothing to do with her decision, but she couldn't. They still had unresolved business between them that prevented her from focusing on anything, on anyone else. She couldn't move on with the present until she put the past to rest.

"Yes."

"I hope you know what you're doing."

Daphne sighed, leaning back on her pillows. "Me, too."

Eight

Daphne walked through the front door of the town house the following night, bearing a shopping bag full of Chinese food. No time like the present to put her plan into action. Except she didn't really have a plan or any real idea what she wanted to accomplish. She knew that she wanted things settled between her and Nathan, whatever that might mean. She could only do that if she spoke to him.

She knocked on Nathan's door, switching her weight from one foot to the other while she waited for him to answer. He came to the door a moment later, wearing a plain white T-shirt tucked into a pair of jeans.

He grinned at her. "Hi, stranger."

"Hi." She swallowed, looking up into his gorgeous hazel eyes. She hadn't expected to feel so awkward around him, but considering what they'd been doing the last time they'd been together, she really shouldn't have been surprised. She sensed no such hesitancy in him, and it annoyed her. Maybe most of all she needed to regain the upper hand she'd held until a couple of nights ago.

"I went a little crazy at the take-out place. I was hoping you'd be able to help me out." She held up the bag as if to prove the veracity of her words. "You haven't eaten yet, have you?"

"No, I haven't eaten yet."

She saw the glint of amusement in his eyes and chose to ignore it. "Good. Meet me in the kitchen in ten minutes."

She turned away from him then, and walked up the stairs to her apartment. She sensed his eyes on her, but didn't turn around to check.

After depositing the shopping bag in the kitchen, she headed up to her bedroom to change. She considered putting on the robe Nathan had given her, but decided against it. That might send him any number of wrong messages. She settled instead for an oversized T-shirt and a pair of baggy sweats.

By the time she got down to the kitchen, Nathan had already begun unloading the various cartons and trays from the bag. "What army were you planning to feed with all this stuff?"

She went to the cabinet to retrieve plates and silverware. "I didn't know what you liked, so I got a little of everything." She placed the plates on the counter and picked up a spoon to begin serving herself.

"So, there was a method to your madness."

She shrugged, feigning a nonchalance she didn't feel. "I was buying dinner for myself; it seemed only fair that I bring you something, too."

She could tell he didn't believe a word she said. Sometimes Nathan proved a bit too astute for her liking. Attempting to focus his attention elsewhere, she asked, "Where's Emily?"

"Asleep, finally. She's teething and refused to take a nap all day. She went down a half-hour ago, probably due to sheer exhaustion. I give her another twenty minutes before she cranks up again."

"Poor baby."

"Poor baby? Poor daddy. My little alarm clock must have woken me up about four times last night."

"Poor Nathan," she said, laughing as he stuck out his bottom lip, looking very much like a little boy complaining of a boo-boo.

Daphne continued to fill her plate with fried rice, dumplings, boneless spare ribs, and shrimp with broccoli. She didn't touch the spicier dishes, which she knew Nathan preferred. That much she'd remembered.

She took her plate over to the little kitchen table and sat down. Nathan followed a few minutes later, carrying the bottle of wine she'd bought and tucked in the bag with the food.

"I take it this is intended for tonight."

"Yes. I'd forgotten about it." She started to rise from her chair.

"Sit. I can handle it." In a few short minutes, he'd opened the wine and poured them each a glass. She took hers from his fingers and sipped deeply.

"How was your day?" he asked, claiming the seat across from her.

"Okay, I guess." She forked a bit of shrimp and rice into her mouth and chewed. She wasn't about to tell him about her visit to the bank to inquire about a loan. She'd quickly learned that it had been Victoria's wealth that had made loaning them money the first time a palatable idea. Without Victoria in the picture, Daphne stood as much chance of borrowing what she needed as she did begging for it on the street.

She could always put up her town house as collateral, but if anything, that would put her in a worse position than she was already in. At least now, she stood to lose only her business; if she couldn't make the loan payments, she could lose her home, as well.

Just the same old story, Daphne had mused as she'd headed back to her office: no one willing to lend you money when you actually needed it. The rich got richer and Daphne just sank deeper into the hole.

"I spoke to a carpenter today about replacing the cabinets downstairs. He'll be here on Thursday to measure. He'll install them sometime next week."

"I'll take Emily to my grandmother's that day."

"There's no need. You can stay up here, if you like."

He raised an eyebrow at that. "You don't mind?"

"Not at all. Since I'm displacing you, the least I can do is offer you somewhere else to stay."

"I see. Emily and I will be happy to take you up on your offer."

"Good." Now that they'd exhausted that topic of conversation, she focused on her plate, trying to concentrate on savoring her meal.

"You didn't ask me how my day was."

She glanced up at him, pausing in her task of bringing her fork to her mouth. "How was your day?"

"Let's see. I changed five diapers, made four bottles, and reached the very messy conclusion that Emily does not like string beans. All in all, a rather productive day."

He grinned at her, and she found his humor infectious. She cocked her head to one side, watching him. "Do you miss it?" she asked. "The star treatment, the entourage, or whatever?" She really had no idea what his life was like.

"I never did have much of an entourage, just a few key hangers-on and yes-people. They all think I'm crazy for giving up my career with my biggest single still riding the charts—not to mention putting them out of work."

"Why did you?"

"I didn't want to wake up one day and realize I'm a forty-year-old has-been. The music industry is definitely a young man's game, and I don't qualify anymore." He leaned back in his chair. "I'm a firm subscriber to the adage that says, leave them wanting more."

"I see." Somehow, his answer disappointed her. She'd hoped his daughter had more to do with his decision than his ego. She should have known better.

"I'd been considering retiring for a while, but when Emily came along, she made the decision for me."

Daphne lowered her head, silently chiding herself for once again jumping to conclusions about him.

When they'd finished their meal, she suggested they go into the living room to open their fortune cookies and finish the bottle of wine. She sat at one end of the sofa while Nathan claimed the other, sitting in such a way that he partially faced her.

An amused smile graced his lips as he surveyed her. His silence and the glint of humor in his eyes disconcerted her. She took a sip from her glass, then placed it on the coffee table on one of the little crystal coasters she kept there.

"Why do you keep looking at me like that?"

"I'm just wondering when you're going to tell me why you're being so nice to me. After the way you bolted out of my apartment the other night, I wouldn't have been surprised if you weren't speaking to me at all."

Daphne snorted. She'd known the moment of truth had to arrive sometime. But what could she tell him, when she didn't know herself what she wanted from him? Her only thought was to echo back at him what he'd told her so many times.

"I suppose I could use a friend right now. My roster is kind of low at the moment. I thought we might start over, if that's all right with you."

"What about Robert?"

He'd never called Robert by his name before. She wondered why he'd waited until now to stand on formality. "What about him?"

"I don't think he likes me very much."

What an understatement! After he'd picked her up on

New Year's Eve, Robert had spent fifteen minutes of their car ride brooding over the fact that she had a man living with her that she hadn't told him about. Although she'd already made the decision not to see Robert again, Nathan's insinuation that she would allow anyone to dictate her actions bothered her.

"Would you let someone you were dating tell you who your friends are?" she asked.

"No."

"Neither would I."

"I guess that's settled, *friend.*"

He tossed her a fortune cookie. She caught it with both hands, brought it down to her lap and broke it in half. "Thanks."

"You know," Nathan began, "they say you're supposed to add the words *in bed* to whatever your fortune says."

"Who says that?"

"I saw it on TV."

"Oh, then it must be right."

"Never mind. What does yours say?"

"Patience and dedication bring big reward."

"In bed," Nathan added.

Daphne swallowed, remembering exactly how big a reward Nathan offered—in bed or out of it. Focusing her gaze on his hands, she asked, "What does yours say?"

"Your sunny disposition pleases others."

He didn't say any more, but in her head she added those blasted words. She looked away from him, determined not to comment on that one.

"And speaking of bed," Nathan continued, "I should get myself into mine. I didn't have a nap today, either." He stood, leaned over, and kissed her cheek. "Good night, Daphne. Thanks for dinner."

He left before she could protest. Not that she really

would have protested. But, true to his word, he'd definitely left her wanting more than the little peck he'd given her.

Daphne pulled one of the throw pillows from the sofa onto her lap and hugged it, sighing. It really would be helpful if she could simply make up her mind what she wanted from him.

The phone rang, and she automatically picked up the extension on the table next to the sofa.

"Hello?"

"Daphne, it's Robert. Sorry I couldn't return your call earlier. I'm getting ready for a trip to Colorado. I'll tell you about it when I get back in two weeks. Will you miss me?"

Sure she'd miss him. She hadn't had a chance to see him since New Year's Eve. Since she intended to break off her relationship with him, she figured that was a conversation best had in person. "I need to see you when you get back."

"I'm counting on it. I've got to go. Take care of yourself. I'll call you as soon as I get home."

Daphne hung up the phone feeling vaguely uneasy. So much of her life seemed unsettled, up in the air—her company, her relationship with Nathan, her lack of one with Robert.

She couldn't do anything about any of it tonight. She rose from the sofa, carried their glasses to the sink, washed the few dishes waiting there, and went to bed.

Daphne hadn't been at her desk more than fifteen minutes the next morning when Sherry buzzed her over the intercom.

"He's baaack."

Daphne gritted her teeth. Though Sherry hadn't said so, there was no doubt in her mind who "he" was. *Ding, ding,*

ding. Round three with Bradley was about to begin. She sat back in her chair, crossed her arms in front of her, and waited for him to present himself.

He appeared a moment later, filling the doorway to her office.

"Bradley, what brings you here so early in the morning?"

"I want to see the books on this place—the accounts, clients, everything."

She should have known. Everything with him boiled down to avarice of one kind or another. He probably wanted to know if he could bleed any more money out of her. Still, she couldn't resist challenging him.

"Why?"

"I'm part owner of this place. I have the right to look at anything I want to."

"For another month at the most. Or are you rescinding your offer?"

"Not at all, but we both know you'll never come up with my asking price."

That was exactly what she feared, but he didn't need to know that. She shrugged. "Suit yourself. All that information is on disk. I'll ask Sherry to bring them into the other office. You can use the computer in there."

"I'll handle it."

Something about the slow grin that spread across his face prompted her to get up from her desk and watch him. He paused at Sherry's desk, canting his hip against it, leaning toward her in a way that was far too familiar for Daphne's comfort. Sherry's burst of effervescent laughter sent a chill through her.

Obviously, Bradley could turn on the charm when it pleased him. And of course, that had to be with her impressionable twenty-one-year-old receptionist. Damn Bradley. Was there any front on which he was not capable of making trouble? She made a mental note to speak to Sherry about Bradley later.

Nathan arrived at the front door of Women's Work just before noon. The offices, decorated in subtle shades of beige, brown, and black, exuded an aura of professionalism and comfort. Nathan wheeled Emily's stroller up to the receptionist's desk. The young woman who sat there watched him expectantly.

"Can I help you?" she asked. "And who is this little cutie?" The girl wiggled her fingers at Emily, who cooed in response.

"This is Emily, and I'm Nathan Ward. Is Ms. Thorne in?"

"Oh, sure. Daphne, I mean Ms. Thorne, is in the office down the hall on the left. If you want, you can leave the baby with me."

Emily gurgled and worked her tiny arms and legs as if she'd heard the idea and liked it. He guessed that settled it. "If you don't mind."

"Oh, not at all. I love kids."

"Thanks." Nathan headed in the direction the receptionist had indicated. He stopped just outside her door. Daphne stood with her back to him, her arms crossed in front of her. Her window faced the glass-and-steel facade of another building, so the view couldn't be what held her enthralled. "Daphne?"

She spun around, took one look at him, and turned back. She sniffled, obviously swiping at the moisture he saw standing on her cheeks. He could count on one hand the number of times he'd seen her cry, so her tears now surprised him.

Before he had a chance to say anything, she turned to

face him again, looking surprisingly controlled. "What are you doing here, Nathan?"

Originally, he'd come out of curiosity. Daphne hadn't told him much about her company, and he'd decided to find out about it firsthand. Now, he didn't intend to leave until he found out what was bothering her. "Emily and I were in the neighborhood and thought we'd take you to lunch."

"Where is she?"

Nathan ignored her question, his hazel eyes skimming over her, taking in the somber navy blue suit she wore. "Are you all right?" he asked.

"I'm fine." She shifted her weight, crossing her arms in front of her. "I'm just busy. I've got to leave in a few minutes to meet a client."

The receptionist's voice crackled over the phone's speaker. "I forgot to tell you, Daph—I mean, Ms. Thorne. Your twelve o'clock appointment canceled."

"Thanks, Sherry."

"You're welcome."

He heard Daphne sigh in response to the cheerful tone in the receptionist's voice. "And turn off the intercom."

"Yes, Ms. Thorne."

Not bothering to hide his amusement, he grinned at Daphne, raising one eyebrow in challenge. "I guess this means you're free."

"Guess so."

"Don't sound so enthusiastic. I might get a swelled head."

"If your head got any more swelled, it wouldn't be able to fit through the door."

"I am going to forget the snappy comeback you just left yourself open for. Where's your coat?"

"Look, Nathan," Daphne hedged. "I really should stay. I've got a ton of work on my desk."

"Which you weren't doing anyway. A little fresh air and sunshine will do you good."

"Fresh air in New York? You've got to be kidding."

Despite her words, he felt her weakening. He took her hands in his and sat down on the desk beside her. "Half an hour. Surely you can spare me that much time."

"Nathan," she said, her voice sounding like a plea. For what? That he would leave her alone—or that he wouldn't?

He chose to believe the latter. He lifted one hand, using his thumb and forefinger to illustrate a tiny space. "Thirty itty, bitty minutes. That's all I'm asking for."

"Well, what have we here?"

Daphne sprang away from him, turning to face the doorway where a man stood watching them. Nathan rose from the desk, noting the mocking expression on the other man's face.

Automatically, Nathan's hands fisted at his sides. His gaze slid to Daphne, who stood watching the man with her head cocked to one side. "Is there something you wanted?"

"Just to let you know I'm leaving. I didn't expect to be interrupting anything."

"You're not. See you around, Bradley."

After casting a scathing look Nathan's way, the other man sauntered away from the door, heading in the direction of the receptionist's desk.

"A friend of yours?" he asked.

"Long story. Are we going to lunch or not?"

He suspected she only agreed to go with him as a means of distracting him from asking any more questions. He decided to allow it, for now. "I guess we're going to lunch."

Daphne retrieved her coat from the back of her door and Nathan helped her into it. They walked out to the receptionist desk, only to find Emily sound asleep in

Sherry's arms. At Sherry's insistence, they left the baby with her, vowing they wouldn't be gone long.

As usual, walking in midtown traffic at midday was like being a salmon fighting its way upstream while all the sturgeon were headed down. Nathan held on to Daphne with a hand on her elbow. "Where are we going?"

"A little place I know." She led him to a park nestled between Lexington and Third avenues. To the left, a concession stand advertised sandwiches, frankfurters, and coffee. Two dozen small wrought-iron tables surrounded a faux waterfall that had been turned off for the winter. A handful of pigeons scrounged for food among the few diners.

He followed Daphne over to the concession stand. "We're eating here?"

"Don't be such a snob, Nathan. You said you wanted fresh air, didn't you?"

Yeah, he'd opened his big mouth and said that. But he doubted that had much bearing on her choice of eatery. He had the feeling she was testing him, and if so he'd failed miserably so far.

"What kind of sandwich would you like?" she asked. "I recommend the ham and cheese."

Given that the only other choices were peanut butter and jelly or a hot dog that looked like it had been roasting since the previous spring, he agreed. He ordered a sandwich and a cup of coffee for each of them. They claimed one of the tables next to the waterfall and sat down.

Nathan unwrapped his sandwich and bit into it. Stale bread, flavorless ham, and the most unpalatable excuse for cheese he'd ever tasted. "Yum," he said.

"Okay, I admit it's not Lutece, but the money from the concession stand keeps the waterfall going in the summer. It's truly beautiful."

He watched her as she broke off a piece of her sandwich

and tossed it to a group of birds. They flocked over it, squabbling, until one bird emerged the victor.

"Haven't you guys ever heard of sharing?" she asked, shaking her head.

She glanced back at him, and their gazes met. She offered him a weak smile and looked away. He wondered what she was thinking, why she'd been so upset when he'd walked in. Did it have to do with that man who'd been in her office? Even if it didn't, Nathan wouldn't have minded flattening the guy simply on principle. But knowing Daphne, she wouldn't have appreciated any such gesture on his part.

"Why did you really come to my office today?"

"You never did tell me what you do. I was curious. What is Women's Work?"

"We're an employment agency for women."

"How did you get involved in that? Last I heard, you wanted to be a teacher like your mother."

"I think that phase lasted for about a year. I wasn't really sure what I wanted to do with myself."

She shrugged, tossing another piece of her sandwich to the birds. "I was the brain of the family. No one ever let me forget I'd started school early and skipped a grade. Everyone always told me I could be anything I wanted. Lacking my sister's artistic ability and my brother's musical talent, I had no idea what I wanted that anything to be."

"Sounds like classic middle-child syndrome to me."

"How would you know?" she teased. "You were the oldest. And besides, you always knew what you wanted to do with your life."

True, he'd always known what he wanted. But he wondered now, if someone had told him fifteen years ago what his life would really be like, if he'd known all the sacrifices and the pitfalls, would he have chucked it all and become a plumber? He doubted it. As a young man, full of himself and so focused on his goal, he knew he wouldn't have listened to anything anyone had tried to tell him.

"Why an employment agency?" he probed. "Mike told me you got a masters in sociology."

"I have an MBA and a masters in social work. I tried the counseling route for a while, but found I wasn't suited to it. Half the time I just wanted to smack my clients on the head and say, 'Snap out of it!' Like Cher in *Moonstruck*. Not exactly the recommended course of treatment."

"So you gave up psychological counseling for employment counseling."

"In a manner of speaking. When Victoria and I decided to go into business together, we wanted to do something that would help women. The welfare laws were changing, making it harder for women to get on public assistance and limiting the time and the conditions for them to stay on it.

"Now no self-respecting woman *wants* to be on welfare to start with. The whole experience is designed to degrade the recipient. Make no mistake, there are people who will do anything to skirt welfare laws, but for those honestly seeking to better their situation, the playing field is worse instead of better."

"What do you mean?"

"In order to keep receiving the same pitiful government check many women have to go to work. The government promises them training, but to do what? Pick up garbage by the side of the road? Some menial job that wouldn't raise them above the level of poverty under any circumstances? And you wouldn't believe some of the programs in place that are really scams promising a 'guaranteed' job that never materializes. Victoria and I wanted to help women break the cycle altogether and find jobs they could be proud of that would enable them to make a decent future for themselves and their families."

"How has it been going?"

"It hasn't been easy, that's for sure. For one thing, most of the jobs we fill are entry-level positions that don't generate much of a commission. Most of the women who come to us are unprepared to do anything, even low-level clerical work.

"And for some of them, they are the only person they know who does work. They have absolutely no support system or anyone to turn to who is knowledgeable about what to do if you have a problem on the job.

"So we started a Professional Women's Network. We meet once a month to exchange ideas, share what's happening in our lives, and figure out ways to help one another advance in our careers. We have a guest speaker come in every month to speak on topics of interest to the women, like how to prepare their taxes, dressing on the job, how to move ahead in their careers. We've had the group in place about a year. The women really love it.

"On top of that, most of these women have kids. Do you have any idea how hard it is to find inexpensive, competent day care in New York? You'd have better luck finding Jimmy Hoffa. So we help subsidize a day-care center available to anyone who gets their job through us." She fed the last of her sandwich to the birds and brushed her hands together, shedding crumbs.

"It sounds like you do good work. So why were you crying when I came in?"

She bit her lip, a gesture he knew signaled he'd broached a topic she didn't want to discuss. "You can imagine that many of the women who come into our office haven't exactly led charmed lives. There's always a story, how they came to be in their particular circumstances. I have one of those faces, I guess. People tend to tell me their most intimate secrets. It just gets to me sometimes."

He covered her hand with his own. "You always were a sucker for a good sob story."

"Gee, thanks." She tried to pull her hand from his, but he held on to it firmly but gently.

"I meant that as a compliment. I've never seen you turn your back on anyone. You put up with me for four years, didn't you? Lord knows that must have been an exercise in futility."

She snorted. "You had your moments."

"Did I?"

She pulled her hand from his. "You know you did. Stop fishing for compliments."

"It's what I do best."

She shook her head, watching him with an expression he couldn't interpret. "Thank you."

"For what?"

She shrugged. "I guess we'd better head back."

"Guess so."

Nathan gathered the garbage from their lunch and carried it to the trash can by the concession stand. Daphne came up beside him and linked her arm with his, leading him back toward Lexington Avenue.

After a few moments, she said, "I have a confession to make."

"Oh?"

"I've never actually eaten there before. I usually go to unwind and feed the birds."

He stopped walking mid-stride and turned to face her. "And you called me a snob for turning my nose up at the place."

She nodded, looking up at him with laughter in her eyes. That expression was worth a year's worth of indigestion.

"May I ask you a question?"

"Sure."

"What exactly do you think that 'cheese' was made of?"

Daphne gave a mock shudder. "I don't even want to know."

When they got back to the office, Emily was still asleep. Nathan quickly rebundled her in her snowsuit and settled her in the stroller. "I guess I'll see you tonight. And I'll take care of dinner."

"In that case, I'd better stock up on the Pepto Bismol."

He grinned at her. "Scoff if you will, but I promise you a meal that will be both tasty and toxin-free."

"I'll believe that when I eat it."

Nathan ran a finger down her nose. "Then, prepare to be amazed." To Sherry, who listened to them as raptly as someone might listen to E. F. Hutton, he said, "Thanks again for watching Emily."

Sherry waved her hand in the air, dismissively. "Anytime. In fact, I wouldn't mind baby-sitting if you've got somewhere special to go." She looked pointedly at Daphne when she said that.

Subtlety was definitely not the woman's middle name. "I'll keep that in mind." He looked at Daphne, who rolled her eyes. She walked to the door and held it open for him.

"Out, Ward. This is a place of business, and I'm not getting any done with you here."

The urge to kiss that sassy mouth of hers, just for good measure, goaded him. But he decided he'd rather have something to look forward to that night.

"I'll expect you home by six," he said, as he wheeled Emily's stroller past her. He smiled a secret smile of anticipation. "And you'd better not be late."

Nine

Daphne opened her apartment door a few minutes before six. Delicious aromas wafted from the kitchen. She smelled apples and cinnamon, which could only mean one thing—pie. Nathan could not have actually baked something. This she had to see.

She hastily hung her coat up in the closet, and kicked off her shoes. "Nathan?" she called, heading in the direction of the kitchen.

"I'm in here," he called back.

She took one look at him in the kitchen and burst out laughing. He wore a white cotton T-shirt with a nude baby casting off its diaper on the front. The caption read: D.A.D. DADS AGAINST DIAPERS. IT'S NOT JUST A JOB, IT'S A DOODY.

He looked at her questioningly, then down at himself. "My sister's idea of a Christmas present."

"I compliment her taste. How is Nina?"

He gave her a disgusted look. "As much of a pain in the neck as ever."

Despite his words, and the ten-year age difference, Daphne knew that Nathan had always shared a close relationship with his sister. She stepped farther into the kitchen. Nathan had laid out a blanket on the floor to her left. Emily lay on her back playing happily with her Sesame Street doohickey with the dangling characters. Daphne stepped around it to stand by the counter. "It smells great in here. What's for dinner?"

He pointed to the steaming plate of food in front of her. "Chicken marsala, wild rice and string beans almondine."

She crossed her arms in front of her chest. "You cooked all that?"

"Nope, it's the special at Carmelo's around the corner." He grinned at her. "If you remember, I never said anything about cooking. I said I'd take care of dinner. I took care of dinner."

Amused, she bit her lower lip. He had her there. "I suppose I should be relieved," she said. "Do you remember the last time you cooked for me? Hamburgers burned so badly, even your grandmother's dog refused to eat them."

He winked at her. "Haven't you ever heard of blackened hamburgers? It's a Cajun specialty." The microwave beeped, signaling the food inside was ready. He went over to it and removed the second plate. "Why don't you go get changed so we can eat?"

"I'll be right back."

Up in her room, Daphne quickly stripped off her suit and stood in front of her closet wondering what to wear. She fingered the sleeve of the robe Nathan had given her. Not yet. She wasn't ready to wear it yet. She wasn't exactly sure what she was saving it for; she only knew tonight wasn't the night. She settled instead for a pair of royal blue lounging pajamas. She slid the silk over her body, straightened her hair into some semblance of order and went back down to the kitchen.

When she got downstairs, Nathan had already seated himself at the kitchen table with Emily on his lap. He did a double take when he saw her. The second time their gazes held and he raised one eyebrow, obviously questioning her choice of attire. She shrugged, walked to the seat opposite him and sat down.

As she arranged her napkin on her lap, she focused on Nathan's child. Awake, she was more beautiful than she had been asleep. Her deep brown eyes were alert and intelligent, looking avidly around the room. The baby's gaze settled on Daphne, and the infant offered her a broad grin.

A sudden well of emotion clogged Daphne's chest, making it difficult to breathe. "Hi, sweetie," she said, her voice sounding strained and foreign. The baby gurgled back at her, waving her arms in the air.

"I think she likes you." Nathan lifted the baby in his arms to rest against his chest. "Emily, say hi to TiTi Daphne," he added, using the Spanish nickname for aunt.

Emily looked up at her father, as if for confirmation. "Da da da," she chanted, grabbing hold of Nathan's nose in one of her little hands.

"Did you hear that?" He loosened the baby's grip and immediately she tugged on one of his ears. "She called me Daddy."

His voice sounded so full of awe that Daphne almost laughed. Being a father suited him, as she'd always known it would.

"I hate to break it to you Nathan, but at this age, she's just making sounds. All babies make the *da* sound, usually even before the *ma* sound. *M* is a more complex letter."

"Tell me about it," Nathan muttered.

"What are you grousing about?"

"Nothing. I know I'm the typical doting father, expecting his offspring to be able to recite the Gettysburg address at a year old. I know it's silly, but I can't seem to help myself."

He didn't appear the least bit repentant, and she found she liked that. Enough children existed in the world for whom no one held out any expectation at all. Why shouldn't he want the best for his daughter? Just because at the moment she was nibbling on his chin?

"Cut it out, you little cannibal." He gently extricated his face from her grasp. "I am not a teething ring."

Daphne focused on her plate, not wanting Nathan to see how deeply his relationship with his daughter affected her. In truth, she envied the woman who'd given birth to Emily, more than she wanted to admit. How any woman could abandon her own child was beyond Daphne's comprehension.

Or how any woman could walk away from Nathan without a backward glance. She realized she might be assuming things. In truth, she had no idea what relationship Nathan had with Emily's mother, if the two of them were in contact or what Nathan felt for her. As of yet, Nathan hadn't said anything about her, and Daphne preferred not to know.

"And now, Miss," she heard Nathan say, "it's time for you to let Daddy eat." Daphne looked up to see him turn and bend over to set Emily down amid the host of toys spread out on the blanket. The baby immediately reached for a plastic Ernie doll and chewed on its head.

"Better you than me, buddy," Nathan remarked, watching his daughter. "You're not eating," he added, when he faced her again.

"I was waiting for you."

"Then, dig in." Nathan picked up his fork and scooped up some rice. "Not bad," he commented, after sampling a bite.

Daphne nodded, but her appetite had fled.

"How was the rest of your day?"

"Good. Surprisingly, I got a lot done. I can see the surface of my desk again. How about you?"

"Emily and I went to our first Mommy and Me class. I'm the only daddy in the group."

"I'm sure you must have loved that."

"Whatever do you mean?"

She dropped her shoulders and cocked her head to one side. He knew exactly what she meant. "You, surrounded by a bunch of young, undoubtedly attentive women. They probably forgot all about their poor little babies and drooled all over you."

"Would that bother you?"

He was fishing again, and she wasn't going to give him the satisfaction of knowing just how much that would bother her. "Not at all. It's none of my business what you do."

He said nothing to that, but the skeptical expression on his face brought one word to her mind: *Liar.*

"How's Emily?" she asked, more to change the subject than anything else.

"She's fine. Looks like she's getting sleepy." He bent down and scooped her up. "I'd better put her in bed. Why don't you check on dessert while I'm gone?"

She waited until he'd gone down the back staircase to scrape their dishes and carry them to the sink. She loaded them in the dishwasher. She'd just opened the oven door when Nathan reappeared. He set the baby monitor on the counter, then joined her.

"How does it look?"

"Fabulous." She grabbed two potholders from the counter and lifted the pie from the rack. "I hope you're not going to try to tell me you baked this."

"Reheating is my specialty. You can thank Mrs. Smith for her expertise with an apple peeler."

She set the pie on the counter. "Now all we need is some coffee to go with it."

"Finally, a job I can handle."

While the pie cooled, Nathan made coffee, and Daphne finished straightening the kitchen. They settled on the living room sofa, their plates in their laps, their coffee cups on the table with the baby monitor standing between them. She glanced at Nathan, who scanned the room, a pensive expression on his face.

He picked up his coffee cup and took a sip. "Mind if I ask you a personal question?"

She swallowed the mouthful of pie she'd been chewing. "Depends on the question."

"How can you afford this place?"

"Actually, I can't. The property taxes are astronomical."

"Not to mention the mortgage."

"Actually, I haven't got one." She wiped her mouth with her napkin. Seeing the questioning look on Nathan's face, she elaborated.

"Believe it or not, I used to live in your apartment. The former owner was a retired businessman. He'd outlived all of his family and he thought of me as a surrogate grand-daughter. He told me he intended to leave me this building in his will. I couldn't allow that, but I knew he didn't want to sell to strangers. This house had been his home for many years. His children had grown up here. He sold it to me for what I could pay, about a tenth of what the building was worth."

She sighed, sitting back on the sofa. Unless her finances suddenly changed, she'd have to sell the building. She didn't look forward to that eventuality with any relish. Despite the knowledge that selling the building for its actual worth would make her a wealthy woman, she loved the comfort and convenience of her home and didn't want to lose it.

She slanted a glance at Nathan. His presence here had saved her this time, though she still didn't know why he'd wanted to rent the apartment from her in the first place. "Mind if I ask you a question?" she asked.

"Not at all."

"Why are you here?"

"I'm eating pie."

"You know what I mean. Why are you living here?"

With a sigh, Nathan put his plate on the table and stood. He walked over to the window and stared out a moment before turning to face her.

"So we're back to that. I suppose you have as much right to know as anyone. You were right, before. In a manner of speaking, I am hiding out."

"From whom?"

"Monica, Emily's mother. For the time being, I've got custody of Emily, and I want to keep it that way."

"Why? Nathan, a baby needs its mother."

She wished she'd never said anything when his jaw flexed and his eyes turned as hard as glass. "Don't you think I know that? Try telling that to Monica. She's the one who abandoned her baby in the care of a man she claims is too irresponsible to take care of himself, let alone an infant.

"Even when she was here, she would disappear for hours, never bothering to explain where she went. She wouldn't even breastfeed the baby, claiming it would prevent her from getting her figure back. Is that the kind of mother Emily needs?"

"Then why don't you sue for custody? Any judge hearing your story would . . ." She trailed off, seeing Nathan shake his head.

"They might, if it weren't for the fact that Monica's father is a Family Court judge, and her brother is none other than the Bronx District Attorney. Tell me I stand any chance of getting custody of my daughter. Not in New York, anyway."

Daphne would be the last person to deny that nepotism, cronyism and favoritism were alive and well in every court system in the land—as well as the notion that mothers alone possessed some special childrearing knowledge that fathers lacked. But it made more sense to her to fight than to hide.

"Even if it weren't for the family connection, what judge in his right mind would award custody of a child to me, a 'singing Romeo,' as Jenny's father calls me? You know, those things they print about me in the paper, they're not all made up."

"I didn't think they were."

"I've done some things I'm not proud of, Daphne. I'm sure Monica and her family of lawyers would dredge up every last one of them to prove I'm an unfit parent. And the worst part of it is, they'd probably be right."

He turned his back to her, shoving his hands in his pockets. Her heart went out to him, but she didn't know what to say. Everything he'd said was probably true—everything except the part about his unfitness as a parent. She knew how devoted he was to his daughter, and in her book that made all the difference.

She rose to her feet. "Nathan—"

Her words were cut short by the sound of the baby crying over the monitor speaker.

"I guess that's my cue to go." He turned to face her, and in his eyes she saw a reflection of so much pain, it stunned her. She wanted to go to him, to comfort him, but her body didn't seem to function.

"Good night, Daphne."

She watched him walk away from her, his hands still thrust into his pants pockets. He hadn't bothered to take the monitor with him. When he'd gone, she sank down on the sofa, listening as she heard Nathan enter his daughter's room.

"Shh, sweetie," she heard him say. "Shh."

She closed her eyes, imagining him rocking the baby, as Emily's crying quieted to a few sniffling complaints.

She heard Nathan say something else, but she couldn't make it out. The sounds became more distant and muffled. He must be carrying her out of the room, she surmised, and shut off the monitor.

Daphne leaned back against the sofa, letting out a breath she hadn't realized she'd been holding. Part of her wished she hadn't pushed the matter. It must have taken a lot for him to tell her the truth about Monica and about his own past.

No wonder he wanted so much to prove to his family that he was a good father to Emily. He needed someone to believe in him, and oddly enough, on that score, she did. She wondered what he'd say if she told him that.

Inadvertently he'd answered her unasked question about his relationship with Emily's mother. Evidently, he'd been willing to marry her as some sort of guarantee of seeing his child. That was a heavy price to ask of any man, especially one like Nathan who valued his own freedom above all else. At least the Nathan she knew had. This new Nathan that she kept getting glimpses of—she wasn't sure she knew him at all.

But she knew she liked what she saw, knew she appreciated his maturity and his enduring concern for her well-being. If she wasn't careful, she'd find herself falling in love with him all over again. Now she had to decide whether she felt like being careful.

"Mijito, quiere aguacate?"

Nathan saw the hint of a grin on his grandmother's face as she stood beside him, offering to cut a slice of avocado onto his plate. She knew very well he couldn't stand avocado, but she insisted on trotting one out at every meal for his benefit. Or rather, for her brand of retribution for his insistence on answering her in English whenever she spoke to him in Spanish.

"I don't like avocado," he said in a voice meant to imply that they'd had this conversation before. "Nelson likes avocado."

His grandmother shrugged elaborately, and sat next to him. "I'm an old lady. I can't be expected to remember everything."

Nathan glanced at his sister, Nina, who sent him an arched look suggesting he only got what he deserved.

Picking up his fork, he scooped up a portion of the rice and beans on his plate. He listened as the women around him made small talk, wondering why his grandmother had asked him to come to lunch today, why his sister was here in the middle of a work day. He figured they'd get around to it soon enough.

His gaze settled on his cousin Yasmin, who pushed her food around her plate rather than eating it. "It's getting to be that time of year for you again, isn't it, Yasmin? When is your tuition due?"

Absolute silence greeted him. He looked up from his plate, scanning the three faces that did their best not to return his gaze. Obviously, he'd inadvertently stumbled onto the reason for the invitation.

He lay down his fork and sat back in his chair. "Okay, what isn't anybody telling me?"

Yasmin darted a glance at him. "I'm not going back to school next semester."

"Not going back? When were you planning on telling me this? After Parsons returned my check?"

"I was planning on telling you today. I was waiting for the right moment."

She'd planned on telling him, not seeking his advice, not valuing his input. "I see. And what are you going to do during this semester off? Backpack through Europe?

Visit the Dalai Lama? Oh, I forgot. People gave up 'finding themselves' in the eighties."

"Leave the girl alone, Nathan," his grandmother admonished. "What's the big deal if she doesn't go back right away?"

"Because people who take time off tend not to finish." Turning to Yasmin, he added, "I thought your degree was important to you."

"It is, but—"

"But what?"

"Nathan, what are you getting so upset about? You didn't go to college at all, and no one took you to task for that."

No, no one had ever taken him to task for anything. No one had ever bothered to question whether he knew what he was doing or to offer advice, even if it would have gone unheeded. He'd never gotten one bit of guidance from anybody. Yet his grandmother saw him as the bad guy for wanting to make sure his flighty nineteen-year-old cousin didn't make a mistake she'd regret.

Nathan gritted his teeth, his exasperation getting the better of him. "And see what a fine specimen of humanity I turned out to be." He stood and grasped his plate in one hand. "Excuse me. I'm going to check on Emily."

He strode to the kitchen, scraped the contents of his full plate into the trash, and left the plate in the sink. Emily was still sleeping soundly when he got to her room. Wanting to leave, but unwilling to wake her, he went out back and sat on the steps leading to his grandmother's garden.

For the first time in a long time, his thoughts turned to his own father, a man he probably wouldn't have recognized if he'd passed him on the street. The last time Nathan had seen his father he'd been eleven years old. Damon Ward had been a jazz saxophonist, a good one, who'd made a name for himself playing with all the greats.

As a child he'd wondered why his father had bothered. Why start a family, only to leave it whenever Quincy or Dizzy or Miles issued the call? As an adult, he realized his father had gotten his mother pregnant and felt obligated to marry her, but not to stay with her, not to make any decent sort of life. He'd disappear for months at a time, claiming to be on tour or working in another state. In all likelihood, he'd probably been shacked up with some woman who didn't come with the baggage of a wife and son and, eventually, another kid on the way.

Two months after Nina was born, his father left for the last time. A year later, when it had become apparent that his father had no intention of returning, his mother had packed up her two children, sold her home, and gone back to live with her mother. No big deal, no fanfare. Like his father had never existed.

Nathan had vowed then that he would never grow up to be like his father, a man whose presence or absence was treated with such utter nonchalance. Nor would he ever subject any woman to the life his father had given his mother, a marriage in little more than name only.

So when he'd returned home to see Daphne and she'd refused to see him, he hadn't pursued her. He'd walked away, viewing her refusal to see him as a rejection of the only kind of life he could offer her.

Absently, Nathan picked at the grass growing at his feet, acknowledging that he'd turned out to be more like his father than he'd ever wanted to be. He'd alienated his own family to the point that even his advice was not welcomed. If it weren't for Monica's jilting him at the altar, he'd be in a similar loveless marriage. Certain kinds of stupidity simply had to reside in the genes.

On the other hand, he had to have gotten his musical ability from somewhere, and his father's final disappearance had made it possible for him to meet Daphne. All in all, he supposed his father hadn't done so bad by him, after all.

Nathan turned, hearing the screen door open behind him. He wasn't surprised to see his sister coming toward him. Aside from his mother, she was the only one in the family who had always tried to understand him.

He patted the seat next to him, and she sat down. "What are you doing out here?" she asked.

"Just sitting."

"Just brooding." She leaned her head on his shoulder. "You shouldn't let *abuela* get to you like that. We both know she's from the old school, set in her opinions of what she thinks is right. She can't understand why at the advanced age of twenty-seven I haven't settled down and had an armload of babies, either."

He put his arm around his sister's shoulders. "Come to think of it, why haven't you settled down?"

"Believe me, if I wanted a man of the permanent variety, I'd have one. But I like my life the way it is. I have a great job, lots of friends—"

"Most of them men, I'm sure."

She punched him on the thigh with the side of her fist. "If you are trying to imply that I sleep around, I don't."

"I never said that. Even if you did, I'm the last one who should judge anyone else's behavior."

"My, we're really feeling sorry for ourselves today. And don't tell me you're sulking because of anything that happened in there. Does this have something to do with Daphne?"

"Du-uh! And I thought you were supposed to be the brains of this operation."

"I am. I only wondered if you're sure how you feel about her."

"I'm in love with her. I always have been. You know that."

"And I always liked her. She never did take too much of your macho crap."

He gave his sister's waist a squeeze. "I thought you were supposed to be on my side."

"I am on your side. But I know how you are."

"How is that?"

"On the surface, you seem like the most easygoing, most laid-back man in the world. But inside"—she poked him in the chest in the region of his heart—"you are one of the most driven men I know."

Nathan laughed. That was as apt a description of him as he'd ever heard.

"Do yourself a favor, Nathan. Take it slow with her. Don't rush her."

"I don't have much of a choice. She's seeing someone else."

"Oh, Nathan, ouch! That must hurt."

"You have no idea." Even now, just thinking about Daphne with that other man made caustic jealousy burn in his stomach like acid.

"You're not giving up, are you?"

He thought of all the subtle and not-so-subtle means he'd used to get under Daphne's skin during the past few weeks. Nathan flashed his sister a grin. "No, I haven't given up."

"Seriously, Nathan," Nina said quietly. "You really hurt her before."

"I know. I only wish I knew how." He looked down, scrutinizing his sister's upturned face. "You know, though, don't you?"

"I have my suspicions. But if I told you, Daphne would have to kill me."

Nathan sighed. Knowing Nina, he'd never get one drop of information out of her if she didn't want to tell him. It was just as well. In truth, he appreciated his sister's loyalty to Daphne.

"I've got to get going. I want to be back home before she gets there." He pulled away from his sister and stood. He held out a hand to Nina and helped her to her feet.

"She got a job."

"What?"

"Yasmin was offered a job working for Donna Karan. She won a competition, and the prize was an internship working at DKNY. You know that's what she's wanted since she used to design clothes for her dolls as a little girl."

"Why didn't she tell me that?"

"She might have if you'd let her get a word in. You know, she really looks up to you, the way you knew what you wanted and went after it. She's trying to do the same thing."

He raised his eyebrows and frowned in a self-deprecating gesture. It hadn't occurred to him that Yasmin thought of him as anything other than a deep pocket she dipped into frequently. "And I chewed her ear off because of it."

"You can be a real jerk sometimes, but I love you."

Nathan regarded his sister, who shared his complexion and eye color, but whose jet-black hair gave her an exotic look. Dressed in a black miniskirt, matching jacket and high heels, she possessed a sophistication, poise, and femininity he never would have expected to find in the little hoyden who'd been able to lick every boy in the neighborhood, including him. She'd been a dirty fighter then. Some things about her hadn't changed one bit.

"All right, I know when you're buttering me up for something. What do you want?"

"Talk to Yasmin again. This time without being so judgmental."

"I think I can handle that." He embraced his sister,

planting a gentle kiss on her cheek. "Take care of yourself, *niña*." He headed through the door, before she had a chance to whack him, her usual response to that variant of her name, that, in essence, called her a child.

"I hate it when you call me that." Her voice rose in volume and pitch as she spoke.

"I love you, too," he called back in the same sing-song voice. Laughing, he went to find Yasmin.

At five-thirty that afternoon, Daphne raised her arms over her head, laced her fingers, and stretched the kink out of her lower back. She'd had a productive day. Despite his threat, Bradley hadn't shown up at the office. She thanked all available deities for that fact. She'd had a hard enough time concentrating on her work with thoughts of Nathan intruding on her throughout the day.

Daphne lowered her arms, remembering the conversation they'd had the night before. He'd told her he was hiding out, but she didn't entirely believe him. Especially since he'd done such a poor job of it. It wouldn't take a good private investigator more than two minutes to find him. That is, if Monica were looking for him in the first place.

Maybe what he really wanted was not a place to hide, but a place to feel safe. A harbor in the storm of his life, as he'd been for her so many times. That thought warmed her, causing something soft inside her to stir to life.

"What are you doing to me, Nathan Ward?" she wondered aloud. But she already knew the answer. He was getting to her, getting under her skin, worming his way back into her heart. She saw no point in lying to herself about what she felt. Caution be damned, she wanted to be with him. She got her coat from the back of her door and slipped it on. As she advanced toward the outer door, she paused, surprised to find Sherry still at her desk. She'd thought everyone else had already gone home.

"What are you still doing here?" she asked Sherry.

"I'm meeting someone a little later. I thought I'd stay and catch up on some work." Sherry's cheeks reddened. Her fair complexion hid nothing.

"A male someone, by any chance?"

"Well—"

"Well, have fun," Daphne called as she continued to the front door. "Don't forget to lock up when you leave."

"I won't."

Humming to herself, Daphne got on the empty elevator car when it came. As she stepped out on the ground floor, she could have sworn she saw Bradley getting onto the car next to hers on his way up. The doors closed too quickly for her to get a good look at him. Tempted to head back upstairs to check for sure, she took a step toward the elevators.

Daphne sighed, letting her shoulders drop. A little paranoia was a dangerous thing. Bradley's looks weren't exactly of the uncommon variety. The man she'd seen could have been anybody. Besides, why would Bradley show up here at this hour of the evening, anyway? Under normal circumstances, everyone in the office would have been gone.

Besides, she looked forward to seeing Nathan with the kind of anticipation she hadn't felt toward anything in a long time She'd be damned if she let some Bradley look-alike ruin her mood.

But when she got home, the house was dark, and Nathan was nowhere to be found.

Ten

Nathan pulled up in front of Daphne's town house a little after nine o'clock that night. He glanced up at the brick facade of the building, which was painted a pale peach. It reminded him of Daphne herself: a contradiction of softness and steel, grit and femininity. A light burned in her living-room window. Daphne was home.

He carried the baby into the house, settled her in bed and went to find Daphne. He'd missed her, missed the dinner he'd intended to share with her. But when he'd called her at home to let her know he'd be late, she wasn't there, and there wasn't any answer at her office, either. He assumed she'd gone out for the evening. Since he doubted he could handle seeing her come home with Robert in his present mood, he'd stayed for dinner at his grandmother's instead.

"Daph—" That was as far as he got in calling her name, before he saw her: sound asleep and curled up on her living-room sofa. She wore his robe, or rather the robe he'd given her—and as far as he could tell, nothing else. Though she'd accepted it from him, he'd begun to wonder if she ever planned to wear it. Had she put it on tonight because she'd expected him to be here, or because she hadn't?

Nathan inhaled, held the breath, then let it out slowly. She looked so soft in slumber, as she always had. Sleep seemed to be about the only time she fully let her guard down. When she slept and when she made love, he amended. She had with him, anyway.

Nathan rubbed the back of his neck with the palm of his hand. How many other men had she lain with? Shared her body with? Loved? She'd practically told him that she hadn't been in love with anyone else, but that didn't mean she'd been celibate, either. Robert's presence in her life gave the lie to that notion. Had she slept with him already? He doubted it, but the mere prospect of it made bile rise in his throat.

Nathan sighed. He had no right to that information. Being asleep, she couldn't give it to him anyway. There was no point in torturing himself further.

He knelt beside her and gave her shoulder a gentle shake. "Sweetheart, wake up."

She mumbled something, but didn't stir. He contemplated leaving her there and getting a blanket to cover her, but the sofa was really too short for her to be comfortable all night. He bent and scooped her up in his arms. Immediately, she burrowed closer to him, burying her nose against the side of his neck. Her warm breath fanned his skin, heating him in other ways as well. She murmured one sleep-softened word: "Nathan."

Nathan exhaled a heavy, desire-laden sigh. "Daphne. Daphne, Daphne." He turned his face and kissed her cheek. "You really are going to be the death of me." Then he carried her upstairs, tucked her in her bed, and went downstairs to spend another sleepless night in his own.

After her stomach growled for the third time, Daphne checked her watch. Nearly two o'clock in the afternoon. Where had the day gone? Unlike the previous few days, she'd barely gotten anything accomplished, and the day was nearly over.

It was all Nathan's fault. She'd been truly surprised to wake up that morning to find herself in her own bed. Only one explanation for that came to her mind. Nathan must have carried her up, because she couldn't remember having gotten there on her own. But since he'd let her sleep, she hadn't set her alarm. She'd awakened a half-hour later than usual, and her day had been thrown off ever since.

She picked up the phone to call the deli around the corner to have something delivered when the line for her private number rang.

She punched the button and held the receiver to her ear. "Daphne Thorne."

"Hi, sleepy head. How are you feeling today?"

She immediately recognized Nathan's sexy voice coming over the line. She sat down and kicked off her shoes under her desk. "I'm fine."

He didn't immediately respond, as if he were waiting for her to say something. Probably to thank him for putting her in bed last night. She shifted in her chair, not knowing what to say to him. She didn't want to seem ungrateful. The last time she'd spent a night on that sofa, she'd awakened with a crick in her neck and a cramp in her lower back. That was Nathan's fault, too. The last time she'd slept on that sofa she'd used Nathan's robes as a blanket.

"Thanks for the lift last night. I don't usually conk out on the sofa like that."

"Believe me, it was my pleasure."

She didn't know what to say to that, either. "So, what can I do for you?" she asked. What she really wanted to know was where he'd been last night. She'd cooked a delicious chicken and pasta dinner, hoping he'd show up in time to eat it. She'd fallen asleep on the sofa waiting for him to get home.

"The carpenter is here and wants to talk with you."

"Put him on."

Within a few minutes, she'd finalized arrangements for the carpenter to come back the following week to install the kitchen cabinets she'd selected. Nathan came back on the line then.

"Everything all set?"

"Yes, thanks. Do you need anything else?"

"Nope. Now that that's over, I think it's time for Emily and me to have a little nap. I'm not too sure what her plans are, but I definitely need one."

"Late night?" She hoped he didn't recognize her fishing expedition for what it was.

"No, but a long one."

That didn't tell her anything. "Well, sweet dreams. I should be home by six-thirty."

"See you then."

Daphne heard the other end of the line go dead. She hung up the phone and tried, without success, to concentrate on her work.

Nathan was setting the table that evening when he heard Daphne opening the apartment door.

"Nathan?"

"In here," he called, pausing in the task of setting the table. "Are you hungry?"

"Famished."

Daphne appeared in the doorway to the kitchen. She'd already shed her coat and her shoes. He let his gaze travel over her, taking in her long skirt and sweater. It was a softer look for her, one that suited her. The more severe suits she usually wore did nothing to complement her gamine face or curvaceous figure.

"What have you got?"

"You have a choice tonight. We can either order a pizza, or we can eat leftovers from lunch today at my grandmother's. What's your call?"

"I vote for grandma. Give me a minute to change, okay?"

"Okay."

She practically skipped from the room, and Nathan wondered about the playful mood she seemed to be in. He checked on Emily, who was playing happily on her blanket on the floor, before filling two plates with the spicy Spanish food his grandmother had sent home with him the day before.

He hadn't heard Daphne's footfalls on the stairs, but when he looked up and saw her standing at the entrance to the kitchen, desire ricocheted through him with lightning speed. She wore the robe he'd given her cinched loosely at her waist. In that instant she'd answered his question of the night before—she had worn the robe for him. Nathan closed his eyes momentarily, praying for strength.

"Is everything almost ready?" she asked.

He didn't know about the food, but he was ready, more than ready. And worse, he suspected she knew precisely the reaction she inspired in him. She'd pinned up her braids, exposing the long column of her throat. He gulped, remembering exactly how sensitive to his touch she was there. It seemed to be an invitation to touch. If he managed to keep his hands to himself during dinner, it would be a miracle worthy of ecumenical scrutiny.

"Just about."

She stepped into the kitchen. "Can I help with anything?"

"No, I've got it covered."

He'd already heated both plates in the microwave. He

carried them over to the table as Daphne claimed the same seat she'd had the last time they'd eaten together.

"This looks great," she said, unfolding her napkin on her lap. "And I'm absolutely starved. I never got to eat lunch today."

"Busy?" He brought a forkful of rice and beans to his mouth.

"Very, but completely unproductive. I don't think I got a thing accomplished today."

"Sounds like the kind of day I have every day. At least you are your own boss. I'm at the mercy of a little two-foot tyrant who always wants things done *now.*"

"Has Emily started to crawl yet?"

"A little. Backwards."

"That's normal. Going backwards is easier than going forward. And believe me, when she starts running all over the house wrecking things, you'll wish she'd never learned to crawl either forward or backward."

A trilling sound from his apartment below cut off the retort he was about to make. He pushed back his chair and stood.

"I'm ringing."

"Excuse me?"

"My phone downstairs is ringing. Watch Emily for me. I'll be right back."

As Nathan headed toward the stairs, Daphne sat back in her chair, watching Emily playing on the blanket. She had been gnawing on Ernie's head again, but apparently bored with that, she threw poor Ernie onto the blanket. "Da da da," Emily chanted. "Da da da."

Daphne decided maybe Nathan was right when he said that Emily had called him Daddy. The baby stared right at her, as if demanding to know where her father went.

"Daddy went downstairs a moment. He'll be right back."

"Da da da," Emily wailed, her bottom lip quivering as if in prelude to tears.

Daphne shook her head at herself. She was getting as bad as Nathan, expecting a seven-month-old to understand what she said.

She got up from the table and knelt on the edge of the blanket next to Emily. She scooped the baby into her arms and settled her against her shoulder. "Don't cry, sweetheart," she cooed. "Don't cry."

Daphne felt tears well in her own eyes as the baby's tiny hands clutched at her neck. She inhaled, breathing in the sweet baby smell courtesy of a recent bath. She sat back on her heels, relishing in the feel of the warm, wiggly body against her own. She stroked her hands over the baby's soft, curly hair, so much like Nathan's in texture, but jet-black in color, like her own.

A puff of baby's breath drifted across her skin, making her throat constrict and her stomach pitch as if she were adrift on a churning sea. Babies always did that to her, made her ache and feel empty at the same time. Holding Nathan's daughter, the sensations were more profound, more devastating, as she'd known they would be.

She lay down on her side on the blanket, cradling the baby in the crook of her arm. The baby yawned and blinked a few times, then brought her index and middle fingers to her mouth and began sucking on them. "Somebody's sleepy," Daphne cooed to the baby. As if to prove her right, the baby closed her eyes and snuggled closer to Daphne.

Daphne rubbed Emily's tiny back, whispering bits of nonsense to her in a soothing voice. She leaned down and kissed the chubby little baby cheek that dimpled when she smiled. She savored every little touch, every caress, because she knew she could never indulge herself like this in front of Nathan. He would see her reaction and question her about it. She didn't think she could handle that without blurting out the truth.

And since she had no idea how Nathan would react if she told him, her secret would have to stay just that.

When Nathan returned to the kitchen, he stopped short, taking in the scene before him. Daphne lay on the blanket with Emily beside her. He watched as Daphne stroked Emily's back in a maternal motion, then she lowered her head and kissed the baby's small forehead, all the while whispering softly to her.

He didn't want to move, didn't want to interrupt this private moment between them. But something about the picture they presented disconcerted him, though he couldn't say what. He leaned an elbow against the countertop and watched them.

As if sensing his presence in the room, Daphne turned to look at him. The beatific smile on her face slowly eased away to become an expression of sadness and, strangely enough, guilt. What did Daphne have to feel guilty about?

Daphne leaned up on one elbow as if to put distance between herself and the child. "She started to fuss while you were gone."

Nathan squatted down beside her, placing his hand on the baby's back next to hers. "I guess I'd better put Her Highness to bed."

Daphne nodded, but didn't quite look at him. He scooped the baby into his arms, cradling her against his chest. "I'll be right back."

He went downstairs and lay the baby in her crib, then leaned his arms on the railing, watching her sleep. What was it about seeing Daphne with the baby that bothered him? Maybe it was that in those few minutes, Daphne had lavished Emily with more affection than Monica had in six months.

He'd never get the answer standing here staring at the baby. He turned out the bedroom light and headed up the stairs.

Daphne hadn't moved from her spot on the floor. She lay on her side with her head resting on her arm. Her eyes were closed, but he didn't think she'd fallen asleep. He lay down next to her, propping his head up on one hand. He inhaled, and the light floral scent of her perfume reached his nostrils. That and the natural scent that was all Daphne. In that instant, his only thoughts of her centered on Daphne as a woman. He laid his free hand on her waist and gave it a gentle squeeze.

"What are you still doing down here?"

She opened her eyes and gazed at him languidly. "Too lazy to get up, I guess."

He stroked an errant braid away from her face, his fingers grazing her cheek. "You know, I never thought of braids as being sexy, until I saw them on you."

"Thank you."

"Wait, what was that? Did you actually accept a compliment from me?"

She raised one shoulder in a feminine shrug. "Could be."

She rolled away from him, onto her back. His gaze traveled over her face, to her throat and lower to the curve of her breasts revealed by the opening of her robe. When he focused on her face again, she regarded him with eyes that had darkened from a dark brown to almost black. The heat revealed in them turned his own excitement up a notch.

"You do know I'm going to kiss you, don't you?" he said finally. If there were any chance she'd rebuff him, he wanted to know it now.

A slow, teasing smile crept across her lips. "Then get on with it, before you talk it to death."

He lowered his head and took her mouth in what he'd intended to be a brief kiss. But Daphne had other ideas. She angled her head slightly, at the same time sliding her tongue past his lips to join with his own. He groaned as her arms slid around him, kneading the muscles of his back in an erotic motion.

He inhaled sharply, his heart thundering like a jackhammer, as she urged him down to her. One of his legs found its way between her thighs. He sank against her, wanting to get closer, but nothing save the removal of their clothing could afford him that.

That thought jolted him out of the sensual haze to which he'd succumbed. He lifted his head and watched her as her eyes slowly drifted open.

"Maybe you'd better get yourself into bed." Before he forgot every ounce of self-control he possessed.

"Maybe," she echoed, but she made no attempt to move. "Maybe I like it where I am now." She cupped the side of his face in her palm, stroking her thumb across his cheekbone.

He closed his eyes, dropping his chin to his chest. "Don't do this to me, Daphne."

"Do what?"

He raised his head and looked at her levelly. "Lead me along when I have nowhere to go. Call me selfish, but I can't share you with someone else."

"I'm not asking you to. I'm not seeing Robert anymore."

He stiffened. His first thought was that Robert had done something to hurt Daphne. "Why not?"

"I didn't think it was fair to date one man when I wanted another. And right now, I'm wondering when he's going to kiss me again."

An important message from the ARABESQUE Editor

Dear Arabesque Reader,

Because you've chosen to read one of our Arabesque romance novels, we'd like to say "thank you"! And, as a special way to thank you, we've selected four more of the books you love so well to send you for FREE!

Please enjoy them with our compliments, and thank you for continuing to enjoy Arabesque...the soul of romance.

Karen Thomas
Senior Editor,
Arabesque Romance Novels

Check out our website at
www.arabesquebooks.com

3 QUICK STEPS
TO RECEIVE YOUR "THANK YOU" GIFT
FROM THE EDITOR

Send this card back and you'll receive 4 FREE Arabesque
novels! The introductory shipment of 4 Arabesque novels – a
$23.96 value – is yours absolutely FREE!

There's no catch. You're under no obligation to buy anything.
You'll receive your introductory shipment of 4 Arabesque
novels absolutely FREE (plus $1.50 to offset the costs of
shipping & handling). And you don't have to make any
minimum number of purchases—not even one!

We hope that after receiving your books you'll want to
remain an Arabesque subscriber. But the choice is yours to
continue or cancel, anytime at all! So why not take us up on
our invitation to receive 4 Arabesque Romance Novels, with
no risk of any kind. You'll be glad you did!

Call us
TOLL-FREE
at 1-800-770-1963

THE EDITOR'S "THANK YOU" GIFT INCLUDES:

- 4 books absolutely FREE (plus $1.50 for shipping and handling)
- A FREE newsletter, *Arabesque Romance News*, filled with author interviews, book previews, special offers, and more!
- No risks or obligations. You're free to cancel whenever you wish... with no questions asked.

BOOK CERTIFICATE

Yes! Please send me 4 FREE Arabesque novels (plus $1.50 for shipping & handling). I understand I am under no obligation to purchase any books, as explained on the back of this card.

Name _____

Address _____ Apt. _____

City _____ State _____ Zip _____

Telephone ( ) _____

Signature _____

Offer limited to one per household and not valid to current subscribers. All orders subject to approval. Terms, offer, & price subject to change. Offer valid only in the U.S.

Thank you!

AN042A

Accepting the four introductory books for FREE (plus $1.50 to offset the cost of shipping & handling) places you under no obligation to buy anything. You may keep the books and return the shipping statement marked "cancelled". If you do not cancel, about a month later we will send 4 additional Arabesque novels, and you will be billed the preferred subscriber's price of just $4.00 per title. That's $16.00 for all 4 books for a savings of 33% off the cover price (Plus $1.50 for shipping and handling). You may cancel at any time, but if you choose to continue, every month we'll send you 4 more books, which you may either purchase at the preferred discount price. . . or return to us and cancel your subscription.

ARABESQUE ROMANCE BOOK CLUB
P.O. Box 5214
Clifton NJ 07015-5214

PLACE
STAMP
HERE

"Not tonight."

"Why not?"

He stroked the side of her face with his fingertips. "Because, sweet Daphne, if I put my mouth on you, I don't know when I would stop, or where I would stop, or if I would stop."

Her tongue darted out to lick the perimeter of her lips. "That doesn't sound so bad," she croaked out.

"No, it doesn't." It's all he'd thought about since moving in with her. "But not tonight."

She pushed him away, scrambling to her feet before he had a chance to stop her. "Good night, Nathan." She tugged on the sash of her robe, tightening it around her. "I trust you'll turn out the lights before you go downstairs."

She'd almost made it to the stairs, when he caught up with her. With a hand on her arm, he spun her around, backing her against the wall. But she wouldn't look at him. With a finger under her chin, he tilted her face up to his.

Even in the dim light, he saw the hurt in her eyes, and it stunned him. It hadn't occurred to him that she would see his refusal to kiss her as a rejection. Didn't she know how much it killed him to keep his hands off her as much as he had?

Bracing a hand on either side of her face, he leaned down so that their faces were only inches apart. "Make no mistake, Daphne Thorne, if all I wanted from you was a quick roll in the hay, I'd be on you so fast you wouldn't have time to breathe."

Her chest heaved as she drew in a breath. "What do you want from me, Nathan?"

"If I told you"—he nodded in the direction of the stairs—"you'd probably run up to your room and lock the door."

"I don't scare that easily."

Maybe not, but he did. He worried he'd jinx himself by

voicing the depth of his feelings for her. He knew she wanted him. She melted in his arms every time he touched her. But he wanted more; he wanted all of her. He refused to settle for less.

But she wouldn't make it easy for him. She slid her arms around his neck, leaned into him, and whispered, "Tell me what you want, Nathan."

As closely as she'd pressed herself up against him, he didn't doubt she knew exactly what he wanted and precisely how much. Unable to keep himself from touching her, he slid his hands down her arms to her shoulders and gently massaged the flesh there.

"I think the more important question is what do you want from me?"

He heard her sigh as she lowered her head to burrow her face against his neck. For a long moment she didn't say anything, but her warm breath floated over his already heated skin and her breasts teased his chest with every inhalation she made. How much of this sweet torture did she think he could stand?

Finally she lifted her head and gazed at him. "I don't know."

He unwound her arms from his neck and took her hands in his. "Until you figure that out, I don't want to rush into anything with you." He kissed the back of each of her hands. "I don't want to hurt you, Daphne, or leave you with any regrets you don't already have."

"All right, Nathan." She pulled her hands from his. "Good night." She turned to walk up the stairs.

"Daphne?"

She paused, but didn't look at him. "Yes?"

"I have this little award thing to go to. Do you want to go with me?"

She spun around, almost tripping on the carpeted stairs.

She braced one hand on the banister. "Are you asking me out on a date?"

She sounded half incredulous, half amused. "If that's what you want to call it."

"When is it?"

"Tomorrow night."

"Tomorrow night? You sure do like to give a person advance notice."

"Sorry about that. Actually, I forgot about it. That was my publicist on the phone earlier, reminding me to show up. So, do you want to go?"

"What about Emily?"

"She's too young to go. I called Nina while I was downstairs and asked her to baby-sit."

"What should I wear?"

"That dress you had on New Year's Eve should do nicely."

"What time should I be ready?"

"The car will be here at seven."

She grinned. "I think I can manage to look presentable by then."

At a quarter to seven the next evening, Daphne stood before the full-length mirror in her room surveying her appearance. She'd pinned up her braids, sprayed on her favorite perfume, and donned her diamond jewelry. She skimmed her hands over her waist, fingering the elaborate beading of her red halter-style dress. Its sweetheart bodice clung to her body like a second skin. The slim skirt fell straight to the floor, though a slit came up to the backs of her thighs.

"Not too shabby," she told her reflection, borrowing a phrase from her sister-in-law, Jenny.

Daphne dropped her hands to her sides. What would

Nathan think? That was the question of the hour. He'd downplayed this "little award thing" he planned to take her to, but she knew better than to assume the evening meant nothing to him or to the career he'd supposedly abandoned. For all she knew, they could be going to the Grammys. Like it or not, Nathan made his livelihood in the public eye. She didn't want to embarrass him or herself.

Daphne sighed. No use wondering about it when she'd find out soon enough. She grabbed her purse and shawl and headed for the stairs. She paused at the top step, seeing Nathan waiting for her at the bottom of the stairs. She knew the precise moment when he noticed her making her descent. His head lifted, and his gaze fastened onto hers. The fiery glint in his eyes told her all she needed to know. As she approached, he extended his hand to help her down the last few steps to stand beside him.

"Do I look okay?" she asked, needing to hear him say it.

She inhaled, waiting for his response, noting the frankly masculine way he appraised her. "Baby, if you looked any more okay, we'd never make it out of this building."

His voice, low and husky, filled her with sexual awareness. Her throat constricted and her breasts felt heavy and sensitive. Unconsciously, she folded her arms in front of her.

He ran a finger along the curve of her cheek. "Why do you do that?"

"Do what?"

He nodded toward her. "Cross your arms in front of you. You aren't hiding anything, quite the opposite, in fact. Don't tell me you're still self-conscious about your breasts."

Her mouth dropped open in surprise, and she snapped it shut. "I have never been self-conscious about my breasts. If I tried to hide them, it's because you were always staring at them."

He laughed, and she knew he hadn't missed her implication that he was still staring. "What can I tell you? Perfection invites admiration."

"Nathan," she warned. "Behave yourself."

"Behave? I don't know the meaning of the word. Besides, you asked me how you looked. I'm merely obliging your request."

He stepped away from her to pose as if for a magazine cover. "You haven't told me how I look yet."

She narrowed her eyes and made a show of looking him up and down. His stark-black tuxedo fit his lean frame as though it were tailored just for him. He wore a white silk dress shirt, which stretched across his chest in an appealing way. But his tie canted slightly to one side. She stepped toward him, lifting her hands to his throat to adjust it.

"I guess I won't be *too* embarrassed to be seen in public with you."

She tried to take a step back, but Nathan's hands had settled on her waist, holding her firmly in place. She glanced up at him and drew in a quick breath at seeing the look of stark desire in his eyes. He blinked and the expression dissolved into a lopsided grin.

"I never did thank you for agreeing to come with me on such short notice," he said.

For the second time, she wondered why he had. He certainly could have asked any number of women better suited to the type of evening he had in store for them to accompany him.

"We couldn't have the playboy of the western world show up without a date, could we?"

She'd meant to tease him, but the fire in his eyes dulled and he stepped back from her, as if she'd struck him. "No,

I guess not," he said, his voice as cold as his gaze on her. "Are you ready to go?"

She nodded. He led her to the door with his hand on her elbow. When he reached for the doorknob, she stepped in front of him, leaning her back against the door.

"Nathan, I'm s—"

"Don't, Daphne. There's no need for you to apologize. If I've been foolish enough to gain the reputation of a man with no character, I suppose that's what I deserve."

Daphne bit her lip. But he didn't deserve it from her. She alone probably knew how undeserved such a reputation had been a lifetime ago. And worse yet, she saw in his eyes that he felt she'd betrayed him. He'd confided in her that he'd made mistakes in his life, mistakes that haunted him, and she'd treated his admission as if it were a joke.

She opened her mouth, hoping to say something to dissolve the tension between them, but nothing came out. She'd hurt him, unintentionally, but that didn't change anything.

"The car is waiting," Nathan said finally, yanking the door open and motioning for her to precede him.

Reluctantly, she started down the front steps, hoping this episode didn't presage disaster for their evening.

Eleven

Midtown traffic, a nightmare on the best of nights, crept along at a pace that made a snail seem like Speedy Gonzales. Nathan watched a gray-haired jogger threading his way through pedestrian traffic along the sidewalk. The elderly man was making better time than they were in the bid to get across town.

He glanced at Daphne, who sat beside him, appearing to watch the traffic outside her window. He'd poured himself a glass of Scotch from the hospitality bar. Now he brought it to his lips and downed a gulp of the dark liquid. He should say something to her, anything to dispel the tension between him. But since no words of conciliation sprang to his mind, he kept his mouth shut.

He'd already said too much. He tore his gaze from her and focused on the scenery outside his own window. Back in her apartment, he'd overreacted. But realizing that Daphne saw him as the rest of the world did had stunned him, saddened him.

He knew Daphne. She could never love a man she didn't respect, and who could respect the man the world knew as Nathan Ward? He'd thought he'd made some headway with her, trying to show her he'd matured beyond the young man who'd left town to go on tour fifteen years ago. Nor was he the persona created for him by a deft public relations hand. But if she could see him, even in jest, as just another playboy, he hadn't accomplished anything at all.

He felt her take his hand a moment later, and he turned to look at her.

"Are you still mad at me?"

He squeezed her hand in his, a gentle smile forming on his lips. "Baby, I told you I wasn't angry with you. If anything, I'm mad at myself for living my life so frivolously."

"Sounds like a case of early middle-age crisis to me."

"It's not that early. In a year and a half, I'll be forty."

"Positively ancient. I'm surprised you can get around without a walker. Maybe we can get the chauffeur to scrounge up a wheelchair and a nice, warm lap rug. We know how easily you elderly types catch cold."

He snorted, shaking his head. "Is that your way of telling me I'm being ridiculous?"

She nodded. "Pretty much."

"An example of your *Moonstruck* method of therapy."

"At least I didn't have to smack you to get your attention."

She'd had his attention all night, even when he'd been staring out the window. He'd cataloged every move she'd made in the periphery of his vision, sensed the warmth of her body next to his, inhaled the subtle floral fragrance of her perfume.

He let his gaze wander over her heart-shaped face, the lush curves of her body. When he'd seen her walking down the stairs toward him earlier, his breath had stalled and his heartbeat had kicked into serious overdrive. He'd stood mutely at the foot of the stairs, rendered speechless for probably the first time in his life.

And now, as he brought his gaze back to her face, his pulse accelerated and his body hardened simply watching her. He'd never seen her look lovelier, and for tonight she was his. He intended to make the most of it.

His left hand was still joined with hers. He brought her fingers to his lips and kissed each in turn. "Have I told you how beautiful you look tonight?"

A grin tilted up the corners of her mouth. "I do remember you mentioning something about that."

"Now who's fishing for compliments?"

"Not me. I've had all the compliments I can stand for one evening."

"Then I won't tell you I'm going to be the luckiest man in the room to have you on my arm."

"Oh, brother. I thought men gave up saying things like that the same time 'Come up and see my etchings' went out of fashion."

She might scoff at him, but he could tell his words flattered her. She glanced out the window, apparently ignoring him, a sure sign he'd gotten to her.

A moment later, her mouth dropped open, and she leaned toward the window as if to get a better look. "Good lord, is this where we're going?"

He turned his head to see what had gained her attention. They'd stopped in front of the Palace Theatre. A crush of photographers flanked the red-carpeted entrance to the building. The car ahead of them had let out a striking couple, neither of whom he knew. They stood posing so the photographers could take their fill of pictures.

On either side of the photographers was a host of spectators, most with cameras, some with signs announcing love of someone or other. They were contained on the sidewalk by police barricades and by policemen and -women who seemed a bit overwhelmed by the task.

He squeezed her hand again. "We don't have to get out if you don't want to."

She leaned back, squaring her shoulders. "What makes you think I don't want to get out?"

"Because you look like someone just offered you a handful of worms." He gave her fingers a gentle tug. "Once we get inside, it won't be like this."

He laughed when Daphne responded, "I sure hope not."

The chauffeur opened the door for them. The minute Nathan alit from the car, Daphne heard the crowd roar to life. She glanced up at the marquee, which read DISC MUSIC AWARDS She took a deep breath, plastered a smile on her face, and grasped the hand Nathan extended to her. She stepped out onto the sidewalk, right into a barrage of camera flashes.

Nathan's arm closed around her waist, steadying her. "Are you okay?" he asked.

"I'm fine, as long as I don't need to see anything the rest of the night."

Nathan's grip on her waist tightened. "Come on, let's get this over with."

He led her forward on the carpeted pathway as both fans and reporters hoping for an impromptu interview shouted his name. He stopped by the one reporter who, Daphne noticed, called him Mr. Ward instead of Nathan.

While Nathan answered the woman's questions, Daphne surveyed the mass of people around her. She'd never understood the appeal of such a public life before. It must be a heady experience, hearing all that applause, being surrounded by all that adulation and knowing it was directed at you.

Nathan handled it all with an equanimity that surprised her. She would have sworn that in the presence of adoring fans, he would have exhibited every ounce of cockiness he possessed. Yet he seemed more preoccupied with her comfort, rubbing his hand over her arm to dispel the goose bumps that had risen on her arms due to the weather.

She focused on the reporter, who seemed barely old enough to legally hold down a job.

"Do you think you'll win?" the woman asked.

Nathan shrugged, seeming completely disinterested in the outcome one way or the other. "I guess we'll know in a couple of hours. Please excuse me. It's cold out here, and I've got to get my lady inside."

The reporter thanked him for his time, and they continued on their way. Once they'd passed under the elaborately decorated entranceway, Daphne drew to a halt, turning to face him.

"You didn't tell me you were up for an award," she accused.

"You didn't ask me. And I'm up for two."

She thought back to when they'd arrived. He'd offered to leave if she wanted to go. She hadn't doubted his sincerity; he would have told the driver to keep going if she'd given the word. She'd been sorely tempted to turn tail and run when she'd seen the crowd awaiting them outside the limousine window. Thank goodness she hadn't given in to that impulse. She wouldn't have wanted to deprive him of accepting an award he undoubtedly deserved.

"Do you think you'll win?" she asked him.

He grinned at her. "What do you think?"

Once inside the lobby of the theater, Daphne glanced around at her fellow attendees, most of whom seemed to be milling around, in no hurry to get to their seats. A more bizarre crowd she'd never seen. Some of the hairdos defied description or logic—and those were on the men. Most of the women dressed in outrageously revealing costumes in shocking colors. Daphne shuddered. Compared to some of them, she might as well have been wearing a nun's habit.

Daphne tightened her grip on Nathan's arm, drawing his attention. "I take it this is the see-and-be-seen portion of the evening."

"Unfortunately. I'd hoped we'd gotten here late enough to avoid this part of the festivities. Do you want a drink?"

She shook her head. "No, thanks. I have a feeling I ought to have a clear head tonight." As she spoke a man with a purple mohawk, full makeup including eyeliner in an electric shade of blue, and several painful-looking body piercings threaded his way past them. Daphne bit her lip to keep from laughing.

"I swear, this business just gets weirder and weirder." Nathan said, shaking his head. "And people wonder how I could walk away from this."

She angled her head to one side and studied him. He seemed completely at ease, but Nathan could be deceptive that way. "Can you really give it up? Won't you miss the applause, the fans? That was an impressive display out there."

Nathan touched his fingertips to her cheek. "There's only one person on this earth I'm interested in impressing."

Daphne swallowed, hearing Nathan's whispered words over the din of the rest of the crowd. He wanted to impress her? Didn't he know he already had? Not only tonight, but with the tender way he cared for his daughter, his candor when he told her about Monica and his past, his patient regard for her own wishes. Slowly but surely, this new Nathan began to come into focus, and she liked what she saw. She more than liked it.

Daphne cleared her throat, not knowing what to say to him. She settled for changing the subject instead. "You never did tell me what kind of award this is. I know the Grammys, the Emmys, the Tonys, but beyond that, I'm lost."

Nathan gave her fingers a gentle squeeze. "I know what you mean. Everyone and his mother seems to give out an award these days. I try to avoid them as much as possible.

Half the time it's more of a popularity contest than a legitimate industry recognition."

"Then why did you come tonight?"

"Because this is a fan-based award given out by *Disc* magazine. There's a poll in the magazine for nominations every September, and later you can vote for your favorite in each category at its Web site."

"God bless modern technology. Are you nervous?"

Nathan squeezed her hand. "No."

The lights dimmed and came up three times, signaling they should make their way inside the auditorium.

Nathan drew his arm around her waist, pulling her closer. "I guess we'd better go find our seats."

An hour later, after numerous speeches, presentations, live performances and commercial breaks, Daphne began to wilt. She'd barely had lunch and she'd skipped dinner entirely as she hadn't been able to get out of her office as early as she'd hoped. She leaned her head against Nathan's shoulder and closed her eyes.

"Don't conk out on me, now," he chided her. "My first category is coming next."

She immediately perked up. "Which one is that?"

"Favorite male R&B performer."

She laced her fingers with his. Despite his earlier nonchalance and his apparent ease at the moment, she could feel the tension in him. He wanted to win, and for that reason she wanted him to win, too. She held her breath waiting for the winner to be announced. When she heard Nathan's name called, she merely stared at him, pressing the fingertips of both hands to her lips.

He leaned closer to her, taking one of her hands in his. "Kiss me, baby," he urged, "so I can go collect my award."

She threw her arms around his neck and pressed her

lips to his. She invested that kiss with all the pride she felt in him, all the happiness that she felt for him. She touched her tongue to his, reveling in his ardent response to her. But, he withdrew from her almost immediately, his hands loosening her grip around him. She blinked and stared up into his smiling face.

He stroked her cheek with the knuckles of one hand. "I'd love to continue this some other time, but right now we're being watched by millions of viewers."

She'd forgotten about the cameras, the audience and the home viewers. She'd thought only of him. And truthfully, she couldn't care if the entire Vienna Boys' Choir stared at them in rapt fascination. "Then let's hope we gave them an eyeful."

He shook his head at her, as he rose to his feet. "Try to stay out of trouble until I get back."

She watched him ascend the stairs to the stage with a stride full of confidence and natural grace. Lord, he was beautiful, and for tonight he was hers. For tonight, they were a couple in the eyes of the world. She planned to use that to her best advantage.

By the time he reached the podium, where a very young, very clingy woman handed him his award, the applause had quieted. Nathan stepped up to the microphone, holding the statuette—a gold CD on an ebony base—in both hands. She listened as he thanked a number of people, but she didn't really hear anything. Not until his gaze locked with hers across the distance.

"There's one more person I have to thank. Someone who, at the beginning of my career, stood by me, believed in me, when everyone else thought I was just another kid with the pipe dream of making it big one day. I owe you more than I can ever repay." He held the award aloft. "But this is for you, sweetheart. Thank you, Daphne."

Daphne sat stupefied as Nathan exited the stage and the

crowd erupted into applause. Several people turned around in their seats to get a better look at her, obviously assuming correctly that she was the Daphne that Nathan mentioned. She ignored them, steepled her fingers and rested her forehead against them.

Why did he keep doing this to her—surprising her with his thoughtfulness? And this time in a public forum, where she couldn't even escape and he wasn't even with her so that she could whack him with something.

If he owed her, then she owed him as well. In those months following the fateful evening when she'd first kissed him, he'd been her rock, her salvation. Her mother had been the glue that bonded their family together. Without her, each of them had begun to fall apart in their own way. Nathan had been there for her, most days picking her up in the morning to drive her to school, seeing her home each night, making sure she never slipped into the depression that threatened to overtake her.

And gradually he'd introduced her to a world of sensual pleasure. He'd taught her about her body, where she liked to be touched and how. His mouth had given her her first orgasm, and his hands had driven her mad with wanting. He'd shown her a facet of herself that she never would have suspected existed. An earthy, sensual side that had blossomed under his tutelage.

And he'd taught her how to please him. She learned every inch of his body, from the birthmark on his left ankle to the tiny scar at his right temple and everywhere in between.

But always, always he'd stopped before they attempted the most intimate act of completion. Considering his reputation, Nathan's refusal to take her virginity confused her. Even at that tender age, she'd equated being in love with making love. And she did love him, more than she'd ever imagined possible.

She knew that in the beginning, he'd thought her too young. He'd tease her about not wanting to give her father any reason to have him thrown in jail, as no one else in her family could stand him or understand her relationship with him. But after they'd been together for more than a year, he still hadn't pressed her to go any further. Did he really want her or didn't he?

By the week before her eighteenth birthday, Daphne had gotten tired of wondering. She'd gone to him, braving the New York City transit system and the chill of the late autumn night to get to his apartment on her own.

He'd opened the door to stare at her in amazement, then growing anger. He leaned one shoulder against the jamb, holding the door open with one hand. "How did you get here?" He never allowed her to come there unless he brought her, afraid for her safety.

"I came by myself." She squared her shoulders, screwing up her courage for what she was about to say. "And I'm not going home this time. I already told my father I was spending the night at Linda Freeman's house. I want to be with you." Finally, she said the words she'd been keeping from him for so long. "I love you, Nathan."

He closed his eyes momentarily, and when he opened them again, the softness in his expression made her heart lurch. "Do you, Daphne?"

"Yes, I do." She dropped her overnight bag on the threshold of the apartment, threw her arms around his neck, and kissed him. He took her to his bed then, divested each of them of their clothes, all the while kissing, caressing, teasing her with his hands and teeth and tongue.

He lay down next to her, stroking his hand over her belly. "Sweetheart, I have a confession to make."

"Now?"

"Yes, now. I want to tell you before we go any further."

He heaved in a deep breath and let it out slowly. "I've never done this before."

"Done what?"

"Made love."

She opened her eyes and looked at him, really looked at him. At first she thought he was joking, but seeing the earnest expression on his face changed her mind. "What are you talking about?"

"I'm saying that I'm every bit as much a virgin as you are."

She stared at him incredulously. "B-but, I thought. I mean, I heard. The way you . . ." She trailed off, not knowing what, if anything, she wanted to say.

"Well, I haven't been a saint, exactly. Before we started dating I'd been with a few girls. I refused to be totally inept sexually. But I never made love to any of them."

"Why not?"

"I've spent the last four years waiting for you to be ready for me. I didn't want anybody else."

Tears sprang to her eyes, and she cupped his face in her hands to kiss him with everything in her heart. And she took him inside her body, feeling no pain, no regrets, nothing but a profound sense of being loved that no words could ever have expressed.

Last night, he'd asked her what she wanted from him, and she hadn't been able to answer him. She knew now what she wanted. She wanted to feel like that again, to feel cherished and desired and loved by him, only him. Over the years, she'd dated, but no one had ever touched her on more than a physical level. No one had ever captured even the tiniest bit of her heart. She'd been kidding herself all these years that she was over him. Maybe, if she was lucky, they'd only just begun.

* * *

An hour later, Nathan let them into Daphne's town house. She'd been unusually quiet ever since he'd returned to his seat. She hadn't balked when he'd taken her hand, but she hadn't looked at him, either. She'd simply sat there, worrying her bottom lip with her teeth to the point that he'd wanted to kiss the spot and make it better.

He hadn't won the second award for favorite song, and when another name was announced, she'd squeezed his hand and whispered, "I'm sorry." But he wasn't. Not about that anyway. All he'd cared about was discovering why she'd slipped into such a silent mood. He still wondered. With Daphne, such complete silence usually equaled anger. But she didn't seem upset with him, only pensive.

She leaned against the wall outside his door. With a hand under her chin, he tilted her face up to him. "Did I upset you with what I said?"

"No, but you didn't have to thank me. Whatever I did, I did because I loved you. You never made me do anything I didn't want to do."

"Maybe not. But I asked things of you that I shouldn't have. I expected you to make sacrifices that I never would have made in return. I didn't see it then, but I do now. I guess it's true what they say: Hindsight is always twenty-twenty."

It was on the tip of his tongue to ask her what had made her shut him out of her life. Had it been one thing in particular or had all his misdeeds simply added up to the point that she'd simply had enough? But he doubted at the moment he could handle what she might tell him, so he let the question die in his throat.

She reached out and cupped his face in her palm. "Whatever either of us did or didn't do, said or didn't say, can't we put it in the past?"

He turned his head and kissed the center of her palm. "If that's what you want."

"That's what I want."

"You'd better get yourself into bed if you plan on going to work tomorrow," he told her.

She surprised him by not arguing. "I know. Good night, Nathan." She leaned up and pressed her mouth to his, a sweet caress that made him want to hold on to her forever. For a moment, he indulged himself, running his hands over her bare back, burying his face against her throat.

Slowly she pulled away from him, walking backwards toward the stairs, a saucy sway to her hips and a teasing smile on her lips. "See you tomorrow."

Nathan chuckled, thrusting his hands into his trouser pockets as he watched her ascend the stairs. That was a threat if he'd ever heard one.

Twelve

Bradley was waiting for her in her office when she dragged herself to work the following morning. She stopped short upon seeing him sitting behind her desk, a scowl on his face, his arms crossed in front of him.

Too bad Sherry hadn't been at her desk to warn Daphne when she came in. Bradley was the very last person she wanted to see right now. She dropped her briefcase and purse in the chair beside the door.

"What do you want this time, Bradley? The Dow Jones not keeping you busy enough?"

"I see you took my advice and wore the red dress."

She merely stared at him a moment, until it dawned on her what he was talking about. He must have seen her on television last night.

She shrugged out of her coat and hung it on the back of her door. "I didn't know you condescended to watch television, much less MTV."

"I had a vested interest in watching this one. And I wasn't disappointed."

"What is that supposed to mean?"

"I saw a different side of you last night, Daphne. One I wouldn't have known existed."

"What *side* is that?"

"I always thought you didn't like men, or more precisely, that you liked women better. I'd always wondered if you and Victoria—"

"That's enough," Daphne said in a voice both quiet and lethal. "I don't care what you think of me, but Victoria deserves better than that from you."

He shrugged, but his cheeks colored and he averted his gaze. *Good,* Daphne thought. Maybe there was some little bit of conscience in the man. But when he looked at her again, with those cold, cold eyes, she knew he was on the attack again.

"I've been wondering something ever since I saw you on TV last night. What turns you on about being with a man like Nathan Ward? Is it money? Fame? I wouldn't have expected you to be so shallow. Then again, I wouldn't have expected you to tongue kiss a guy on national television, either."

Daphne gritted her teeth. She'd sooner give herself a root canal than discuss Nathan with Bradley. "Unless you have something of value to say, I suggest you leave before I have you thrown out. And this time, I'll bypass building security and go straight to the NYPD."

Her threat, as idle as the last, didn't faze him one bit. He rose from her chair and straightened his suit jacket. "This has been fun, but I've got to get to work."

He walked toward her, stopping only inches in front of her. Daphne glared up at him, but that didn't seem to faze him either. A feral grin turned his features into an evil mask. "Don't threaten me, Daphne. I'd hate to see you put in jail for false arrest. Imagine what all those nice government agencies who send you referrals would think about that."

He touched his fingertips to her cheek and, startled, she smacked his hand away.

He chuckled, not with humor, but with the satisfaction of knowing that he'd rattled her. "See you around,

Daphne," he said, resuming his advance toward the door. "Time is getting short for you, isn't it? Do let me know if you ever come up with the money to pay me."

After he'd gone, Daphne sank into her chair, rested her elbows on her desk, and put her head in her hands. What a ridiculous position to be in: needing money and sharing her home with a man wealthy enough to solve her problem ten times over.

But she couldn't ask Nathan for the money. She didn't doubt that he would give it to her. Knowing him, he'd insist on giving her the whole hundred thousand and refuse to take any of it back. That was the problem; she didn't want to be beholden to him. That, and her pride. How could she ask him for the money without telling how much of a mess she was in? She couldn't, so she wouldn't even try.

She sat back in her chair, and tried to concentrate on her work. Anything to divert her from the problem at hand. Tonight when she got home she'd retreat to her room and weigh her options, figure out what to do.

But one question nagged at her the rest of the day: How had Bradley known she'd be at the awards ceremony in the first place?

Nathan glanced at the kitchen clock for the fourth time in half an hour. Daphne was late. With Robert out of the picture, he didn't worry that she wouldn't be coming straight home. Besides, he'd seen the promise in her eyes last night as she bid him good night. She'd gone to bed as he'd suggested, but he didn't expect her to be that easy on him tonight. He counted on her not being so easy tonight.

But, where was she? He went to the kitchen window and looked out. Darkness had already fallen on the city.

Despite Daphne being a grown woman who could take care of herself, he still worried. Then he saw her, trudging down the street as if she, not Atlas, bore the weight of the world on her shoulders.

He huffed out a breath. For a moment, he wondered what the odds were that Daphne would come to him and share her burden, whatever it was. He doubted he could count that high. No, Daphne would handle her problems the way she always did: by herself. That would leave him in the uncomfortable yet familiar position of wondering exactly what it was that bothered her, and maybe comforting her if she'd let him.

He opened the door to her apartment to her, and waited with arms outstretched. He welcomed her into his arms, surprised she went into them so readily. She lay her cheek against his chest and her fingers gripped his shoulders. He held her, swaying slightly.

"I guess I don't have to ask how your day went."

"Rotten, awful, downright stinkola."

He couldn't help laughing at her assessment. "Stinkola? That bad?"

"Worse."

He rubbed his hands up and down her back. "Want to tell me about it?"

As he'd expected, she shook her head. "I'd rather not, if you don't mind. I don't even want to think about it."

Nathan sighed. Would it kill her to need him, just a little bit, to depend on him, just a little bit? "Why don't you take off your coat and come into the kitchen? Dinner's almost ready. Are you hungry?"

She sighed, stepping back, out of his embrace. "I'm not going to be very good company tonight. I think I'll just grab something and eat it in my room."

"Don't you dare. Not after I risked life and limb and electrical appliances to cook dinner for you tonight."

She blinked and a broad grin broke across her face. "Get out! And the kitchen is still standing?" She went to the archway that separated the two rooms. She glanced at him over her shoulder. "What did you make?"

"See for yourself."

He leaned against the counter as she went over to the stove, donned an oven mitt, and lifted the lid off the biggest pot. "You made water?"

"I'm waiting for the water to boil to cook the pasta. If you look in the other pan you'll find the sauce for the spaghetti."

She replaced the first lid and lifted the second. "Doesn't look too bad." She leaned down and sniffed. "Doesn't smell too bad." She got a spoon from the dishwasher and dipped it into the sauce. She brought a tiny sample of it to her lips. "Not bad at all. Classico Roasted Garlic?"

He shook his head. "Four Cheese. There's a loaf of garlic bread heating in the oven."

"I'm impressed." She rinsed the spoon and set it down in the sink. "You've discovered one of the three man-proof meals."

"I beg your pardon."

"Just a bit of woman wisdom. If a man invites you over for dinner, more than likely he'll cook one of three things: steak, spaghetti, or anything grilled. They're considered man-proof, because even a man can't mess them up."

"Thanks a lot. Your confidence in my gender's culinary skills is completely underwhelming."

She laughed, and he relaxed a little. "How long until it's ready?"

"About fifteen minutes."

"I guess I can't let you eat your first meal alone. I'll go get changed and be right back."

When she came back a few minutes later, he wasn't surprised to see her dressed in the black robe again. She stopped by the small playpen he'd bought for Emily that morning.

"I hope you don't mind if I keep that up here for when Emily and I are around. Now that she's mobile I'm afraid to leave her on the floor if I'm busy."

"I don't mind at all. Just remind me not to tell you 'I told you so.' " Daphne leaned over and stroked her palm over Emily's hair. "Hi, sweetheart," she cooed to the baby. Emily gurgled back at her, offering her a juicy baby smile.

Nathan watched the two of them, remembering the unease he'd felt the night before. Emily had pulled herself into a standing position, holding on to the railing of the playpen. Daphne hovered over the baby, stroking her hands over her small back. But she made no move to pick her up, which Emily obviously wanted.

"You can take her out if you want to," he volunteered. "It's time for her last bottle anyway."

With seeming reluctance, she lifted the baby out of the playpen and settled her against her shoulder. She turned to him, a wary expression on her face. "Do you want me to feed her?"

"If you wouldn't mind." He handed Daphne the bottle he'd already warmed.

"No, I don't mind."

She went to the table, taking the seat he usually occupied, which meant her back was to him. "Ssh, sweetie," he heard her say.

"She likes it if you sing to her."

Daphne glanced at him over her shoulder. "She probably likes it when *you* sing to her. My voice would probably shatter her eardrums and every window in the house."

Nonetheless, a moment later she started to sing "You are my sunshine," in a voice both low and soothing. Though she'd never had any training that he knew of, her voice was melodious and strong, a testament to the musical ability that ran in her family.

He closed his eyes a moment and listened to the bittersweet lyrics of the song. How many times had he experienced the sensation the song spoke of—dreaming of her, only to wake and find himself alone?

Abruptly, she stopped singing, and pivoted on her chair to face him. "I can't believe it. She's out already."

"I told you she likes to be sung to. Either that or that voice of yours has rendered her comatose."

She gave him a droll look. "Thanks a lot."

"Hey, you said it first."

She rolled her eyes at him. "Do you want me to put her in bed?"

"No, I'll do it. Everything's ready. Why don't you serve yourself? I'll be right back."

It took him only a few minutes to get Emily settled and return up the stairs, but in that time, she'd filled plates for both herself and him. He joined her at the table, unfolding his napkin in his lap.

"So what's the official verdict?" he asked as she scooped a forkful of pasta and sauce into her mouth.

She took a moment to chew and wipe her mouth with her napkin. "I told you I liked it before."

"I know, but I thought you were just being nice to me."

She grinned at him. "You should know better than that."

"I should." He let the conversation drop, concentrating on eating his own food and watching Daphne. They lapsed into silence, and he wondered if she'd fill the void by telling him about her day if he remained quiet.

She didn't. By the time they finished their meal, she hadn't said one additional word without his prompting her first. Nathan sat back from the table, wiped his hands on his napkin, and dropped it onto the table.

"Ready for the movie?" he asked.

She slanted a glance at him. "What movie?"

"Your favorite. *The King and I* is on A&E tonight. Starting in about—" He glanced at his watch. "Seventeen minutes."

He watched a grin spread across her face. "Seventeen minutes? We'd better clean up quick."

"I'll clean, you pop the popcorn."

"You've got a deal."

Fourteen minutes later, they carried the popcorn, sodas, and the baby monitor into the living room. Nathan settled on one end of the sofa while Daphne found the remote and switched on the appropriate channel. She sat on the opposite end of the sofa, drawing her legs up underneath her.

"What are you doing all the way down there?" he asked her.

She shrugged. "Getting comfortable?"

He shook his head. "Come here." She didn't budge, merely raised one eyebrow in challenge. The sofa wasn't long, but it was deep. He rested one bent leg against the back of the sofa, leaned over and grabbed her waist. He pulled her toward him. He settled her against him so that her back was to his front. "Better?" he asked.

She nodded. "Except I can't reach the popcorn."

He handed it to her. "Anything else?"

"Ssh, the movie's starting."

Nathan relaxed against the arm of the sofa as the opening credits began to roll and the overture from the movie began to play.

He reached around Daphne to grab a handful of popcorn. "What do you like so much about this movie, anyway?"

"A scantily clad Yul Brynner running around, and you have to ask what I like about this movie?"

"That's why you made me sit through this thing so many times? I'm shocked."

"Hush. You were probably too busy staring at Rita Moreno to care what I was looking at."

"Nah, she's too skinny in this one. I liked her better in *West Side Story*. She's got a little meat on her bones. 'A boy like that would kill your brother,' " he sang, mimicking an interpretation of the actress done by a popular comic. " 'Forget that boy and find another.' "

She giggled, such a rare sound for her that he squeezed her to him. "So you have the hots for Yul?" he teased. He found it impossible to be jealous of a man who had been several years Daphne's senior in the movie and dead now besides.

She nodded. "Actually, he reminds me of you. All that posturing and posing." She rested her hand on his thigh and gave it a squeeze. "But deep down, he was a good guy."

She glanced back at him, and he didn't bother to hide the shock he felt. "If you're going to start singing 'Something Wonderful,' I'm leaving."

" 'He may not always do—' " she began, imitating the King's wife.

He turned her face toward the television screen with a finger on her chin. "Watch the movie."

"Spoilsport."

Laughing, he wrapped his arms around her waist, intending to behave himself. But after a few minutes of her hair brushing his cheek and her sweet scent tickling his nose, he lost the battle for self-control.

His hand strayed upward, first to span her rib cage, exploring the delicacy of her bone structure. Then higher, to trace the fullness of her breasts with his fingers. He cupped one breast in his palm, kneading the soft flesh in his hand. He inhaled sharply, his nostrils flaring, as he heard a soft moan escape from her lips.

"Do you like that, baby?" he whispered against her ear. She didn't give him an answer, and he didn't really expect one. He knew her breasts were exquisitely sensitive. He slipped his hand under the cover of her robe to repeat the same exploration of her bare skin. She gasped, her back arching, as he found her nipple and rolled it between his thumb and index fingers.

He took the popcorn from her and placed it on the table. Then he turned her so that she faced him, kneeling between his legs. He cupped her face in his palms, pulling her down to him so he could kiss her.

His lips claimed hers, his tongue delving into the sweet, warm recesses of her mouth. She leaned into him, tilting her head to one side, giving him better access to her mouth. His hands moved up her back to cup her shoulders in his palms and pull back the collar of her robe with his fingers.

She pulled away from him, sitting back on her heels. "What are you doing?"

"I want to see you." He slid his fingers beneath the collar of the robe and pushed it from her shoulders. It banded around her upper arms, effectively imprisoning her arms by her sides. The silky material stretched low across her breasts. It didn't take much coaxing for the thin material to part and bare her breasts to him.

For a moment, he could only stare at her. She was so lovely, she took his breath away. All that smooth dark skin, tipped with even darker aureole. His hand began a slow, thorough perusal of the flesh he'd uncovered.

He covered one full, soft breast with his hand, squeezing gently. It swelled against his palm, as he knew it would. He slid his hand across to her other breast, to draw a circle around her nipple with his thumb. All the while, he knew she watched him, waiting for his reaction. He cupped one breast in the palm of his hand and gazed up at her.

"You're even more beautiful than I remembered," he said finally. He stroked his thumb across her distended nipple, then leaned down and took it into his mouth, tracing his tongue along the same path.

"Nathan," she moaned, her fingers digging into his sides.

Hearing his name on her lips only enflamed him more. He nipped her soft flesh with his teeth and felt her jerk in reaction.

He lifted his head to look at her face, while circling his palm over the offended area. Her eyes were closed, her head tilted back on her shoulders. He leaned down to trace a path of gentle kisses along the column of her throat.

"Did I hurt you?" he whispered against her ear.

She buried her face in the side of his throat. "No."

He cupped her chin in his palm, tilting her face up to him. She opened her eyes, eyes that had darkened to nearly black. He traced one finger down the side of her face. "Don't hide from me, Daphne," he chided.

"I'm not. I-we—"

That's as far as he let her get before he covered her mouth with his own. His hand slid around her back, holding her to him. But he wanted more. He wanted to feel her bare flesh against his. He broke the kiss, leaned back and yanked his T-shirt over his head. He tossed it to the floor, then pulled her back into his arms.

"Nathan," she called, this time in protest, as he shifted them on the sofa so that his back braced against the arm of the sofa and she lay on top of him.

"Shh, baby," he soothed. "I just want to feel you next to me." He groaned as she relaxed against him, her soft body molding to his harder one. Her cheek lay against his shoulder and her hands were trapped against his chest. He grinned wickedly, knowing she couldn't see his face. In this position, he could do anything he wanted, and she couldn't do a thing to stop him. His hands slid down to cup her buttocks in his palms, bringing her in intimate contact with his erection.

She squirmed against him, driving him to the brink of what little control he had. But she wasn't trying to arouse him, he realized; she was trying to get enough leverage to lift her head.

She gazed down at him, a soft smile on her lips. "I thought you wanted to take things slowly between us."

Nathan sighed. She couldn't do anything, but she could bring him to a screeching halt nonetheless. "I do remember saying something stupid like that." He touched his lips to hers briefly. "I do want to take things slowly, but I can't seem to help myself when I'm around you."

He captured her mouth again, this time for a longer kiss full of tenderness and yearning. When he raised his head, he cupped her face in his hands. "Go to bed, Daphne." If they kept this up, no power on earth would keep him from joining her.

She bit her lip, and by the hungry way she looked at him, he knew she was contemplating that eventuality. "Now."

She sat back, adjusting her robe into some sense of normal wear, then leaned down to touch her lips to his. "Good night, Nathan," she whispered.

She started to withdraw from him. He caught her hand in his before she could rise fully from the sofa. "Why'd you stop me?"

A sad little smile curved the corners of her mouth. "I don't want you to have any regrets, either."

She pulled away from him, and he let her go, watching her as she walked toward the stairs. Didn't she know the only regret he'd have is if he messed things up with her again? Maybe it was time he proved to her that his interest in her was more than merely physical.

She'd barely reached the first step when he called to her again.

"Daphne."

She stopped her advance, turning to face him. "Yes."

"I have to fly to L.A. tomorrow night. One of those commitments I couldn't get out of. I don't want to take Emily with me. Would you watch her for me?"

She didn't say anything for a long moment, and he tensed waiting for her response. "What about your grandmother?"

"She's got the flu. And Nina has some big project at work she's trying to finish over the weekend."

He hoped he'd told those outrageous lies with some semblance of a straight face. Nina had actually volunteered to come stay in his apartment while he was away, and his grandmother, as always, was healthy as a horse.

"How long will you be gone?"

"Hopefully, just for the day. Will you miss me?"

She shrugged, but a mischievous smile turned up the corner of her lips. "I'll have to think about it."

He chuckled, knowing she would, even if she refused to admit it. "So, would you mind taking care of Emily for me?"

"Of course I'll watch Emily if you need me to."

"I'll see you tomorrow, then."

Without responding, Daphne turned and walked the rest of the way upstairs.

"Your cab is here."

Nathan heard the driver's impatient honk, the second time in five minutes that he'd blown the horn. He'd finished packing ten minutes ago, but hadn't risen from his

spot on the bed. Going into the other room would signal
that he really intended to leave. He hadn't been ready to
admit that yet. He didn't have much of a choice, though.
He'd committed to this project a long time ago, and backing out at the eleventh hour wasn't his style.

He'd agreed to record the duet, which would serve as
the closing song for an animated movie, thinking Emily
would one day get a kick out of hearing her dad's voice
on a children's film. It hadn't occurred to him at the time
he'd signed on the dotted line that Emily would be too
young to travel with him.

He never would have suspected Daphne would be back
in his life, either, and that he would be loath to leave her.
Hindsight might be twenty-twenty, but foresight was blind
as a bat. He sighed, stood, and slung his bag over his
shoulder. Time to get his show on the road.

He stopped at the archway to the living room and
dropped his bag to the floor. Daphne stood by the front
window, looking out. She held Emily, who feasted on one
of Daphne's many braids. Daphne turned to face him.
"You'd better go before he leaves without you."

"If he knows what's good for him, he'll shut up and
wait." He crooked a finger at her. "Come here."

She walked toward him, offering him his daughter. He
wanted to hold Emily, but he wanted Daphne, too. He held
the baby in one arm and pulled Daphne closer with his
other arm around her waist. The two most important people in the world to him, he squeezed them both to him.
Daphne's response was to mold herself closer to his side;
Emily's response was to gnaw on his chin.

He chuckled, and Daphne pulled away enough to look
at him. "Help," he cried playfully. Emily's tiny fingers had
a death grip on his face.

Laughing, Daphne took the baby from him. He leaned
down and kissed his daughter's cheek, then stroked his

palm over her soft, curly hair. "You behave yourself," he admonished her.

Nathan straightened. "Do you think there's any chance she'll listen?"

"None whatsoever."

He smiled, cupping Daphne's chin in his palm. "You behave yourself, too," he whispered, before lowering his head and claiming her mouth with his own.

The cab's horn sounded again. Daphne slowly withdrew from him, her gaze lowered. "You'll miss your flight."

He'd miss them, Daphne in particular. No matter what, Emily would always be his; his hold on Daphne was much more tenuous. Suddenly, it seemed as if he were leaving forever instead of only one day. He knew in that moment, that any life that included him being away from her for long stretches of time was absolutely out of the question.

She stepped away from him. "Don't worry. I'll take good care of her, Nathan."

She'd obviously misinterpreted his melancholia. He didn't want to leave her thinking that he doubted her ability to look after his daughter. "I know you will." He stooped to pick up his bag. The car horn sounded again as he gave Daphne one last, brief hug.

When he pulled away he winked at Daphne. "That man is definitely not getting a tip."

Thirteen

Daphne pulled up in front of her father's house at a little before four o'clock on Sunday afternoon. She'd called Elise to tell her she wouldn't be able to come by early and help cook dinner, but hadn't explained why. She wondered what her sister would say when she walked through the door with Nathan's child in tow. Probably nothing that could be repeated on the front page of *The New York Times*.

She parked the car and retrieved a sleeping Emily and her baby bag from the backseat. Before she got even halfway up the walk, Alyssa ran out to meet her.

"Who is this little cutie?" Alyssa asked, scooping the baby out of Daphne's arms before she had a chance to protest. Alyssa didn't wait for an answer. She started back toward the house, cradling the baby in her arms and speaking to her in a singsongy voice. Daphne had to quicken her pace to keep up with her niece.

By the time they reached the house, Elise stood in the open doorway, her arms folded across her chest and a very unamused expression on her face. Alyssa squeezed past her mother and went into the house. Daphne wasn't so lucky. Elise moved to block her path as Daphne turned to close the front door behind her.

"Is there something you want to share with me?" Elise asked when Daphne raised a questioning eyebrow.

"You know very well that's Nathan's daughter."

"What are you doing with her? is more the question. And where is he?"

"He had to go out of town and asked me to watch her. Satisfied?"

"No. Don't you see what he's doing? He's sucking you into that life of his. How long before you spend more time wondering where he is than you spend with him? How long before he runs off altogether, chasing after some dream of fame or glory?"

"It's not like that, Elise. He's retired from his career."

"Really? Tell me, what's he off doing today?"

Daphne sighed. "He's out in L.A. recording a song."

"So much for giving up his career, wouldn't you say?"

"Is that the test of whether or not he cares for me? Whether he's willing to give up his livelihood for me? Well, he didn't do that for me; he did it for his daughter. He didn't want Emily raised by someone else."

"So the man is capable of doing one thing right," Elise said grudgingly. "Are you in love with him?"

She knew the answer her sister wanted to hear, but she couldn't give it to her, not if she were honest with herself. "I'm getting there."

"Oh, Dee." Elise shook her head, a sympathetic look in her eyes. "I hope he doesn't break your heart. I was there the last time. It wasn't a pretty sight."

Daphne leaned against the wall as Elise turned and walked into the house. No she didn't suppose it had been a pretty sight. Devastated by Nathan's departure, she'd withdrawn into herself, refusing any effort to comfort her. She and her sister had always been close, but she'd shut Elise out, unwilling to discuss Nathan with her at all. Elise probably resented Nathan for that, too.

Daphne huffed out a breath. She doubted Elise had finished on the topic of Nathan, either. So much for a pleasant evening spent in the bosom of one's family, too.

"Da da da."

Daphne looked up from her paperwork to focus on Emily. Daphne had brought the portable playpen into the office, set Emily and several assorted toys in there with her, and was trying to get some work done. That had been twenty minutes ago.

Daphne had come in early to catch up on a few things. All she'd succeeded in doing was reading the same column of figures a dozen times.

"Da da da," Emily repeated.

Daphne put down the pen she'd been chewing on rather than using. "I know. I miss him, too." Nathan had called her last night to tell her that the recording session hadn't gone as smoothly as he'd hoped. He wouldn't be making it home before morning.

Between thoughts of Nathan and the baby who beckoned her, she really wasn't going to get anything accomplished today. She should have stayed home and told Sherry to call her if she needed anything. Conceding the battle, she kicked off her shoes, skirted around her desk to where the playpen stood, and lifted Emily out of it.

"Come on, sweetie," Daphne cooed, settling the baby against her shoulder. "I'd hate being in that little playpen, too." She grabbed a couple of toys from the playpen and sat on the floor, snuggling the baby on her lap. "So what are we going to do now?" She held up the plastic Ernie. His face was caved in on one side from Emily's love bites. "Look what you did to poor Ernie."

Emily grabbed Ernie and drooled on a new spot on his head. Daphne laughed, stretching out on the carpet with

Emily sitting on her stomach. She drew her knees up to serve as a backrest for the baby.

She lifted one of Emily's little feet encased in a tiny StrideRite prewalker. Last night, she'd lain with Emily on Nathan's big bed playing "This Little Piggy" with that foot. She closed her eyes recalling the guilty pleasure she'd felt feeding her, bathing her, simply knowing that the little girl depended on her for everything.

And every time she'd thought about Nathan, she'd cringed a little inside. She should have told him. She should have told him years ago about their own child, but she hadn't had the heart to do it. Not when it had been over nearly as soon as it had begun. Not when she'd already been losing him anyway.

As his career had started to heat up, their relationship had started to cool down. He'd gone from playing the occasional gig to working steadily at one club or another. She'd hardly seen him anymore, and when she had, he seemed as if he were merely putting in time until he could get back to what he really wanted to do.

Or worse, he expected her to tag along behind him like some groupie and watch him perform. She'd plastered a smile on her face while other women flocked around her, pretending to befriend her, telling her how lucky she was to be with him. But the minute they'd thought she wasn't looking, they'd make a play for him.

To her knowledge, Nathan had never taken any girl up on her offer, but it didn't do her ego any good to know that if he ever sought to replace her, he wouldn't have to go looking; the women already flocked to him.

She'd been losing him, but rather than hold on more tightly, she'd let him go. She never could have competed with what had been his dream for as long as she'd known him. Nor had she wanted to. She'd had her own dreams, vague and unfocused as they had been. A life spent at the beck and call of any man had never been something she would have put up with.

Nor would she ever have tried to keep a man by virtue of bearing his child. If it hadn't been for the miscarriage, she would have told him about the baby. She wouldn't have had any choice. But she never would have expected him to stay with her because of it.

He'd already made his choice, anyway, by leaving town without so much as a word of warning to her, without so much as a good-bye. What more evidence would she have needed that the priorities in his life had shifted?

The sound of the outer office door opening pulled her from her reverie. She assumed Sherry had come in, and paid no more attention to the sound. She focused her attention on the baby instead. Emily gurgled happily, still munching on Ernie's dented head.

"Well, isn't this interesting."

Daphne tilted her head back to stare up into the cold, hard eyes of Bradley Davenport. Daphne immediately rolled into a sitting position, yanking her calf-length black skirt down to cover her legs. "What do you want, Bradley?"

Bradley braced his shoulder against the door frame. "He's even got you watching his brat for him now. How long before he gives you one of your own to play with?"

Daphne clutched the baby to her as she rose from the floor to stand behind her desk. She had enough sense to admit he frightened her. She was completely alone with him in a twenty-story office building at a time when no one else, save her equally defenseless receptionist, was likely to show up. Even useless building security didn't come in until eight-thirty. She wanted as much space and as many objects between them as possible. Unconsciously, she glanced toward the door and the escape it could provide her.

She focused her attention on Bradley again, who braced both hands on her desk, leaning closer to her, a derisive smile lining his lips. "If you're worried that I'll try to ravish your precious body, don't be. I told you I'd be back to finish looking over the records on this place. That's all I'm here for."

He straightened away from her desk, adjusted the jacket of his light gray suit, and strolled out of her office. A few moments later, she heard the door to Victoria's office shut.

"So glad to know I amuse you," she muttered under her breath. But she still hurried to her door, closed it, and locked Bradley on the other side.

By ten o'clock that morning, Daphne decided to give up the ghost and go home. Her mind wasn't on work; her thoughts were scattered, and she had yet to hear one word from Nathan as to when he might be able to get home. She packed Emily's things in her bag and readied herself and the baby for the frigid temperatures outside. She would leave the playpen where it was. She settled Emily into her little red-and-white stroller, and started out of her office door.

The sight that greeted her as she approached the reception desk made her pause. Bradley sat on the edge of Sherry's desk, facing her. She couldn't hear their conversation, but their body language spoke of the kind of intimacy not usually associated with computer keyboards and Xerox machines.

At that moment, Bradley lifted his head and gazed at her with a look of such utter triumph, it made her stomach wrench. She knew that if he hadn't already slept with Sherry, he was certain he could if he wanted to. And all to get back at her, for what reason she couldn't begin to fathom.

But it all made sense: the night she'd sworn she'd seen

Bradley in the elevator and Sherry had claimed to be waiting for someone, how Bradley had known she would be at the awards show. Sherry must have told him, because Sherry was the only person Daphne had told. She hadn't thought about that before.

Daphne shifted her gaze to Sherry. The instant their eyes met, Sherry's cheeks colored and she looked away. "Damn," Daphne muttered under her breath.

"Sherry, would you take the baby and ring for the elevator for me?"

Reluctantly, Sherry slid from her seat, and without looking directly at Daphne, wheeled the stroller away. To her surprise, Bradley got up and held the door open for her.

After Sherry left, Bradley closed the door and leaned his back against it. "Was there something you wanted to say to me?"

In all the time she'd known him, she'd never seen Bradley angry. His attacks, though malicious, were bloodless, lacking any real emotion. At the moment, he practically radiated with anger.

"You know damn well there's something I want to say to you. I don't know what kind of twisted game you're playing, but leave Sherry out of it."

"What I do or don't do with Sherry does not concern you."

"She is my employee and my friend. Of course it's my concern." Especially since Daphne had allowed Bradley to come into her sphere in the first place. She'd made up her mind to warn Sherry about Bradley, but she'd gotten so absorbed in her own life, she'd never gotten around to it. And now Sherry would pay the price for it.

"Stay away from her. She's a child. A baby. She hasn't even finished college yet."

"She's a grown woman with a mind of her own. And

if you try to turn her against me, I will make things very unpleasant for you."

Yeah, like he was such a bundle of joy now. "Leave her alone," Daphne repeated.

He yanked the door open and held it. "Don't you have an elevator to catch?"

Resigned to the reality that nothing she said would have one iota of effect on Bradley, she left. Sherry was the one she should be talking to anyway. She stalked past Bradley, and strode toward the bank of elevators almost directly across from her office door.

Sherry had been squatting next to the baby's stroller, talking to her in the high-pitched voice adults reserve for infants. When Sherry noticed Daphne approaching, she stood and smoothed her hands over her skirt.

"I took the blanket off. She was getting hot in there."

Daphne ignored her comment. In a soft voice, full of concern, she asked, "Why didn't you tell me you were seeing Bradley?"

"I knew you wouldn't approve."

Daphne let out a breath. Of course she wouldn't have approved, but what did that have to do with anything? "I'm not your mother to approve or disapprove of what you do. But I'd hoped I was your friend."

Sherry darted a glance at her. "You are, it's just that . . . I knew you two didn't get along. I know you don't like him."

"With good reason."

Sherry did look at her then, a spark of defiance flashing in her blue eyes. "He isn't like that with me."

Daphne shook her head. Why would he be? Any man bent on seduction knew how to behave nicely. But she also knew that telling Sherry that Bradley was using her would probably fall on deaf ears. At the very least, Sherry seemed infatuated with Bradley; at worst, she imagined herself to be in love with him.

Nor did she miss the irony of holding such a conversation with Sherry, when not one day ago, she'd been on the receiving end of similar comments from her own sister. Perhaps Sherry wasn't the only one deluding herself.

Daphne cupped her hand around Sherry's shoulder. "Just do me a favor, okay? Remember that if you ever want to talk, I'm here."

Sherry nodded. "I hear the phone ringing."

Daphne didn't hear a thing and knew Sherry simply wanted to escape from her. "Go ahead," Daphne said, feeling defeated.

Daphne bent down to readjust the blanket around the baby. She'd have better luck trying to discuss the theory of relativity with Emily than she would trying to convince any woman that the man she loved was no good for her.

Hours later, after she'd tucked Emily into bed, Daphne went up to her room, taking the baby monitor with her. Driven by the need to do something, she'd started sorting through the clothing Victoria had left her. The items she intended to keep already hung in her closet. Most of the other items she'd give to Goodwill. The suits she packed up to give to a friend of hers who ran Suited for Success, a company that provided interview clothing for poor women. Victoria had stipulated in her will that Daphne couldn't use any of the clothing for her own business; she'd never said anything about donating them to someone else's.

But the task was over much too quickly. With nothing else to occupy her mind, the events of the day nagged at her, haunted her. She sat down on her bed, gazing at the mirror across from her. The shiny silver glass reflected back a woman with bowed shoulders and dead eyes. None of the hauteur that Daphne Thorne was famous for. She had nothing to be haughty about, at the moment. Her entire life seemed to lay in shambles at her feet. And it was all her own fault.

She'd accused Nathan of being prideful, but she bore the guilt of the same sin. If she hadn't been so worried about her own image being damaged, she'd have asked Nathan for the money or, if not him, her brother. Then, she wouldn't be in this mess. She wouldn't have left an impressionable young woman vulnerable to Bradley's advances.

Something on the dresser caught Daphne's eye. An envelope. The letter Jonathan Craig had given her the day she'd discovered the contents of Victoria's will. She'd stuck it in her coat pocket that day and tossed it on her dresser when she'd gotten home that evening. She'd avoided opening it until now.

No time like the present to find out whatever message it contained. Maybe something to make her feel better about the situation she found herself in.

She leaned forward to pluck it from its space beside her perfume bottle. Settling back, she slid her index finger under the flap to open it. Inside was a single sheet of Victoria's stationery. She unfolded it and began to read the body of the letter.

If you are reading this, you must be wondering why I saddled you with Bradley as a partner in Women's Work. I know you two never got along, though you were gracious enough never to tell me so to my face. You may not believe this, but he wasn't always as you know him. As a young boy, he was shy and so sweet, you wouldn't have recognized him. We made him what he is, his father and mother and I, constantly fighting and wrangling over what was supposedly best for him. In his own way, he's had a hard life, too.

I know I have no right to ask this of you, but please look after him for me. He doesn't have anyone else, at least no one else of any substance. No one who could possibly guide him back from the path of enmity that he's chosen. In life, I could never seem to do anything right by him. Even in death, I can't give up on him. I'm counting on you.

Daphne glanced at Victoria's signature, just as a big teardrop splashed onto the page, marring the perfect, proportioned script of Victoria's handwriting. Daphne hadn't realized she was crying until she saw the drop of water seeping into the page. She swiped at her eyes before folding the letter and returning it to its envelope.

Daphne understood the guilt Victoria must have felt over her role in what she'd seen as Bradley's fall from grace. She sensed the pain Victoria must have felt knowing that nothing she did ever reached him. She'd expressed both sentiments to Daphne while she'd been alive. But had she honestly hoped that anything Daphne could do at this point would work some miracle and reform Bradley?

Daphne knew she didn't have it in her to accomplish that. She felt the weight of that burden anyway. *Always your friend,* Victoria had written. Her friend, yes, but she asked too much, more than Daphne could give. How could Victoria expect her to want anything to do with a man who treated her with such contempt? A man who would use a young woman merely for revenge? Bradley would destroy everything they'd built as blithely as he would get a shoe shine on the corner. What kind of legacy would that be for Victoria?

Suddenly she felt exhausted, tired beyond anything she'd ever experienced before. Too many decisions, too many wrong choices, too much pressing down on her shoulders, bowing her spirit.

She didn't want to think about it anymore, any of it. She wanted to wash it all away, to be cleansed of everything, both the past and the present.

And, God help her, she wanted Nathan. She didn't want him to do anything, she just wanted him to be here, to hold her, to make her feel safe. She needed him, and it scared her that she did. Especially since he wasn't here. All Elise's predictions of doom and gloom came back to taunt her. Could she ever really depend on him to be there for her?

She rose from the bed and, taking the monitor with her, went downstairs to Nathan's apartment. After checking on the baby, she went to the master bathroom and stripped off her clothes. Leaving them pooled on the commode lid, she stepped into the shower, turning the water up full blast. She shivered, even though the water raining down on her was warm.

Nathan let himself into his apartment, dropped his bag to the floor, and tapped the door closed with his foot. He hadn't managed to get a flight out of LAX until four o'clock that afternoon. It was after midnight now, and all he wanted was to kiss his daughter, make sure Daphne was all right, and fall into bed someplace for a good eight hours.

Lord, save him from the divas of the world. A recording session that should have taken a few hours at most had dragged on for more than a day—thanks to the machinations of the other half of his duet, a twenty-year-old wannabe who thought one hit album made her a star. What made it worse was that the powers that be put up with that crap, encouraged it even. The more bad behavior one could get away with, the higher up the musical food chain you could assume yourself to be. Nathan had never resorted to such nonsense as a means of asserting his personal power. A professional did his job and went home. He was exactly where he wanted to be.

Finding Emily was easy. She lay on her side in her crib, sucking her preferred two fingers. Not wanting to wake her, he readjusted her covers, kissed his own fingers, and touched them to her cheek. "Sweet dreams, sweetheart," he whispered as he turned out the light in her room.

Now, to find Daphne. He checked his room, but she wasn't in his bed, where he assumed she'd slept for the past two nights. He called her name, but got no response. The only sound in the apartment came from the direction of the master bathroom—a whooshing noise that indicated Daphne must be in the shower.

He knocked on the door, but getting no answer, he poked his head inside. The water was on full tilt, and it had to be hot; the bathroom mirror had fogged over and a layer of steam clouded the room. Perspiration instantly broke out on his own forehead from the heat. He could see the outline of Daphne's body through the glass shower walls. She probably hadn't heard him come in.

Not wanting to alarm her, he intended to back out the door and wait for her to come out. Then he heard Daphne sniffle.

Concerned, he stepped farther into the bathroom. "Daphne?"

"Nathan!" Another sniffle followed her surprised exclamation. "I-I'll be out in a minute." Her voice sounded strangely high pitched and strained.

"Are you sure you're okay in there?"

He got no answer at all that time. Genuinely worried, he opened the glass door and a gust of steam escaped. Daphne stood with her back to him, her arms wrapped around her middle, her forehead resting against the tiled wall. He knew instantly that she wanted to hide from him, not her body, but her emotions. She didn't want him to see her crying.

"Sweetheart, what's the matter?"

"Please, please, go away," she whispered.

But in her voice he heard a plea for him to ignore her words and come to her. He didn't hesitate. He stepped into the shower, sliding his arms around her, pulling her flush against him. The water, nearly hot enough to scald, instantly saturated his clothing, plastered his hair to his scalp, soaked through his shoes.

Daphne didn't fight him, she simply held herself rigid, refusing to relax against him. He leaned down to whisper in her ear. "Baby, tell me what happened."

He sensed the tension in her, the war inside her whether or not to confide in him. Finally, she sagged against him, lowering her head. "I've made such a mess of everything."

She sounded so anguished that his heart ached for her. "How did you do that?"

She shook her head.

"Tell me."

"I . . . Bradley . . ."

Nathan stiffened. He remembered the man he'd seen in her office. He wanted her; that much Nathan knew. And if Daphne was crying, only one possible reason for her tears sprang to his mind. It filled him with such rage that his hands tightened around her.

"Did he touch you?" She said nothing, only shaking her head, whether in denial of his question or as a refusal to answer him at all, he didn't know. "Did he hurt you?"

She remained damnably silent. He wanted to shake her and make her answer him. He turned her in his arms so that she faced him. "Daphne, tell me. Did he hurt you?"

Her response was to wrap her arms around his neck and

press her nude body against him. She stared back at him with darkened, troubled eyes. "Make love to me, Nathan," she murmured.

How was he supposed to say no to that? The expression in her eyes went beyond the simple desire he'd seen there so often. She needed him, and as many times as he'd wished that she would, he couldn't complain about the form it took. He would give her physically that which she would not accept from him any other way.

He stroked his hands down her bare back to rest on her hips. "Is that what you want?"

"Yes." Her hands slid down to the closure of his shirt, trying unsuccessfully to unfasten the buttons. He ripped it off his body instead. The silk was ruined anyway. He tossed it over the shower wall. It landed on the other side with a sodden plop.

Then her hands were on him, sliding around his back to bring him closer to her.

"Daphne," he groaned against her ear. Between the heat of the water and the warmth of her body, he felt as if he'd been set afire. He hugged her to him, his hands straying over her back, and lower to cup the soft flesh of her buttocks in his hands. She nipped his shoulder in response, and it sent a jolt of pure pleasure sizzling through him.

She leaned up and pressed her open mouth to his. Her tongue slipped inside his mouth, probing, teasing, taunting him in a way that made him groan into her mouth and made his fingers tighten their grasp on her. Her fingers dug into the muscles of his back, a sensation both pleasurable and painful at the same time. Her hips undulated against his, bringing him fully, achingly erect.

He'd never seen her like this, this frantic, this out of control. Again, he wondered what had happened in his absence to affect her this way. But he couldn't think beyond giving her the release she needed.

With his hands at her shoulders, he pressed her back against the shower wall. He divested himself of the rest of his clothes in the same hasty manner.

His eyes were on Daphne the whole time, watching her as she watched him bare himself to her. His gaze traveled over her face to the long, delicate column of her throat, and lower, to her full breasts, narrow waist, and gently flaring hips.

She leaned against the shower wall, her gaze traveling over him. Her eyes reflected back to him a hunger that rivaled his own. When he stood before her totally nude, fully erect, she whispered, "You're more beautiful than I remembered, too."

He smiled at her assessment, but his hands trembled as he reached for her. Despite her claim that this was what she wanted, he had no idea if he was doing the right thing by her. But neither was he prepared to stop now, not unless she wanted him to.

He cupped her breast in his hand, kneading the soft flesh with his fingers. "Are you sure, baby?"

The ragged moan that escaped her lips gave him all the encouragement he needed. He bent his head and took her nipple into his mouth. She gasped and her hands rose to cup his head, holding him to her. Her fingers threaded through his hair, setting off electric sparks along his scalp.

But it wasn't enough. The urge to taste all of her nearly overwhelmed him. He kissed his way down her body, using his tongue and teeth and lips to sample every inch of her.

Kneeling before her, he parted her with his fingers, baring her sweet flesh to him. He touched the tip of his tongue to her most sensitive core. She jerked against him, moaning his name.

The scent, the taste of her, drove him wild. He ached to be inside her, but this was Daphne's time, his time to give her what she needed. He urged her legs wider apart and slid two fingers inside her. He withdrew them, then thrust into her again, in imitation of the more intimate act he craved.

"Nathan!"

Hearing her urgent cry, he angled his head to look up at her. He replaced his mouth with his thumb, stroking back and forth over her engorged flesh. "What is it, baby?"

"I want you."

He rose to his feet. "You have me, baby." He flexed his fingers inside her to prove his point.

She hit him on the shoulder with the side of her fist. "You know what I mean."

And he knew from the breathlessness in her voice and the restlessness in her body that she wasn't far from coming apart in his arms. He buried his face against her throat, placing a series of kisses along her neck. "Come for me, Daphne," he murmured. "Let me make you feel good."

She did just that a moment later, arching against his hand, her fingers digging into his sides. He covered her mouth with his own, taking her cries into his mouth, holding her until the spasms that rocked her body faded to small tremors.

She sagged against him, and he wrapped both his arms around her, cradling her against his chest. "Are you all right?" he asked.

She nodded against his shoulder. He held on to Daphne with one hand and shut off the water with the other. "We'd better get out of here, before we both turn into prunes." He lifted her in his arms and carried her to his bed.

Fourteen

Hours later, Daphne stood by Nathan's bedroom window, looking out at the night sky. She wore the red robe Nathan had bought for her, one of the ones he'd sworn he intended to take back to the store. She'd found it and the others hanging in his closet a moment ago when she'd gone in search of something to wear. She should have known he'd never returned them, but finding them had surprised her anyway.

He surprised her. She hadn't expected him to understand her need for simple release. She hadn't known what she wanted herself until he was there, filling her with the most exquisite sensations imaginable. Then he'd carried her to his bed and held her until she'd fallen asleep in his arms.

She glanced over her shoulder at the bed where Nathan lay. His head rested on his own pillow, but his arm stretched out across where she'd lain, as if he was reaching for her in his sleep.

This was the man she'd spent the last day doubting—doubting that he cared for her, doubting that he was any good for her. With no more provocation than the reprehensible behavior of another man, she'd forgotten everything she'd come to know about him and had painted him with the same damning brush.

As she watched him, he began to stir, first feeling

around with his hand that lay on her side of the bed. Abruptly, he lifted his head, seeming to search the room until his gaze settled on her. He propped his head on one hand, watching her.

"What are you doing up?" he asked.

"Just thinking." She turned back to the window, hoping to forestall his inevitable question regarding the direction of her thoughts. He said nothing for a while. She relaxed until she felt the heat of his nude body behind her as his arms came around her waist.

"What about?"

She picked the least of her sins to tell him about. "It seems I owe you an apology."

"What for?"

"I used you to make myself feel better."

"Well, as the song goes, 'If it feels this good being used, go on and use me up.' "

"I'm serious, Nathan. I've never done anything like that before."

She let her eyes drift closed, as he stroked the side of her face with the backs of his fingers. "Baby, what makes you think I did anything I didn't want to do?"

"Maybe not, but you couldn't have gotten much satisfaction—"

"Believe me, I got plenty of satisfaction watching you climax in my arms." His lips touched down on her shoulder, warm and moist, sending a shiver of pleasure rushing through her.

"Why didn't you—" She almost said "make love to me," but that wasn't really accurate. He had made love to her, taking nothing for himself. "Why didn't you—"

"Come inside you?"

"Yes."

"For one thing, neither one of us had the foresight to

bring a condom into the shower. Until a few days ago, I didn't even own any."

That admission shocked her down to her toes. "You, Nathan? You didn't own any condoms?"

He sighed, and his breath fanned across her cheek. "You want to know the last time I had sex? A year ago, the night Emily was conceived. Before that, I don't even remember."

"You don't have to explain yourself to me."

"I know I don't. But I want you to know I haven't spent the last fifteen years seducing half the female population on the planet. In truth there have been very few women since you, Daphne."

That left her to wonder why Emily's mother had been one of those women. Especially since Monica had been living with Daphne's brother at the time. "Then why did you—?"

"Why did I sleep with Monica?" She sensed a reluctance in him, an unwillingness to share that part of his past with her. She heard him exhale, as he rested his chin on top of her head.

"I wish I had a better answer for that. I was feeling sorry for myself and she was there. She told me that things were over between her and Michael. But the fact is, I should have exercised some of my renowned self-control, and I didn't. Chalk it up to one more mistake for the great Nathan Ward."

She turned in his arms to face him. Cupping his cheeks in her palms, she stood on tiptoe and pressed her lips to his. "I don't care, Nathan. I don't care who you've been with or what you've done. I was curious, that's all, but I had no right to ask you. I told you I wanted to put the past in the past and I meant it. So, if you insist on beating yourself up, don't do it on my account."

She kissed him again, and this time his arms closed

more tightly around her, banding her to him. One of his hands rose to cradle her head as he deepened the kiss, sliding his tongue into her mouth to mate with her own. She melted against him, running her hands over his shoulders, his back, anywhere she could reach. Moisture pooled between her thighs in anticipation of what was to come.

He lifted his head and stared down at her. His eyes had turned that remarkable shade of green she knew so well. "Come back to bed with me," he whispered, his voice rough.

She shook her head. She wanted to stay there by the window, where she could see him. Moonlight filtered in through the window, painting his skin a silver hue. She lowered her gaze, tangling her fingers in the dark brown hair that furred his chest.

She turned him so that his back faced the window. "Sit," she said. She pushed against his shoulders, not hard enough to topple him, but he seemed willing to oblige her. He sank onto the cushioned window seat, bracing his hands on either side of him.

"What are you doing?" he asked.

"Finishing what we started."

She untied the sash of her robe and slid the silky garment from her shoulders. It slithered soundlessly to the floor. She watched his gaze follow its path and travel back up again to settle on her face.

"Come here," he said, reaching for her.

She pushed his hands away and knelt between his spread legs. "Not yet."

Grasping his shaft in both hands, she took him into her mouth, reveling in Nathan's uninhibited groan of pleasure. But she wanted more. She wanted to give him back the ecstasy he'd given her. She wanted to make him tremble with it, to call out her name as she'd called out his when her orgasm overtook her.

She slid one hand lower, to cup his scrotum in her palm. She squeezed gently, eliciting another groan from him.

His hand locked around her wrist, trying to stop her. "Baby, don't," he growled. "I can't take too much of this. I want to be inside you."

She wanted him inside her, too. She'd planned on it. She retrieved the condom she'd stashed in her pocket soon after she'd risen from Nathan's bed. She rolled it on to him, knowing he watched her. When she glanced up at him, his gaze was so hot, so intense, that it sent a shiver through her.

She rose to her feet, and he pulled her onto his lap to straddle him. She lowered herself onto his shaft, her muscles contracting as she filled herself with him.

"Oh, God," Nathan groaned, as his arms closed around her, pulling her against him. She buried her face in the side of his neck. For a moment it was enough for him simply to hold her.

Then, slowly, sensuously, she started to move over him. His hands grasped her hips, guiding her, helping her set a rhythm. He thrust into her, and she moaned, her back arching, her head lolling back on her shoulders.

One of his hands rose to cradle her head; the other cupped one of her breasts in his palm. He lowered his head and took her nipple into his hot, hot mouth, teasing her tender flesh with his tongue.

"Nathan," she cried out.

"I'm here, sweetheart."

He thrust into her again, sending shafts of pure pleasure rocketing through her body. She inhaled, drinking in air, breathing in the scent of their lovemaking that permeated the room. A sheen of perspiration coated her skin as her movements became more rapid and less deliberate. It was too much, this growing ache inside her that yearned for completion.

And suddenly she was afraid, terrified of losing what little control she had, of losing herself in him. Afraid most of all that she wouldn't please him.

"Nathan," she whimpered, against his neck.

He cupped her face in his palms, forcing her to look at him. "Don't fight it, baby. Let it happen."

"Come with me," she pleaded.

He grinned. "Wild horses couldn't stop me."

She pressed her mouth to his, kissing him with all the passion inside her. She trembled as his hands made a slow, erotic journey down her body to settle on her hips. Holding her in place, he thrust into her again and again, making her writhe, making her call out his name.

"That's it, baby," he growled against her throat. "That's it."

He thrust into her again, and she lost it. Her entire body shook, as wave after wave of ecstasy rippled through her. And beneath her, she felt Nathan's body shudder. He buried his face against her throat, crushing her to him, as the tremors in his body overtook him. Daphne clung to him, stroking his back, feeling him tremble beneath her fingertips.

When he could breathe somewhat normally again, Nathan raised his head. He touched his lips to Daphne's temple. "Thank you."

She raised her head to look at him, a puzzled expression on her face. "For what?"

He stroked her braids away from her face. He didn't know what to say now that he'd opened that particular can of worms. He'd felt her tense up and start to withdraw from him. He didn't know why, but at the moment he didn't want to question her about it. All that mattered to him was that she'd let it go, she'd trusted him.

"That was you here a moment ago, wasn't it? That woman who rocked my world off its axis."

She lowered her head, but not before he saw the huge grin on her face. "Did I?"

"You know you did. Just like I rocked yours."

She lifted one shoulder in a feminine shrug. "You might have nudged it a little bit."

"Liar." He cupped her breast in his palm and stroked his thumb over her nipple. Daphne closed her eyes, as a soft gasp escaped her lips. He leaned closer to her and whispered in her ear, "All I have to do is touch you and you melt."

"Egotist," she shot back. But when she opened her eyes and looked at him, all the humor in him died a quick death. Her dark brown eyes had darkened to almost black. And in them he saw a renewed desire he was powerless to ignore. She rocked her hips against him and he felt himself surge to life, still inside her.

He wanted her again, too, but not here. "Hold on to me," he said. She obliged him, wrapping her arms around his neck and her legs around his waist. He stood, intending to carry her to his bed. Then he heard her moan his name against his throat.

"What is it, baby?"

"I'm not making it to the bed."

Tangling his fingers in her braids, he pulled her head back so that he could look at her. Her eyes were closed, and her teeth clamped on her lower lip. He lowered his head and took her lip into his mouth, stroking his tongue over the offended spot.

She moaned and moved against him, and he lost it. Angling her hips to better receive him, he drove into her like a madman. She convulsed around him almost immediately, her muscles contracting around him, her nails scoring his back. He groaned and let his own release overtake him, a powerful wave of exquisite sensation that actually left him weak.

Somehow he made it to the bed and collapsed on it with Daphne on top of him. He lay there for a long time, simply holding her. She snuggled against him, her hands against his chest, her cheek resting on his shoulder. He'd thought she'd fallen asleep, until she lifted her head and looked down at him.

"You, Mr. Ward, are absolutely awesome."

He brushed her braids over her shoulder. "You're not so bad yourself, kid." He cupped her face in his hands and brought her lips down to his for a brief kiss.

"You'd better get some sleep if you plan to go to work tomorrow." He waited, hoping she'd say she had no plans to go into her office. He no longer believed Bradley had done anything to harm Daphne physically, but he'd damn sure shaken her up emotionally. He didn't want her confronting him again alone, but he doubted she'd allow him to accompany her to the office without a fight.

Daphne sighed. "I'd love to go in late tomorrow, but I've got an appointment out of the office first thing in the morning."

Hearing that, another plan began to form in Nathan's mind. He laid Daphne back on the pillows, disposed of the condom, and rejoined her. He pulled the covers over them and settled her against his chest. "Then go to sleep, sweetheart," he crooned.

When he was sure Daphne was asleep, he slipped from the bed, checked on the baby, and went to the phone in the living room and dialed Michael's number.

"This had better be good," Michael said in greeting.

"It is. How early can you be over here tomorrow morning? I need someone to watch Emily."

"Since when do I look like a baby-sitter to you? Get Daphne to watch her."

"If I wanted Daphne to know, I wouldn't be calling you, would I?"

Nathan heard the rustling of sheets in the background, and imagined Michael sitting up in bed. "All right, Ward. What's going on?"

"Some guy in Daphne's office got out of line with her, and I intend to straighten him back up."

Without hesitation, Michael asked, "What time do you want me there?"

"Eight o'clock."

"I'll be there."

Nathan hung up the phone and went back to bed. Daphne lay on her side, facing away from him. He slid in behind her and pulled her against him, stroking his hands over her soft, lax body. It was a long, long time before he finally drifted off to sleep.

Nathan opened the door the next morning to find a sleepy-looking Michael staring back at him. Nathan huffed out an annoyed breath. "You're late."

Michael covered his mouth and yawned. "You're the one who called me in the dead of night. You woke Jenny up, and I had to find some means of distracting her from asking what you were calling about." He yawned again. "Let's just say I didn't get much sleep last night."

"Well, wake up. I'm not going to leave Emily with you if you're going to be asleep two minutes after I leave."

"I'm fine. Give me the baby."

Nathan handed his daughter to Michael. "She's bathed, fed, and changed. All you have to do is make sure she doesn't bump into the furniture while she crawls around."

"Yes, Dad," Michael teased. "And if I do a good job can I borrow the car tonight?"

Casting a sour look at Michael, Nathan went to the coat-rack to retrieve his jacket. Out of the corner of his eye he saw Michael come to lean against the wall beside him.

Michael shifted the baby in his arms. "You're not going to do anything stupid, are you?"

Nathan slipped on his jacket. "Probably."

Michael sighed. "Look, I completely understand how you feel. But Daphne is not going to appreciate what you're doing. You know that."

"Yeah, I know. But what do you want me to do, Mike? The bastard made her cry. I can't have that. Tell me you would do anything differently in my position."

"I'm not saying I would. But when Daphne finds out about this, I want to be able to say I tried to talk you out of it."

"Chicken," Nathan accused.

"Damn straight. I don't want her tearing a strip off me over what you do. I like my hide the way it is."

Nathan snorted. "If Daphne asks, you didn't know anything about it." He walked over to where Michael stood, leaned down and kissed Emily's cheek. "Just take care of my daughter. And you, Miss"—he waved a finger at Emily—"behave for Uncle Mike."

Nathan let himself out the door and loped down the outside stairs.

When he got to Daphne's office, Sherry wasn't at her desk, which was one thing in his favor. Sherry would probably call Daphne if she saw him. He planned to be in and out before Daphne ever found out.

He stalked down the hallway to Bradley's office, stopping in the doorway. Bradley was seated behind his desk, as Nathan had expected he would be. Nathan wanted to smash his fist in the man's face, just on sight. But despite what he'd told Michael, all he intended to do was give Bradley a warning.

Bradley looked up, a derisive expression coming over

his face. He leaned back in his chair, swiveling slightly from side to side. He steepled his fingers in front of him. "Well, well, well. If it isn't Nathan Ward in the flesh. What can I do for you today?"

Despite his nonchalant pose and flippant attitude, Nathan sensed an undercurrent of pure hatred in Bradley that their one brief meeting couldn't explain.

Nathan stepped forward, glaring at Bradley with all the contempt he felt. "It's not what you can do for me, it's what I can do for you. A bit of friendly advice. Leave Daphne alone."

"Sorry, *friend,* but I can't help you there." Bradley stood and braced his hands on his desk. "I take it Daphne hasn't told you about our very special partnership, so let me fill you in. If she really wants to get rid of me, she knows what she has to do. And since she hasn't done it, I'm figuring she must not mind my, um, company. So why don't you run on home and when I'm through with her, you can have her back."

Nathan didn't miss his implication that some sort of sexual relationship existed between the two of them. He didn't believe that for a moment. Anger speared through him, white-hot and quick as lightning.

One moment, he was standing on the opposite side of the desk. The next, he'd vaulted over it, knocked the chair out of the way, and had Bradley against the window, his hands locked around Bradley's throat.

He wasn't smirking now. In fact, Nathan noted with a surge of satisfaction, every bit of color had leached from Bradley's skin. Nathan leaned in so that his face was only inches away from the other man's. "Nobody talks about Daphne like that," he said in a low, deadly voice. "Nobody."

Then he heard a sound that made him freeze in place and the blood run cold in his veins.

"What is going on here?"

Hearing the outrage in Daphne's voice, he gritted his teeth and prayed for strength. He let go of Bradley, who sagged back against the window, coughing.

Nathan turned to Daphne and opened his mouth to speak. She silenced him with a narrow-eyed look that sent a chill of alarm through him. She wasn't merely angry with him, she was furious.

"Don't bother to explain. I know exactly what's going on here. You thought you'd avenge my honor by coming in here acting like a caveman. Real mature, Nathan. Real mature."

She turned and started toward the door. Nathan watched her walk away, not sure what to do or say. Or maybe he should avoid doing or saying anything more with Daphne in her present mood. He felt a short-lived moment of hope when she paused at the open door and turned back. "Bradley, are you all right?"

"I'm fine."

Brows drawn together, Nathan's head snapped around. He'd have sworn Bradley would use this opportunity to make him look worse in Daphne's eyes. In response to his stare, all Bradley did was shrug.

"As for you, Nathan," Daphne said, drawing his attention. "You have five minutes to get out of my office before I have you arrested for trespassing. And that's not a threat, it's a promise." With that, she marched from the room. A moment later he heard the door to her office slam.

Nathan was out the door a second later. He went to her office door and knocked softly. "Daphne, it's me, Nathan. Open the door."

Absolute silence was the only response. God, he hated Daphne's silence. It infuriated him, as it always had. "Daphne," Nathan yelled, "open this door before I break it down."

For a moment, Nathan contemplated actually putting his shoulder to the door, but all he'd accomplish would be to anger Daphne further. Sighing, he resigned himself to the fact she wasn't going to speak to him. He shoved his hands in his trouser pockets and walked out of the office. She might be able to avoid him here in the office, but at home, he wouldn't let her get off so easily.

When Daphne's cab pulled up in front of her town house that night, Nathan was sitting outside on the front steps, head down. He looked so forlorn, the temptation to feel sorry for him assailed her. She bit her lip, steeling herself against that emotion.

She, not he, was the injured party. He'd not only humiliated her with that display of territoriality, he'd put her in an even worse position with Bradley. She'd missed Bradley's departure after she'd closeted herself in her office, but Sherry had told her he'd left looking angry and determined. The question was, determined to do what? File assault charges against Nathan most likely.

Daphne paid the driver and got out of the car. As she walked, Nathan's head came up. She ignored him, marching up the stairs and through the unlocked doorway. She slid off her coat and hung it on the coatrack.

She felt Nathan watching her, but she refused to look at him or speak to him, which is what she knew he was waiting for. He wanted some indication of the level of her anger with him. Right now, it was still off the scale. If he expected civil conversation from her, he'd have to wait until later.

She turned to walk up the stairs to her apartment, but Nathan blocked her path.

"Aren't you going to say something?"

She glared up at him, her eyes as frigid as the weather outside, remaining completely silent.

Nathan dropped his hand, moving out of her way. "Before you go, would you mind telling me what exactly you are so upset about?"

"You mean aside from the fact that you nearly choked the life out of another human being today?"

"If there was another human being in the room, I must have missed him."

"And what about Emily? What is supposed to happen to Emily if you get thrown in jail for assault?"

"We both know that if he planned to file charges against me, I'd have had a visit from our friends in blue by now. If you ask me, he's more likely to be interested in a payoff to keep his mouth shut. He can go hang himself if he thinks I'll give him one thin dime, so what's the problem?"

"The problem is, Nathan, that I do not need you to fight my battles for me, literally or figuratively."

She started to walk past him, but he caught her by the waist, pulling her back against him. "You definitely needed something last night," he said softly against her ear. "And since I'm the man who gave it to you, I have every right to want to protect you."

She tried to move away from him, but his grip around her waist tightened. "What is he to you, Daphne? What hold does he have on you?"

She knew she couldn't get out of explaining her relationship to Bradley. Things had gone too far already. She didn't have the money, and, short of taking Bradley to court, there was no other way to get rid of him. Worst of all, she feared what Nathan would do the next time Bradley got out of line. She didn't doubt there would be a next time.

Daphne let go of the breath she'd been holding. "He's Victoria's stepson and my partner. For one hundred thousand dollars, which I don't have, he'll go away and leave me alone. Or that was the deal until this morning. I don't know what he'll do now."

"How much do you have?"

"About sixty thousand dollars."

"Does that include the money I gave you?"

"No. I told you that's not my money. It's in the bank."

"Let me help you, Daphne. At least let me do that for you."

She nodded, feeling utterly defeated. "All right."

"I'll have a check for you first thing tomorrow morning."

"Thank you." She extricated herself from him and walked out of his apartment without looking back.

Fifteen

Daphne stalked into Bradley's office the following morning, slapped the envelope containing Nathan's certified check for one hundred thousand dollars on the desk, and stood back, crossing her arms in front of her. "There's your money. Now get out."

Bradley leaned back in his chair, looking up at her, an unreadable expression on his face. "I don't want your money."

"That's too bad, because you're going to get it. Don't let the door hit you on the way out." She turned, intending to go to her office and try to get some work done that day. Before she'd taken two steps, Bradley stood in front of her, blocking her way.

She stopped in her tracks. "Lay one finger on me, and I'll have Nathan back here in a flash. And this time I won't care what he does to you."

Bradley raised his hands as if in surrender. "I just want to talk to you."

"So talk."

"Sit down . . . please."

She looked at Bradley, really looked at him. A line of purplish bruises was visible above the collar of his shirt. Despite her dislike for Bradley, she couldn't help feeling a pang of guilt at the evidence of what Nathan had done to him.

She crossed to one of the chairs facing his desk and sat down on the edge. "You've got five minutes."

Bradley walked behind his desk, but didn't sit. He stood by the window looking out. "Do you remember the first time we met?"

Daphne blinked. He wanted a stroll down memory lane? What for? "Of course I remember. It was at Victoria's Christmas party six years ago. What has that got to do with anything?"

"You were wearing this outrageous black dress. And you wore your hair down then, not in braids. I practically dragged Victoria over to where you were for her to introduce me to you."

"And . . . ?"

"And, I thought you'd pat me on the head and offer me some cookies and milk."

"You were my partner's stepson. How was I supposed to treat you?"

"I wasn't a child. I was a twenty-five-year-old man, and I was infatuated with you."

She folded her arms in front of her. "I see, I dented your little ego, and you decided to behave as badly toward me as humanly possible."

"Something like that. Then, I found out that you were Victoria's best friend and business partner."

She supposed that automatically tainted her in his eyes. "What did Victoria ever do to you to make you hate her so much?"

"Victoria destroyed my parents' marriage."

Daphne shook her head. She'd heard the story of Victoria and Bradley's father years before. "Victoria didn't know your father was married until she'd already fallen in love with him. She told him she wouldn't have anything more to do with him while he was married to someone else. It was your father's decision to end things with your mother so that he could marry Victoria."

Daphne waved her hand in Bradley's direction. "And who are you to talk, anyway? You destroyed her marriage to your father. He divorced Victoria because you made it impossible for them to get along. He chose you instead of her. So, who was the villain of that piece?"

Bradley shook his head. "My father divorced Victoria because he thought she was having an affair with Jonathan Craig."

Daphne narrowed her eyes at Bradley. "Why would he think something like that? Victoria and Jonathan were never anything more than friends."

"Because that's what I told him."

Daphne stared at him, shocked by what Bradley revealed. "Bradley, how could you? Victoria was never anything but good to you. She treated you as if you were her own son, and that's how you repaid her?"

He shoved his hands in his trouser pockets. "I never expected him to believe me. As far as my father was concerned, Victoria walked on water. He always sided with her against me. But when he confronted her with my accusation, she got angry and walked out. So, he assumed I'd been telling the truth."

Daphne lowered her head and closed her eyes. What a convoluted mess! Bradley must have been all of eight years old when his parents divorced. She could imagine him as a young boy, desperate for his father's love and willing to do anything to get it. But he must have been an adult when he'd told the lie that ended Victoria's marriage—old enough to know what consequences such a story would bring. And what did it matter now? All of it was water under the bridge, a past none of them could go back and change.

She lifted her head. "Why are you telling me all this?"

"As an apology of sorts."

"Why?"

Bradley snorted. "Having another man's hands around your throat gives you a bit of perspective."

Daphne almost laughed. Having grown up a child of privilege, she supposed Bradley was used to having other people take whatever he dished out. Nathan's violent response must have scared the bejesus out of Bradley. For the first time, she wondered what Bradley had said to provoke Nathan to such uncharacteristic fury.

"And besides," Bradley continued, "I've been informed by someone I do care about that if I don't get my act together, she won't have any more to do with me."

Daphne's eyebrows lifted. "Sherry?"

Bradley nodded. "Despite what you think, I'm not using her. If anything, I'm, well, I . . ."

He trailed off, leaving Daphne to fill in the rest. Bradley was falling in love with Sherry? Daphne sighed. "So, where does that leave us?"

"I don't want your money. I never thought you'd come up with it in the first place. That was before I knew Nathan Ward was in the picture." He picked up the envelope and handed it to her.

No, he'd just wanted to torment her with the possibility of losing everything she cared about. She snatched the envelope from his hand and stuffed it into her purse. As much as she hated to admit it, she couldn't force him to take her money. "What *do* you want from me?"

"I don't know. Maybe I can find something useful to do around here."

Daphne stared at Bradley, shaking her head. If he didn't know, she certainly didn't know, either. But she thought of the letter Victoria had left for her, asking her to take care of Bradley. She knew she couldn't turn him away if he wanted to stay and was willing to behave himself.

"I'm not making any guarantees," Daphne told him. "You have done some pretty awful things and, frankly, I don't trust you. It's only for Victoria's sake and for Sherry's that I'm relenting at all." That and the fact that she really didn't have any choice. Daphne shook her head, at a loss of what else to say. "Just stay out of my way."

Not waiting for a response from him, she walked out of the office. Sherry was standing in the hallway, gripping her hands together. She'd probably listened to every word they'd said.

"Thanks, boss."

Saying nothing, Daphne tilted her head toward Bradley's office. Sherry flew past her to get to Bradley.

"How'd I do?" she heard Bradley ask Sherry, but whatever response she gave was muffled by the door closing behind her.

Daphne didn't know what to expect when she arrived home that night. She and Nathan had barely spoken to each other that morning when they'd gone to the bank together for the check. Just as she'd suspected, he'd insisted on giving her the full amount, and wouldn't listen to her plans to pay him back.

Finding Nathan out on the steps again surprised her. Night had fallen more than an hour ago. She felt rather than saw his gaze roaming over her. She stopped on the bottom step, not knowing what to say to him. All the anger she'd felt had dissipated. If she were honest with herself, she knew she'd been more upset with him for putting himself in the position where Bradley had something to hold over him than anything else.

"Hi," she said, finally.

"Hi."

"What are you doing out here?"

"I'm letting the apartment air out. The carpenter was here to install the cabinets this afternoon."

She'd forgotten she'd scheduled the work to be done today. "How do they look?"

"Why don't you go in and see for yourself?"

She did as he suggested, walking past him to enter the town house. After hanging her coat on the coatrack, she went directly to the kitchen. Five newly hung white cabinets gleamed in the rays of the overhead light. Now if she only had a stove and a refrigerator to put in their proper places, she'd have a decent kitchen. They would both be delivered on Saturday.

Hearing Nathan's footfalls behind her, she turned to face him. "It looks great, don't you think?"

Nathan shrugged in response, shoving his hands in the front pockets of his jeans. "I hope you don't mind that I paid him. I couldn't get through to you on the phone, and you didn't leave me a check."

"No, I don't mind." She turned away from him, going to the nearest cabinet and opening the door. "Where's Emily?"

"I took her to my grandmother's this morning after you left."

"I see." She'd exhausted all the inane conversation she could come up with. She turned around to face him, bracing her hands on the counter behind her. "Nathan—" she began, not knowing what she wanted to say.

He came to her, wrapping his arms around her. "Don't say anything, Daphne. I'm sorry. I honestly did not go there with the intent to bash his head in. Maybe I shouldn't have shown up in the first place, but I'll be damned if I'm going to stand by while someone else takes advantage of you."

She slid her arms around his waist, holding him to her. "You scared me. I've never seen you like that before. You with your hands around someone's throat."

Nathan chuckled. "I scared myself, too. I've never laid a hand on another person in my life." He kissed her temple. "What did he say when you gave him the money?"

"He wouldn't take it."

Nathan pulled away from her. "He wants more?"

She shook her head. "He doesn't want any. He doesn't want to give up his partnership in the company." She slanted a glance up at Nathan. "I agreed to that."

"You what?" With his hands at her shoulders, he set her away from him. "You're kidding me, right?"

"No."

Nathan walked away from her, going to stand by the archway to the kitchen. He ran his hand over his hair in a gesture of exasperation.

"I don't understand you, Daphne. Two nights ago, I came home and you were a wreck. You couldn't even tell me what he did to make you so upset. I've seen firsthand what a jerk the guy can be. Is that what you want to subject yourself to?"

"No, but—" She stopped, not wanting to explain to Nathan the obligation she felt because of Victoria's letter. "You once said I was a sucker for a good sob story, and I guess you were right. Besides, I'd rather have him where I can keep an eye on him."

She bit her lip, knowing how Nathan would react to her next bit of news. "Bradley is having some sort of relationship with Sherry."

"With that little girl? I really should have pounded him into the carpet."

"It wouldn't have helped. She thinks she's in love with him."

"Good, God." Nathan shook his head. "And this is the sort of man you want to have around you?"

No, she didn't want him around, but she honestly didn't see any other way. "It's my company, Nathan. I have to run it as I see fit."

"Then, all I can say is that I think you're making a mistake."

"If it is, it's not the first one, and I'm sure it won't be the last."

Nathan exhaled a heavy breath. "Are you hungry?"

Daphne blinked. "Excuse me?"

"Are you hungry?" Nathan leaned his shoulder against the wall. "We are never going to agree on this, and, truthfully, I'm tired of talking about it. Do you want to go out to dinner with me?"

"I'd like that." She knew Nathan wasn't finished on the subject. He could be more tenacious than Elise when it came to chewing a subject to death. But if he was willing to put it aside for a while, so was she. "Where do you want to go?"

"I have a place in mind." He winked at her. "Go put on something pretty for me and we'll go."

Daphne lifted her eyebrows as her gaze traveled over Nathan. He wore a faded pair of jeans and a T-shirt. "I suggest you do the same."

"Meet you in the kitchen upstairs in fifteen minutes," Nathan promised.

"Make it twenty," she said as she slid past him out the doorway.

She went up to her bedroom, and on impulse, grabbed one of Victoria's outfits from her closet—a scarlet crepe de chine dress that crisscrossed over her breasts and dipped almost to her waist in the back. The form-fitting skirt ended at mid-thigh. The matching shawl-collared jacket was lined with heavy black silk, making it warm enough to wear outdoors without an overcoat.

After a brief shower, Daphne donned the outfit, added black stockings and her favorite black satin pumps with three-inch heels, and considered herself ready.

Nathan stood at the center island of the kitchen when she stepped through the double doors. He'd been raising a glass of juice to his lips when she arrived. As she walked toward him, he slowly lowered it to the counter. She came around to his side, holding out her coat for him to help her into it.

He did so, then grasped her shoulders and turned her around to face him. "You look . . . incredible."

His husky declaration sent a thrill of pleasure through her. She let her gaze roam over him. He wore all black, except for his tie and an olive green jacket, the same color his eyes darkened to in passion. Was that a coincidence, or had he worn it deliberately to get to her?

Daphne swallowed. "You don't look so bad yourself," she teased. But not even a glimmer of a smile appeared on Nathan's face. Instead, he placed a finger under her chin and tilted her face up to his.

He lowered his mouth to hers, kissing her with such tenderness that it made her ache. Then, slowly, he pulled away from her, watching her with a hint of a smile on his lips.

"What was that for?"

"I didn't want to have to wait all night to kiss you." Out on the street a car horn sounded. "Our chariot must be awaiting us outside."

With a hand on her waist, Nathan started to guide her toward the stairs. "Why aren't we taking your car?"

"If I were still driving the Jag, I would."

She had noticed that she hadn't seen his car in a while, but had never asked him about it. "What happened to it?"

"I traded cars with my cousin, Nelson. His wife just divorced him, taking everything except for the family car neither of them wanted. The brown Volvo across the street."

She stopped where she was and stared at him incredulously. "You traded a two-hundred-thousand-dollar car for one that probably didn't cost fifty thousand when it was new?"

"I haven't got much use for a two-seater anymore."

Daphne shook her head. "You're crazy."

"You already knew that." Nathan took her hand. "Come on. If we're late Armando will give away our reservation."

Daphne looked out the window as the limousine pulled up in front of a small white stucco building with a red-and-yellow canopy. As the driver helped her out of the car, she read the words spelled out in big red letters: RINCON DEL MUNDO—corner of the world. As they stepped into the dimly lit eatery, she felt as if they'd stepped into another world. Save for Nathan, herself, and the tall, gray-haired man approaching them, the restaurant appeared to be virtually empty.

"*¡Hola! ¿Como estas?*" the older man said, embracing Nathan.

Daphne stood to the side, looking around, as the two men continued to greet each other in words most of which had not been covered in her high school Spanish class.

Nathan stepped back and slung an arm around her waist. "Daphne, this is Armando, the owner of the restaurant."

"Welcome," Armando said. The next thing she knew, she was enveloped in a bear hug that nearly knocked the breath out of her. "*Mi casa es su casa.*" Armando stepped back and winked at Nathan. "I love saying that."

After they'd shed their coats, Armando led them through

the dimly lit restaurant. Although several chandeliers hung overhead, most of the light in the room came from the candles that burned on each table. The pristine white walls were decorated with a variety of frescoes, the most prominent of which depicted a bullfight complete with bull, toreador, and a crowd throwing roses into the arena. The strains of a solo guitar playing "Malagena" drifted through the restaurant.

They stopped at a semicircular booth set in a little alcove by a large window.

"I hope this is to your liking."

Daphne looked at the elaborately decorated china set out on a white tablecloth. Next to the table, a bottle of wine chilled in a crystal bucket on a stand. "It's lovely." She allowed Armando to help her slide into one side, while Nathan entered from the other.

"Perdoname, un momento," Armando said, by way of excusing himself. "I need to check on your dinner." He bowed slightly before heading toward the front of the restaurant.

"Would you like some champagne?" Nathan asked.

"Yes, please." She watched Nathan pour the bubbly liquid and accepted the glass he handed to her. She took a deep sip, savoring the sweet wine. "Thank you."

Nathan took a sip from his own glass, then placed it on the table. "What do you think?"

Daphne glanced around the room. "The paintings are exquisite, and Armando is a character." She focused her gaze on Nathan's face. "What did he say to you when we came in?"

"He said you were much too pretty to be seen with a bum like me."

Daphne grinned. "Well, I have to agree with him there."

"Me, too."

She rolled the stem of her champagne flute between her

fingers. "What did Armando mean when he said he had to check on our dinner? We haven't ordered anything yet."

"Armando has a habit of telling you what you're going to eat, rather than asking you what you want."

"Is that why we're the only ones here?"

"We're not. Besides, it's early. The dinner crowd doesn't usually show up before nine o'clock."

"Then why are we here so early?"

"To avoid said dinner crowd." Nathan chuckled, then picked up his glass and took a sip. "Going out isn't the same for me as it is for most people. Once people recognize me, they have no compunctions about coming up to me, asking for autographs or for me to pose for pictures with them. I've had people pull up a chair to my table and begin talking to me as if I'm their long-lost friend—regardless of who I happen to be with. I put myself in the public eye, so I don't suppose I have much right to complain about it. But I wanted to be able to take you out without anyone interrupting us or having a hundred pairs of eyes staring at us."

She supposed his notoriety did make it difficult to carry on a normal life. She hadn't really thought about it much. The only other time they'd been out together it had been in his milieu, where everyone vied for attention rather than shunned it.

"I see you two are getting along well." Daphne turned to see Armando heading toward the table, an ebony serving tray in his hands.

Armando placed the two dishes he carried at the center of the table. "For your appetizer, I bring you *Camarones a la Plancha,* shrimp grilled with lemon, wine and sherry. And just for you, my *Especial a la Armando.* Enjoy." He smacked his tray as if it were a tambourine, then turned on his heel and left.

"What do you want to try first?" Nathan asked, unfurling his napkin on his lap.

"What do you suggest?"

"How do you feel about squid?"

"I like squid fine, as long as they stay in the ocean where they belong."

"I guess octopus is out of the question, then."

"Oh, yeah. I'll stick with the shrimp, thank you."

Nathan shook his head. "One of these days I've got to teach you how to eat."

As they ate, the restaurant began to fill. Armando strolled through the tables, strumming on an ornately carved guitar. He serenaded the diners with Spanish love songs in a lilting tenor voice.

"I think I'd come here just to hear him sing," Daphne said as a waitress served their main course, a delicious paella made from yellow rice and various types of seafood from shrimp to mussels.

"That's why most people come here. Before he opened the restaurant, Armando was a featured tenor with the Metropolitan Opera."

As if on cue, Armando came over to their table. It took her a moment to recognize the melody of the song, "Lady in Red," but the words he sang were Spanish.

When the song ended, Armando bowed slightly. "That was beautiful," Daphne said as she applauded.

"How about a song from you, Nathan?" Armando prompted, offering Nathan his guitar. "Sing a song for your lovely lady."

She'd almost forgotten that a million years ago, before he'd started on a solo career, he'd played guitar for his band.

Nathan accepted the instrument, strumming his thumb over the strings. Armando pulled out their table enough to accommodate Nathan settling the guitar on his lap. He grinned at her. "Are you sure you're up for this? I haven't played in years."

She nodded, wondering what he'd sing for her. He began to play, and immediately she recognized the opening bars to "Now and Forever," the song he'd written for her so many years ago. Emotion, both bitter and sweet, washed over her, as he sang about a love destined to last forever and promises neither of them had been able to keep.

But they'd both been little more than children then, kids playing at being grownups. They'd probably never stood a chance, even if all the other things had never happened to drive them apart.

And now, fifteen years later, were they really any better off?

He looked down at the guitar as he played the final notes of the song. When he lifted his head again, there was a lopsided grin on his face. "How was that?" He handed the guitar to Armando.

She simply stared at him a moment, not knowing what to say. Then the quiet of the room was shattered by the sound of applause. She glanced over her shoulder in surprise at her fellow diners, most of whom were staring back in her direction.

And then suddenly a crowd of people enveloped their table. Most of them only wanted to say hello or shake Nathan's hand. Others wanted autographs on cocktail napkins or little bits of paper. You'd swear the Pope had come to this little Greenwich Village restaurant, instead of a man who grew up not fifty miles from where they sat.

And all the while, he had his arm around her, or held her hand, or touched her in some way that reassured her that he was with her, and all the others were extraneous.

She wondered if he had done it on purpose, called attention to himself and her to show her what life in public was like for him—what life would be like for her if she

were with him. He could have refused Armando's offer.
He could have sung anything to her. But in choosing a
song anyone would recognize as his, he'd issued an invitation to all these people to notice him.

At the same time, she realized how deeply he'd touched
people's lives with his music. He'd once said he regretted
living his life so frivolously, but there wasn't anything
frivolous about making people happy or helping someone
forget their cares, if only for the duration of a song.

After a while, when everyone else had gone back to
their tables, he took her hand and kissed the back of it.
"Are you ready to go?"

"Yes."

After bidding Armando good-bye, they headed out into
the frigid winter night.

ONCE AND AGAIN

"Very funny," She wore his hand. "Come in"

Sixteen

It had started to snow while they were in the restaurant. By the time they pulled up in front of Daphne's town house, a thin white blanket covered the streets. The wind had picked up, swirling snow in every direction. Tomorrow it would all be an ugly black mess piled up at the curb, but for tonight, it was beautiful.

When the driver opened the door, Nathan helped Daphne out. He left her standing on the sidewalk while he tipped and thanked the chauffeur-bodyguard, who'd kept vigil over them all night from a spot at the bar. Crowds, even innocuous-looking restaurant patrons, could sometimes turn ugly with a celebrity in their midst. If Nathan had been alone, he never would have bothered with such precautions, but he wouldn't take any chances with Daphne's safety.

Once he got her inside the house, he took her coat from her and hung both hers and his on the coatrack. When he turned around, Daphne was right behind him. She wrapped her arms around his neck and pressed her soft body to his.

"So, Mr. Ward, what's it going to be? Your place or mine?"

"Both. You go to your place, and I go to mine."

"Very funny." She took his hand. "Come upstairs with me."

He lifted her hand to his lips and kissed the back of it. "Not tonight."

"Don't start that again." She slid her hand down his chest to his belly, and lower, to cup his erection in her palm. "Don't try to tell me you don't want me, Nathan, 'cause I'm not going to believe you."

God, he wanted her. In every way a man could want a woman he wanted her. But more than her body, he wanted her love. He feared he'd never get it if he made it too easy for her. With them sharing the same house, it would be too easy to end up sharing the same bed, with no thought to anything beyond gratifying each other physically.

The first time, she'd come to him out of need, and he'd accepted that. He'd already made up his mind not to touch her again until he had some inkling that she felt more for him than simple caring.

She leaned down and nipped the tip of his earlobe, and he closed his eyes, letting the pleasurable pain wash over him. With the way she worried that lip of hers, her penchant for biting him in all the right places had never surprised him.

She cupped his face and brought her mouth to his. Her tongue, warm and sweet, slid into his mouth. Unable to help himself, he gave into temptation, sucking on it, eliciting a throaty moan from her. He broke the kiss and set her away from him. "Daphne, please—"

"Please what? Please you? I'm trying to."

She reached around in back of her, and he heard the rasp of the zipper of her dress as she eased it down. The fabric immediately parted, revealing her bare breasts.

Nathan drank in the sight of her, from the siren's smile on her lips to her full breasts and nipples that had already peaked. The urge to touch her, to taste her, nearly overwhelmed him. He pulled her against him, wrapping his arms around her waist. "Don't do this to me, Daphne."

"I just want to love you, Nathan," she whispered against his neck. "Don't you want me to love you?"

He wanted that more than anything in the world. His fingers tangled in her braids, tilting her head back, forcing her to look at him. "Do you love me, Daphne?"

"Yes."

She answered without hesitation, but in his mind, he discounted her answer. She'd probably agree that Ross Perot was the Easter Bunny if he asked her right now. But he also knew there wasn't enough willpower in the world to keep him from making love to her right now.

He unzipped her dress the rest of the way then smoothed it down over her hips. She stepped out of the dress and kicked it aside. That left her bare except for a pair of lacy red panties, a pair of black, thigh-high stockings, and a pair of high heels. "Have mercy," Nathan muttered under his breath.

Daphne laughed a throaty little chuckle, raising one eyebrow provocatively. "I don't plan on having any mercy at all."

She had his jacket off in no time flat. Then her hands went to his tie, loosening and then removing it. She tossed it aside and began unbuttoning his shirt. He leaned back against the wall, resting his hands on her waist, letting her have her way.

But once her hands went to his belt buckle, he stopped her. Covering her hands with his own, he said, "Come inside with me."

He fished his keys out of his pocket and let them into his apartment. He kicked the door closed and backed her up against the hallway wall. He braced a hand on either side of her. "Now, where were we?"

"Right here." She wrapped her arms around his neck

and brought his mouth down to hers. He picked her up and carried her into the living room only a few feet away.

He sat down on the sofa, cradling her in his lap. He ran his hand over her breasts, her belly, and lower to skim the waistband of her panties. She sucked in her breath and her muscles contracted beneath his fingertips. Lifting her with one hand, he pulled her panties over her hips and down her legs. For a moment, he simply stared at her, admiring the perfection of her almost-nude body.

"See anything you like?"

Nathan chuckled. "I'm beginning to think there's a little bit of the exhibitionist in you, Daphne Thorne." He used his thumb to stroke the most sensitive flesh between her thighs. "You like being naked in front of me."

"I do. I like the way you look at me." Her voice was low, breathless, and so sexy that his own heartbeat quickened.

"How do I look at you?"

She exhaled a long, sigh-laden breath. "Like you can't wait to get naked, too."

And he couldn't. Ever since he'd decided to make love to her, he burned to be inside her. He laid her down on the sofa and stood to shrug out of the rest of his clothes. He retrieved the condom he'd left in his pants pocket, put it on, then covered her body with his own.

He adjusted them so they lay side by side, facing each other. "Where were we again?" He skimmed his hand down her body, lingering at all the spots he knew would excite her. "I keep losing my place."

"There's a good one," she murmured, when he cupped her derriere in his palm and squeezed.

He would have laughed, except it took too much energy just to breathe. He pulled her on top of him so that she straddled his body and thrust into her. His whole body shuddered as her warm, moist sheath enveloped him.

"Why, Mr. Ward," she murmured, "I do think you like having me on top."

"All the better to touch you"—he cupped the underside of one of her breasts in his hand—"and taste you"—he circled his tongue around its aureole—"my dear."

Daphne gasped and rocked her hips against him, and the time for humor had passed. He grasped her hips, lifting her up slightly and set her down again, setting a slow, deliberate pace. He wanted this time with Daphne to go on forever.

A thin sheen of perspiration had already broken out along his skin and hers, too. He inhaled, breathing in the aroma of their lovemaking. Her soft hands were on his chest, teasing his nipples. When she lowered her head to stroke her tongue to one of them, every ounce of restraint deserted him.

He thrust into her. She moaned his name, which only drove him closer to the precipice. He didn't know how much more of this sweet torture he could take. And she, too, seemed to be ready to topple over the brink. He watched her face as he thrust into her again. Her eyes squeezed shut and her body trembled with the power of her release. She collapsed against his chest and he let his own orgasm overtake him.

He lay there for a long time, rubbing his hands up and down her back, as he waited for his heartbeat to settle down and his breathing to return to normal.

He squeezed her side. "Sweetheart, are you okay? Daphne?" He lifted his head so that he could see her face. Her eyes were closed and her breathing had evened out.

Daphne was sound asleep.

Nathan chuckled. "I thought I was the one who was supposed to roll over and play dead." He turned his head and kissed her cheek. He closed his eyes, savoring the warmth of her lax body laying on his. He'd get up in a moment and take her to his bed. But a minute later, Nathan had fallen asleep himself.

The next morning, Daphne walked into a thankfully empty office. Sherry had called her at home to tell her that she wouldn't be in until that afternoon. She hoped that meant Bradley wouldn't be in, either, or that perhaps he'd remember he had a job somewhere else and leave her in peace.

Daphne sat at her desk, steepled her fingers in front of her, and rested her cheek against them. She really should get to work, but the only thoughts that congealed in her brain were those of Nathan.

Last night, he'd made wild, passionate love to her. This morning, she'd woken up snuggled next to him in bed. He must have carried her there after she'd fallen asleep on top of him. And when she'd risen to get ready for work, he'd followed her into the shower and made such sweet love to her that it had left her weak and trembling in his arms.

She sighed, sitting back in her seat. He'd asked her if she loved him, and she'd told him the truth. She did love him, now more than she ever had before. But she knew by the skeptical look that had come into his eyes that he didn't believe her. She didn't know what to do about that. She accepted the fact that he loved her, though he'd never said so. He'd shown her in so many ways that she didn't need words. Why couldn't Nathan see how much she cared for him?

The phone rang, ending her opportunity for reflection. With no one else in the office, she had no choice but to answer it.

"Women's Work, Daphne Thorne speaking."

"Hi, Daphne, it's me, Robert. Did you miss me?"

"Robert!" she exclaimed. She hadn't given him one thought since he'd left. "When did you get back?"

"Last night. I called you at home, but you must have been out. I see you haven't been listening to your answering machine."

"No, I guess not."

"I need to see you. Tonight. Can we meet for dinner?"

"I'd like that." They made arrangements to meet at a popular East Side restaurant.

"Maybe we can go listen to some music afterward. There's a concert series going on at the IBM building this month. I think it's Beethoven tonight."

"Um," Daphne hedged, not wanting to get his hopes up for a continuation of their relationship, but not wanting to blurt out her true reason for seeing him tonight. "Let's play it by ear." She realized the unintentional pun in her words when she heard Robert's soft laughter. "You know what I mean."

"You're the boss lady," he said. "We'll do whatever you want."

"See you at six-thirty," she said. She hung up from him and immediately dialed Nathan's number to let him know she'd be home late that night. The machine came on, and she left a message. She hoped Nathan would get home before dinnertime to hear it.

Robert was waiting for her at the bar when she stepped into the dimly lit restaurant on Fifty-third Street. He stood as she approached, placing a kiss on her cheek in greeting. "You look fabulous," he said, eyeing her up and down. "Something is different about you."

She said nothing to that. "You look great yourself." And he did. He seemed to have lost weight and his skin was tanned a deep bronze. "I thought you said you went out of town on business."

He helped her into a seat and sat next to her. "I did. Two weeks of intensive surgery. They flew in these women and little girls from India who'd been burned by men throwing acid in their faces. It seems in that country if a woman rejects a man's advances, he takes revenge on her in that way. Barbaric, if you ask me."

Daphne had to agree. But perhaps no more barbaric than a million other practices forced on women around the world every day. "You sound as if you enjoyed yourself."

"It's the most satisfying work I've ever done. And as a thank-you, the hospital sent us down to Mexico for a medical convention. Little more than an excuse to lay in the sun and sip margaritas for a couple of days, hence the tan." He picked up his glass and took a sip of his drink. "What have you been up to while I've been gone?"

Luckily, the appearance of the hostess forestalled her answer. She led them to a table for two on the opposite side of the room. After taking their drink order and providing them with menus, the hostess left them alone.

"Anything look good to you?" Robert asked, scanning the menu.

Daphne took a deep breath. She wanted to put an end to this charade before it went on any longer. "Before we order, there's something I have to tell you."

He put down the menu, a look of concern in his brown eyes. "What is it?"

"I wanted to tell you this before you left, but there wasn't any time. I wanted to tell you face-to-face." Daphne sighed. She'd never had to have this type of conversation before. How did one go about letting a man down easily?

"You're seeing someone else, is that it? That guy who lives downstairs from you, no doubt. What's his name?"

"Nathan. Nathan Ward."

"Nathan Ward? *The* Nathan Ward?" Robert shook his head. "You didn't tell me *he* was my competition. But then there really wasn't any competition, was there?"

She shook her head. "No."

She studied his face. He didn't seem particularly upset or even piqued at her for wasting his time. In fact, he seemed amused, which unaccountably annoyed her.

Robert sat back in his chair. "I have a confession to make, too. I met someone while I was in Colorado, another doctor. She lives in California but she's relocating to New York next month. I didn't really pursue anything with her, thinking you were back here waiting for me. I guess I don't have to worry about that anymore."

"I hope things work out for you. You deserve it."

"Hold on. You sound like you're leaving."

"I am. I made this date with you under false pretenses. There's no point in continuing it."

He covered her hand with his own. "I came out to dinner with a friend. We're still going to be friends, aren't we?"

Daphne beamed up at him. "I think that doctor from California is a very lucky lady."

"So is Nathan Ward. Looks, money, fame, and you. No guy deserves all that." He picked up the menu. "Now, what do you want to eat?"

After dinner they walked over to Madison Avenue to catch the last hour of the concert. Having grown up with a mother who taught piano both at school and in her home, Daphne knew most of the pieces by heart. When the concert ended and the applause died down, Robert helped her from her seat.

"I suppose I'd better get us a cab. I don't want to be accused of not seeing you home properly again."

She tried to decline, knowing Nathan would probably have a fit seeing her coming home with another man, this man in particular. But Robert was adamant, and she finally relented. When they reached her town house, Robert even stepped out of the car with her, embracing her in a brotherly hug.

"Take care of yourself, Daphne," he said. "Give me a call sometime."

"I will," she promised. "You do the same." He climbed back into the cab, and she headed up the stairs.

As she suspected, Nathan was waiting for her when she walked in the door. He stood with his shoulder braced against the doorjamb to his apartment, his arms crossed in front of him. His hazel eyes glinted green in the dim light of the foyer.

"What were you doing with him?" he said without preamble.

Just as she never would have allowed Robert to dictate to her who her friends could be, she wouldn't allow Nathan to do so, either. "I went out to dinner with a friend. I left you a message on your answering machine telling you that." She shrugged out of her coat and hung it on the coatrack.

"Yes, but you neglected to tell me who that *friend* was, didn't you?"

Hearing the accusatory tone in his voice, she narrowed her eyes at him. "What exactly are you saying, Nathan?"

"I called your office at six o'clock hoping to catch you before you went out. Sherry said you'd already left. It's nine-thirty now. Plenty of time for dinner—and other things as well."

"We stopped by the IBM building for the tail end of a concert, not that it's any of your business."

"The hell it isn't. You got out of my bed this morning. That makes it my business."

"Robert has been out of town for a while. I went out with him to break up with him."

"Then that has got to be the chummiest breakup I've ever seen."

Daphne huffed. She supposed she should have been more forthright with Nathan to begin with, especially since she knew he doubted the strength of her feelings for him. "If you must know, we decided to stay in touch. He's met someone else. What do you want from me, Nathan? A signed affidavit that nothing happened? Blood? Well, forget it. I've already bled for you."

"What is that supposed to mean?"

"Nothing."

Nathan watched her as she started to walk toward the stairs leading up to her apartment. Judging from the look of horror that crossed her face when she realized what she'd said, it was definitely something. He stepped in front of her, blocking her path. "What do you mean you've already bled for me?"

"Nothing." She tried to move past him to go upstairs to her apartment, but he wouldn't let her pass. "Nathan, please. I didn't mean anything. I want to go to bed."

She tried to skirt around him to get to the stairs. He grasped her upper arms, holding her in place. "Last night you practically begged me to make love to you, but tonight you want to go to bed alone?"

"Tonight I'm tired. Nathan, let go of me."

"Not yet. Not until you tell me what has you so upset."

"Nothing."

"I'm not letting you go until you tell me."

She sagged against him, resting her forehead against his chest. "Can't you leave the past alone?" she whispered.

"No, baby, I can't. Not if it hurts you this much." With a hand under her chin, he tilted her face up to his. "At least tell me one thing. Why wouldn't you see me when

I came back? Why did you shut me out of your life all those years ago?"

"I didn't. You were the one who walked away."

"I didn't walk away, I went on tour. You know that. I got a call saying that the opening act had backed out at the last minute and could we fill in. What was I supposed to say? Hold on a minute, I have to ask my girlfriend if I can go? It was either get on the bus or get left behind."

"Yes, that's what you told me."

"And you didn't believe me?"

She pushed away from him. "I don't know what I believed. Does it matter anymore? It was fifteen years ago."

"Yes. It matters to me. It's always mattered to me."

"You could have fooled me. I would have sworn all your new friends were what mattered to you. When you finally did call me to tell me where you were, that's all you talked about. All the fabulous new people you were meeting, how everyone treated you like a king."

"What was I supposed to tell you about? My band was opening with the hottest act going. Wasn't I supposed to be excited?"

"But you never once told me you missed me. Or that you loved me."

"I thought that was obvious. I thought you knew how I felt."

"Forgive me if I needed a reminder."

"Then why did you refuse to see me when I came back?" He'd come back specifically to see her. His sister had called him and told him that Daphne was in trouble. He hadn't questioned her word. He'd risked everything to come back and see her, and her father and brother had met him at the door and told him that Daphne said to go away.

"I couldn't. I couldn't face you."

"Why not?"

She turned her face up to his and he saw such pain reflected in her eyes that it stunned him. "Because, fifteen years ago, I was pregnant with your child."

He took a step back, reeling as if she'd slapped him. Daphne had been pregnant with their child? Oh, God, he'd had no idea. He sank down on the steps, for a moment too nonplussed to say anything.

He looked up at Daphne to see tears streaming down her face. He took her hand, pulling her onto his lap. He smoothed her tears away with his thumbs. "Why didn't you tell me?"

"I had planned to, the day you left town. I went to your grandmother's house and she told me you'd gone off somewhere. She didn't know when you'd be back."

He could imagine how she'd felt, going to find him, learning that he'd disappeared just when she needed him most. He hadn't even left his grandmother a phone number where he could be reached.

"What happened to the baby?"

"There wasn't any baby."

No, there couldn't have been. If she'd carried the pregnancy to term, he would have known about it; the whole neighborhood would have known about it. That left only one other option in his mind. He lifted his head and scanned her face. "What did you do, Daphne?"

"What do you mean?"

"I mean, what did you do? If there was no baby, you had to have done something. You don't become unpregnant without doing something. What did you do?"

She pushed off his lap and stood. "Are you asking me if I had an abortion? Is that what you want to know? Why shouldn't I have? You weren't there. For all I knew you weren't coming back."

He recognized that response as a nonanswer. She hadn't said what she'd done, only what was within her rights to do. If she'd aborted his child, he wanted to hear it from her own lips. He rose to his feet and faced her. "What did you do?" he repeated.

"Nothing. I didn't do anything."

She pulled away from him, heading up the stairs to her apartment. For a moment, he watched her go. Maybe he should accept that she'd given him her answer in her own way. Maybe he should accept the fact that at that time she'd hated him enough to destroy their child. But he couldn't. The Daphne he knew wasn't capable of destroying anything.

By the time he stirred himself to action, she'd already made it to the landing. She fumbled with her keys, trying to get the door to her apartment open. He stepped up behind her and took the keys from her trembling fingers.

With his hands at her shoulders, he turned her to face him. She wouldn't look at him, until he tipped her face up to his with a hand under her chin. In her eyes he saw a look of such total defeat that his heart ached for her. He held her gaze a moment, wishing to convey to her silently that whatever she told him would be all right. He couldn't blame her for anything she'd done fifteen years ago. But she lowered her head, saying nothing.

He wrapped his arms around her waist, pulling her into his arms so that her forehead rested against his shoulder. "Daphne, why can't you tell me the truth?"

"I fell, all right, I fell. I was upset and I wasn't watching where I was going, and I slipped on one of the steps in my parents' house and fell the rest of the way down the stairs."

She drew in a long, ragged breath. "I thought I was okay, but the next morning, I started bleeding, and it wouldn't stop. I went to the hospital and the doctor told me I'd lost the baby. He said the fall probably didn't have anything to do with the miscarriage, but I . . ."

She stopped, and he filled in the rest for her. She'd blamed herself for losing their child. Which meant she'd wanted it. Even though he'd deserted her, she'd wanted his child.

He didn't know what to say to her. While he'd been having the time of his life, she'd been going through hell. No wonder she hadn't wanted to see him. He'd been such a fool, only seeing what he wanted, never considering what she needed. He'd told her once that he'd asked too much of her. He hadn't known at the time how true that statement was.

He stroked his hands over her back in a soothing manner, saying nothing, hoping his silence would prompt her to keep talking.

"I stayed at the hospital as long as they would let me; then I took the subway home. I pretended I had the flu for a couple of days so no one would question me about staying in bed."

"You didn't tell anyone?"

"Who was I going to tell? My father? He was still grieving over losing my mother. Sometimes I think he's still grieving. Or how about Elise? She was busy planning her wedding to Garrett. She barely knew I was alive. Or Michael? He was still so angry. All I would have needed to do was give him a focus for all that rage. No, I never told anyone."

"I'm sorry, baby. I'm so sorry you had to go through that alone. I would have been there for you if I'd known. Nothing mattered to me as much as you did. Nothing."

Daphne shuddered, as all the hurt, all the humiliation, washed over her as if it were yesterday, not fifteen years ago, that she'd been pregnant and alone and scared. All the unexpressed grief at the loss of their child welled up inside her, overwhelming her with its depth. All the anger at him and herself and at fate for taking away both the man she'd loved and the child she'd wanted.

She clung to him, needing his warmth and his strength, and hating herself for needing them. After a moment, she pulled away from him, wiping her eyes with the back of her hand.

"That's easy to say now, isn't it? But the truth is, you weren't there. The truth is, I was completely alone at the worst time of my life. And you know what? I made it through just fine. So you go on home, Nathan. I don't need you now, either."

He lifted his hand to touch her cheek, but she turned her face away from him. He dropped his hand to his side. "Don't do this, Daphne. Don't shut me out. I don't deserve that."

"Maybe not, but I want you to go. I've been kidding myself thinking this time could turn out any better than the last one. We might be older, but we are still the same people. Nothing has really changed."

"I hope I've changed. I know I'm not the same kid who could walk away without a second thought. You were right about that. I should have told you. I shouldn't have left without at least leaving you a note. But you know something? I'd hoped you loved me enough to understand."

He took her hand, and for a moment she stood there letting the warmth of his skin seep into her cold flesh.

"I left you alone all these years because I knew I had nothing to offer you, nothing you wanted, anyway. I can't walk away this time, Daphne. I can't."

"You don't have any choice." She pulled her keys from his hand. "The stove and the refrigerator will be delivered tomorrow. There's no need for us to see each other anymore."

The sound of Emily's crying reached Daphne's ears. "Your daughter is calling you."

"Damn," Nathan muttered. He took a step down the stairs. "This isn't over, Daphne."

"Yes, it is," she whispered, but not loud enough for him to hear her. It had to be over, now, before she fell any more in love with him than she already had. He'd broken her heart once, and she'd barely survived it. A second time would surely be fatal. It would be best if she got Nathan out of her life before he totally destroyed her.

She managed to unlock the door and ran up to her bedroom. She threw herself on her bed and buried her face against her folded arms.

But how did she go about getting him out of her heart?

Seventeen

Daphne awoke the next morning to the sound of someone rapping on her bedroom door. Her eyes burned and her stomach churned and her back ached from the uncomfortable position she'd slept in. She raised her head and lifted her hand to her temple. A dull ache throbbed there and it took her a minute to orient herself.

Had last night really happened? Had she really told Nathan about their child? Had she banished him from her life, just as she had fifteen years ago? She wished it were all part of a horrible dream, but she looked down at herself, realizing she still wore the same clothes she'd had on the day before.

And who else but Nathan could be knocking on her door right now? She heard him call her name, obviously trying to rouse her. Last night she'd been so caught up in her own emotions, she hadn't seen the folly of trying to rid herself of a man who had full access to her house.

She rose from the bed and, like a bent old woman, hobbled over to the door. She turned the knob and pulled the door slightly ajar.

"Yes?"

"The deliverymen are here, and I have to go."

She'd hoped he'd come to check on her to see if she was all right. She'd hoped he realized that she'd only said what she had last night because she'd been consumed with the past and not thinking clearly. His brusque comment dashed any hope of that. "I'll be right down."

He walked away without another word. She pulled a pair of jeans and a T-shirt from her dresser and put them on. Barefoot, she padded down to Nathan's kitchen. The two deliverymen had already uncrated the refrigerator and were sliding it into place. But she didn't see Nathan, and her spirits plummeted, thinking he'd already left before she had a chance to speak to him.

Then she saw him, coming out of his bedroom in the back, holding the baby in his arms, walking toward her with purposeful strides. He carried Emily's diaper bag over one shoulder. Both he and the baby were dressed for the cold weather.

"Where are you going?"

"Out. You told me to go. I'm going."

But she hadn't meant it. She'd been angry and hurt, and she'd lashed out at him because of her own turmoil. He had to know that even then, she hadn't really expected him to leave. "About last night—"

"Yes, about last night. I think you made your feelings quite clear. I never had a chance to voice mine."

"What did you want to say?"

"You once told me that you wanted to put the past in the past, but that's not entirely true, is it? You want to be able to cling to those things you can hold over my head as examples of how I've wronged you. You want to blame me for leaving you fifteen years ago. But the truth is, if I'd known you were pregnant, I never would have gone. And if you'd told me you'd miscarried the baby, I wouldn't have gone back. I had a right to know, Daphne. No matter how you felt, I had a right to know."

"Why? Because you were the baby's father?"

"No, because I loved you and you owed me the chance

to make things right with you. I had a right not to be made into the louse who left Daphne Thorne high and dry, not when I didn't have a clue what was going on with you.

"And rather than face me with that truth when I did come back," he continued, "you hid behind your family and sent me away. So when you start doling out blame for what happened back then, make sure you save just a little bit of it for yourself."

He walked away from her, out the open front door. A mixture of emotions ran through her as she watched him leave. She deserved everything he'd said to her, and probably more.

She'd spent the last fifteen years trying to hate him for leaving her, but she'd never quite succeeded in doing that. Maybe because she'd always known she'd born as much onus as he for the way their relationship had ended. It had been easier to lay all the blame on him. Then she never had to examine her own role, never had to admit that on that day she'd made the worst mistake of her life.

Her knowledge that he'd be back was her consolation. But nighttime fell and morning broke and still Nathan hadn't come home.

Nathan sat on the back stairs of his grandmother's house, shredding blades of dead grass between his fingers. His grandmother and his sister still hadn't gotten back from church, and Emily slept in her crib upstairs. For the first time in two days, he was blessedly, thankfully, alone.

As soon as he'd walked in the door with Emily, his family had sensed something wasn't right with him. They'd spent the last forty-eight hours staring at him as if he were a specimen in the zoo. They knew something bothered him, but as of yet, no one had tried to worm it out of him.

He heard the screen door open, and knew his short reprieve had ended. Nina came out of the house wearing a pair of jeans and a bulky cardigan sweater that had once belonged to him. She sat next to him, wrapping the sweater around her more tightly.

"You're going to have to pick a better spot to do this brooding of yours. The cold might not bother you, but I'm tired of freezing my buns off just to talk to you."

"What's up?" He put his arm around her, rubbing his hand over her arm to warm her.

"You're what's up. She finally told you, didn't she? Why she wouldn't see you fifteen years ago."

"Yes. She'd been pregnant with my child. She miscarried the baby." He glanced at his sister. If she was surprised by his revelation, she didn't show it. "But you already knew."

"I'd suspected she might have been. I saw her in the drugstore buying a pregnancy test. I didn't know what to do. It took me a week to get up the nerve to tell you. And by then you were gone."

Nathan sighed. And when he'd finally gotten around to letting anyone know where he was, it was too late. Daphne had already lost the baby.

"And you can't forgive her for not telling you?"

"It's not a matter of forgiveness. Forgiving someone is what you do when you feel they have wronged you. And I don't fault her for what happened."

"Then what is it?"

Nathan shrugged. "Maybe it's crazy, but I feel like I'm grieving for a child I never knew, never would have had a chance to know."

"Kind of like me when we found out Dad had died? I

was a wreck. You didn't think there was anything strange about that."

Nathan found his first smile. "Well, you know how overemotional you women get."

"Watch it, bub." She punched him on the arm. "I still know how to hit you where it hurts."

"I've noticed."

"But, seriously, Nathan, what are you doing here? You should be with Daphne. She needs you as much as you need her."

"According to Daphne, she doesn't need anyone, especially not me."

"And you paid attention to that? You've left her alone for two days. You haven't even called her, have you?"

"No, I haven't."

"And she's probably going through hell right now, wondering when you're coming back."

"Maybe."

Nina rolled her eyes and shook her head, obviously disgusted with him. "Go home, Nathan. Take that sweet little baby of yours and get out of here. Grab Daphne and hash this thing out and move past it."

He didn't know whether Daphne would welcome him or want to kick him out altogether. But Nina was right about one thing: His home, his life, was with Daphne. He'd been away long enough.

"And for God's sake, make yourself presentable," Nina continued. "This scruffy look is definitely not you."

Nathan rubbed his fingers over his stubbly chin. He hadn't shaved in two days. "That bad, huh?"

"I've seen cave drawings of troglodytes that were better groomed than you are."

"Gee, thanks, sis."

"Hey, I call 'em how I see 'em."

He gave his sister's shoulders a squeeze. "How did you get to be so wise?"

Nina stood, gathering her sweater around her. "All I have to do is look to you, dear brother, to figure out what *not* to do."

She winked at him before walking up the few steps to the house and disappearing inside.

Daphne sat on her living-room sofa, sipping the last dregs of the hot chocolate she'd made a half-hour ago. The now-cold liquid tasted bitter on her tongue. She loved Nathan; she missed him. No comfort food she knew of could change the fact that he chose to be apart from her rather than with her. In the past two days she'd vacillated between fury at him for being gone so long and despair that he would never come back.

She put her cup down and stood, feeling restless. She should have left for her father's house fifteen minutes ago. She'd resigned herself to going, as not showing up would certainly cause speculation about the reason for her absence. She hadn't gathered enough impetus to make it out the door.

She paced around the living room, stopping by the bookcase in the corner. A small purple package caught her eye, and she pulled it off the shelf. She held in her hand the video from Nathan's song, "Always." Jenny, who'd been in the video with Nathan, had given it to her when it first came out. Until now, it had remained on her shelf with the shrinkwrap intact.

She slit the wrapping open with her fingernail as she walked over to the television set across the room. She knew she'd only torture herself to watch it, but she put it in the DVD player anyway. Nathan had told her that this song had become his biggest seller. At the time, she'd felt a little jealous having any song eclipse the one he'd written for her.

But as the music began to play she could see why. The melody, sweet and haunting, perfectly complemented Nathan's smooth tenor voice. And the film itself was beautiful. The whole video seemed as if it were shot through some kind of scrim that gave it an ethereal quality. Nathan, dressed in gray, stood by a large window. As he sang, images, faint at first, then growing in intensity, danced across the television screen—like memories fading in and out, momentarily blocking out the present.

The lyrics spoke of a lost love, while the pictures illustrated the doomed relationship—sensual, seductive images of Nathan and Jenny together. One picture in particular gave Daphne pause, a scene in which all you saw was Nathan's back and over his shoulder you saw Jenny's face. The expression on her face, one of pure rapture, made Daphne wonder what Nathan had been doing at the time to cause such a reaction in Jenny.

Daphne sighed. Being jealous of Jenny was beyond ridiculous. Jenny doted on Daphne's brother to the point of being downright disgusting.

When the disc drew to an end, the credits flashed on the screen, superimposed on the final moments of the video. She didn't know why it surprised her to see that Nathan had written the words to the song, but it did. Was theirs the doomed love affair he'd sung about? Was that how he remembered their time together? Or was every word, every nuance, designed solely to sell more records?

The sound of a car door slamming outside reminded her she had somewhere to be herself. She'd left her coat on the rack downstairs. She'd just shrugged into it when she heard a key turning in the lock to the front door. A second later, Nathan came in, carrying a sleeping Emily in his arms.

What a powerful image that was: Nathan and the baby coming home to her. For an instant, her pulse accelerated and her breath stalled in her lungs. Her gaze roved over him, taking in every inch of him. When she looked at his face, his eyes reflected the same hunger she knew he must see in her own.

"Daphne," he whispered.

She ran to him, all the misery of the last two days forgotten. Nathan pulled her into his arms with his free hand. He lowered his mouth to hers, and all the heat, all the hunger she'd seen in his eyes poured out into his kiss. She kissed him back, giving him all the love, all the passion she held inside.

When he pulled away from her, he touched his fingertips to her cheek. "Let me get the baby settled, and we can pick up where we left off."

Something about his words disconcerted her. She took a step away from him. "I have to be at my father's house. They're expecting me."

"I'm sure your family will understand if you don't show up this one time."

Daphne shook her head. "No. I'd better go." She skirted around Nathan and walked out the open front door without looking back.

Hours later, Daphne sat behind the desk in her father's study. She'd come in here mainly to escape Elise's curious, too-perceptive eyes. She knew Elise suspected that something bothered her, but Daphne wasn't in the mood to put up with her sister's acrimony where Nathan was concerned.

Daphne surveyed the room. Nothing in it had changed since she was a child. The same heavy tomes crowded the bookshelf; Mr. Bones, her father's life-size human skeleton, still wore the same top hat her father had bestowed on him the New Year's Eve Daphne had been eleven. If anything, the only addition to the room was more clutter and a heavy coat of dust, as this was the one room her father never allowed her to clean.

The whole room seemed frozen in time, stagnant, the same way her father's life had stalled the day her mother had died nearly twenty years ago. He'd excelled at his career as a biology professor, but to her knowledge, her father hadn't had one date, hadn't even looked at a woman in all that time. He'd sealed off that part of himself capable of loving in more than a platonic way.

At first it had been understandable. For a long time, Daphne couldn't have imagined that any woman could take her mother's place. But as the years had passed, she'd wondered about her father's lack of interest in the opposite sex.

She knew that her mother wouldn't have wanted him to spend his life locked away from love. She would have wanted him to be happy. But "happy" was not an adjective that leaped to her mind when she thought of her father.

She supposed that was why she'd always felt compelled to look out for him, because she sensed a profound loneliness in him that the years had done nothing to erase.

She wondered how much of his disinterest stemmed from a fear of betraying her mother's memory, and how much was due simply to habit he'd fallen into, one he didn't have the will to break?

And suddenly, she knew what bothered her about Nathan coming home today. How many times had he come to her, after some escapade or other, without apology, without explanation, just expecting her to accept that whatever was important to him mattered more than her own feelings? How many times had she allowed him to get away with that because, more than anything, she wanted to be with him? That wasn't exactly what had happened today, but it was close enough to disturb her. She refused to put up with that anymore. If they couldn't move beyond the same old patterns, they had doomed their relationship before it had really begun.

"What are you doing in here?"

Daphne's head snapped around. Elise stood in the doorway, her hands braced on either side of the frame. She beckoned her sister inside with a wave of her hand. "Come in."

Elise sat on the edge of one of the chairs facing her. Daphne couldn't manage to muster a cheerful face for her sister. She knew Elise had picked up on her mood when she folded her arms in front of her and asked, "What's Nathan done now, not that I really want to know."

Daphne focused her gaze on her sister, annoyance rising in her. "You know, there's one thing I've never been able to figure out, Elise. What did Nathan ever do to you? Why do you hate him so much?"

"It's not what he's done to me; it's what he did to you. How am I supposed to feel about a man who got you pregnant and deserted you?"

Daphne blinked. "You knew about the baby?"

"Of course I knew. We were sisters; we shared a room. I never said anything because, well, I didn't know what to say. When Nathan left, I tried to be there for you, but all you did was push me away."

If that were true, Daphne had never seen it. She'd been too miserable at the time to pay attention to anything but her own agony. But she couldn't have her sister thinking Nathan had abandoned her when he hadn't.

"Nathan didn't walk out on me. He didn't know about the baby. I never told him."

"Oh, Dee, how could you not have told him? He had a right to know."

Daphne smiled ruefully. The same words Nathan had

said to her. Wonders never cease! Nathan and Elise finally agreed on something.

"I had a miscarriage when I was two months pregnant. That's why I didn't tell him. He wasn't here for me to tell him anyway."

Daphne sighed, shifting in her seat. "Well, I finally did tell him," Daphne continued. "His response was to disappear for two days. Then he waltzed back home expecting everything to be all right. Things are definitely not all right."

"What are you going to do about that?"

"I don't know. Don't get me wrong, Elise. I love Nathan. I want him back. But if I let him get away with this, there will be no living with him. He'll think he can get away with anything."

Daphne leaned back in her chair, folding her arms in front of her. "It's too much like before. All he'd have to do was give me this little smile or touch me and I'd forgive him." She glanced up at her sister noting the incredulous look on her face. "What?"

"Well," Elise began, "when I think of women who have no resolve where men are concerned, your name doesn't immediately top my list."

"I, unfortunately, am as vulnerable as the next woman." Daphne huffed out a disgusted breath. "Frankly, I talk a good game, but when he came in that door, I threw myself at him like a lovesick teenager."

Elise laughed. "So you want to punish him because you have no self-control?"

"No, I want to punish him for knowing I have no self-control and using it against me." Daphne put her elbows on the desk and rested her chin against her folded hands. "Actually, I don't want to punish him at all. I just don't know what to do."

Elise's eyebrows lifted. "Are you asking me for help?"

"I guess so. Yes. Why does that surprise you so much?"

"You never have before. The high-and-mighty Daphne Thorne actually needing someone else. Shocking."

"What is that supposed to mean?"

"Come on, Dee, ever since you were a little girl you were so standoffish with everyone, everyone except Mom. And when poor Nathan came along, you treated him like dirt. Every girl in the neighborhood was after him, but he only had eyes for you. I honestly felt sorry for the guy. You seemed to revel in making him miserable for having the nerve to be attracted to you. I can't tell you how surprised I was when you finally relented and went out with him."

Daphne stared at her sister, her mouth agape. "If that's true, why did you dislike him so much?"

"I never did, not until I thought he'd abandoned you." Elise lowered her head. "I'm not proud of it, but I was jealous. You were close to him in a way that you would never allow yourself to be with me. I think that's why I came down on you so hard when I heard he was living with you. In the last few years we'd really gotten to be friends. I saw him as a threat to that."

Daphne shook her head, smiling ruefully. "You know, it's funny, I didn't come to you because you were so involved with planning your wedding, I didn't think you'd want to be bothered."

Daphne lifted her shoulders and let them fall with a sigh. "I guess that makes us both pretty pathetic, huh?"

"Mmm," Elise agreed.

"Let's not do that again, okay?"

"It's a deal." Elise leaned back in her chair. "While we're having this love fest, would you mind a little sisterly advice?"

"Not at all."

"Before you judge Nathan too harshly for his disappearance, maybe you ought to take a look at your own role in things. I'd lay odds that the reason he left is because you pushed him away, or you shut yourself up in your apartment and refused to speak to him."

Daphne snorted. Her sister knew her better than she thought. "Actually, a little of both."

"Oh, Dee, didn't you consider how he'd feel when you told him? No man worth anything wants to find out years later that he'd abandoned a woman when she was pregnant with his child. What did you expect him to do? Thank you for keeping the secret all this time? If I'd done something like that to Garrett, two *years* later I'd still be wondering what happened to him, never mind two days."

No, she hadn't thought about how Nathan would feel. Her only concern had been whether or not he would blame her for losing the baby. He'd said it himself before he left, but it hadn't sunk in until now. "I've made a real mess of things, haven't I?"

"Yup. But that's what we humans do. We make mistakes. The only unforgivable errors are the ones we don't bother to correct. Use some of those lofty brain cells you are supposed to possess and figure out a way to make things right with him." Elise rose from her chair and exited the room, leaving Daphne to contemplate her words in solitude.

When Daphne pulled up in front of her town house later that night, she noted the light burning in Nathan's window with a spurt of hope. If Nathan was awake, then maybe they could settle things between them. Although Elise's words echoed in her mind, she had no idea what she'd say to him.

She got out of the car and let herself into the building. Disappointment flooded her as she realized Nathan wasn't waiting at his doorway to greet her. It would have made things easier for her, but she supposed some things weren't meant to be easy.

She slid off her coat and hung it and her purse on the coatrack. When she turned around, he was standing right where she'd hoped he'd be. Her gaze roved over him, taking in every inch of him, from the black T-shirt that stretched across his chest to the jeans that clung to his long legs, and back again.

Their gazes met, and for a moment she held her breath, wondering what he was thinking. She didn't realize she'd been retreating from him until her back hit the wall. She'd hit the wall in a metaphoric way, as well. She couldn't put it off any longer.

"It seems I owe you another apology."

"For what?"

"I've spent the last fifteen years blaming you for how our relationship ended. I've come to realize I should have been looking a little closer to home."

His brows drew together. "What do you mean?"

"The real reason I didn't tell you was because I didn't want you to blame me for losing the baby. I let you go, rather than risk your censure. I wanted to blame you for leaving, but I never considered that I was the one pushing you away."

She studied his face to gauge his reaction to what she'd said. His eyes were hooded, his expression unreadable. He exhaled a breath. "Come here," he said finally.

She walked toward him on unsteady legs. As she approached, he welcomed her into his arms. She sank against him, resting her cheek on his chest.

Nathan stroked his hands over her back. "I'm not interested in assigning blame, Daphne. It really doesn't matter anymore who did what. I just want to finally put the past behind us and move on."

She lifted her head and gazed up at him. "Then I need to know you are not going to pull a disappearing act every time the whim strikes you. I need to know I can count on you."

"And I need to know that you are not going to withdraw your love from me every time I do something that upsets you. I need to know that you are not going to keep shutting me out."

A sad little smile curved the corners of her lips. For the second time that day, she said, "I guess we're pretty pathetic, huh?"

He touched his fingertips to her cheek. "Pathetic, no, but we do need to trust each other. That's the issue we've been dancing around, isn't it? We've both been reluctant to let go and believe that what we share now has a chance. I know I have been."

She nodded. "So have I."

"That stops now, Daphne, because if it doesn't, there really is no hope for us at all. Can you trust me, Daphne?"

She nodded. "I always have. And just to set the record straight, I never really faulted you for leaving to pursue your career, though a little warning would have been nice. And I didn't tell you I'd miscarried the baby, not because I didn't think you'd stay, but because I knew you would. You would have blown your big opportunity, and you would have grown to hate me because of it. The only thing I ever blamed you for was loving your music more than you did me."

"It wasn't that, Daphne. If I was guilty of anything, it was of taking you for granted. I couldn't imagine that you wouldn't always be there for me. We had something so special, I couldn't imagine losing it until it was gone." He tugged on a braid, one that nature had streaked gray. "I won't make that mistake again."

She hit his shoulder with the side of her fist. "You'd

better not." She looked up into his eyes, saw the green
fire glinting there. They had some things to work out between them, but for tonight, the time for talking had
passed. She leaned up and pressed her mouth to his.
"Make love to me, Nathan," she whispered against his lips.

She felt no hesitancy in him this time, as his mouth
claimed hers for a ravishing kiss. Her fingers tangled in
the soft, curly hair at his nape. His hands slid down to
cup her buttocks, pulling her roughly against him. A groan
of pleasure rumbled up through his chest as she pressed
her hips against him. Her hands went to the back of his
shirt, trying to free it from the confines of his waistband.

Her eyes flew open in surprise when he pushed her back
against the opposite side of the doorway. "Oh, no you
don't, Daphne Thorne. This time when I make love to you,
I'm going to do it properly. In my bed."

Wrapping his arms around her hips, he picked her up
and carried her to his room. He set her down beside his
bed. His hands roamed up her body, under her sweater,
over the lacy black bra she wore. He lifted her sweater
over her head and tossed it aside. His hands settled on her
rib cage, his thumbs drawing a lazy pattern over her
breasts.

"God, I've missed you," he whispered. "I missed touching you and tasting you."

Daphne gasped as he lowered his head and took one of
her nipples into his mouth, stroking her sensitive flesh with
his tongue. "I've missed you, too," she managed to get
out.

His hands roamed over her body, stroking her, teasing
her, driving her crazy. He divested her of her clothing until
she stood before him nude. She looked up at his face. His
gaze was so intense that she had to look away from him.

He cupped her chin in his hand, tilting her face up to
him. "I thought you liked the way I looked at you."

"Don't tease me, Nathan. Not this time."

He recognized the urgency in her voice, the same yearning he felt in his own body, the same need for completion. He laid her on the bed and quickly shrugged out of his own clothes. Then he joined her on the bed, covering her with his body. She cradled him between her thighs, wrapping her legs around his waist.

He thrust into her, reveling in the feel of her soft flesh enveloping him. She arched against him, taking him deeper into her body. He groaned, lowering his head to bury his face against her throat. Her hands were on his back, stroking him, loving him, making him crazy. It was too much, this exquisite tension that built in his body, tautening his muscles, demanding release.

And beneath him, Daphne was just as restless. He lifted his head and looked down at her. Her eyes were closed, her teeth clamped on her lower lip. Her chest heaved as she moved against him, meeting the slow, deliberate pace he'd set.

He leaned his weight on one elbow, using his other hand to cup her breast in his palm. "Come for me, Daphne," he whispered. He lowered his head and took her nipple into his mouth, laving it with his tongue.

"Nathan," she cried, her body contracting around his as her nails dug into his shoulders. And his own release overtook him, arching his back, making him shudder with the most powerful climax he'd ever experienced.

He collapsed on top of her, and she held him to her as they both recovered. "I love you, Nathan," she murmured against his ear.

He raised his head and looked down at her, a teasing grin on his face. "Now you tell me, after I did all that work."

"You're not finished yet," she said. She cupped his face in her hands and brought his mouth down to hers.

* * *

"Nathan, would you please hurry up? Your grandmother will be ninety before we make it to her eightieth birthday party."

Daphne paced around Nathan's bedroom, bouncing the baby in her arms. She'd managed to bathe and dress both herself and Emily, and Nathan still hadn't gotten out of the shower. Daphne looked down at the baby. "I swear, your dad is worse than a woman."

Emily didn't respond, not even with her usual gurgles and coos. Daphne put her hand to the baby's forehead. She didn't feel warm, but Daphne sensed that Emily wasn't quite herself either. "What's the matter, sweetie?" Daphne asked, bouncing the baby on her hip. Emily clung to Daphne's neck and sucked on her tiny fingers.

Daphne tucked her hair behind her ear to keep it out of the baby's grasp. Two weeks ago, she'd taken her braids out and had her hair styled in a shoulder-length bob. Sighing, she touched her hand to her own forehead. Maybe it was she who was out of sorts. She felt flushed and achy in an odd way. Her period, which had been due two days ago, had yet to make an appearance. Being late or missing a period altogether wasn't that unusual for her. Ever since she'd turned thirty-five, her menstrual cycle had been a little wacky. But the only other time she'd felt like this she'd ended up going to the drugstore for a pregnancy test.

"Nathan," she called impatiently. The sooner they got there, the sooner they could come home. She intended to tell him about her suspicions tonight.

But he was already right behind her. His arms closed around her, and he nuzzled her neck. "Have I told you how delectable you look today?"

"No, not yet."

His hands slid down to ride her hips. "What do you say we let Emily play in her crib a few minutes while we play in ours?" She closed her eyes and sucked in her breath as Nathan pushed up the hem of her skirt and fondled her. "How about a quickie before we go make nice to the relatives?"

She pulled away from him. "We're late as it is. And if you think I'm letting you take anything off considering how long it took you to put it on, you're mistaken."

She'd meant to sound indignant, as a means of discouraging him. Instead she'd sounded downright bitchy. She sighed. "I'm sorry, I didn't mean to snap at you. Can we just go?"

"Sure, baby. Anything you want."

But the damage had already been done. She noticed Nathan scrutinizing her as they put on their coats. The entire way in the car he was uncharacteristically silent. But she didn't want to tell him yet. Not until they were alone and would be for a while. On the way home, she'd stop at a drugstore. Then they'd know with some reasonable certainty whether or not she carried his child.

Nathan's family was a diverse population of young and old, male and female and every color of the human rainbow. And they were all crowded into his grandmother's small house.

Dinner was a potluck buffet as diverse as the people who ate it. Daphne had baked a ham using her mother's favorite mustard-and-brown-sugar glaze. Someone had taken it from her the moment they'd walked in the door. The meat had been carved and laid out on an attractive platter. Daphne served herself a slice as she filled her plate. Nathan tried to feed Emily, but she didn't seem interested in food. After a while, Nathan took Emily upstairs to put her down for a nap.

Some of the younger cousins had cranked up the stereo, moved the living-room furniture to the side, and begun to dance.

Nathan came up behind her. "What is this sacrilege," he said, feigning outrage.

She glanced back at him. "What did you expect them to play? Your songs?"

"God, no. But I wouldn't mind something where people actually sang instead of screamed objectionable things at the top of their lungs."

"You're showing your age, Mr. Ward."

"Yeah. Soon I'll be old enough to write my autobiography, *As Crotchety as I Wanna Be.*"

Daphne laughed, but she spotted another of Nathan's cousins out of the corner of her eye, standing by the stereo.

He winked at her when she turned her head to face him. "Enough of that crap." A couple of seconds later, the sounds of Brian McKnight's sultry voice filled the room.

Nathan wrapped his arms around her waist and nuzzled her ear. "Great," he muttered. "Now they play the competition."

"Behave yourself," she warned.

"I don't know the meaning of the word. Come out back with me for a minute."

"It's freezing out there."

"I'll keep you warm."

She didn't doubt that. "I want to check on Emily first." Even with the monitor on, with so much noise in the house, she might be awake and no one would hear her.

He kissed the side of her neck. "Just don't take forever."

"I won't," she promised, then headed up the stairs to check on the baby.

* * *

Five minutes later, Nathan sat on the steps leading to his grandmother's garden, wondering what was taking Daphne so long. He wanted a moment alone with her. He knew something had been bothering her from early this morning, but she hadn't said one word to him about it. If he'd done something to upset her, he wanted to know now, before she stewed over it any longer.

He heard the screen door open behind him. He stood, surprised to see his grandmother walking toward him, not Daphne. "What are you doing out here?" he asked. He took her hand and helped her sit on the top step before retaking his seat.

"Nina tells me you come out here to brood. What do you have to trouble you today, Nathan? I'm the one who just turned eighty."

"I wasn't brooding. I was sitting out here, thinking how lucky I am."

"Luck, nothing." Nathan's grandmother waved her hand dismissively. "Ever since you were a baby, we knew you had talent. You used to sing along with the radio while you were still in diapers. Of course, none of us knew what you were singing."

Nathan put his arm around his grandmother. "You know, growing up, I always wondered why you never kept a tight rein on me like you did the girls. You never offered me any advice or tried to guide me in any way."

She lifted her shoulders in a helpless gesture. "What did I know about the music business? What was I supposed to say? I gave you the best advice I knew how—I said 'knock 'em dead.'"

"And you did. You left home playing with a band, but it was you the record companies wanted, you who they made a star. And that band you first, what do you say, opened for? Where are they now? Who knows? They had a few songs, then what?"

Nathan smiled at his grandmother's assessment. He hadn't realized she'd paid that much attention to his career, especially not back then.

"You had the courage and the talent and the drive to succeed while others fell by the wayside. And now, you have a beautiful baby daughter and you have Daphne, though I better see an engagement ring on her finger the next time I see her. Whatever you have, *mijito*, you've earned. And I am so very proud of you."

He hugged his grandmother as she planted a warm, moist kiss on his cheek. *"Gracias, Abuela."*

Nathan's grandmother leaned back and threw her hands up as if in exasperation. "Now he speaks Spanish to me."

Hearing the door to the house open, Nathan swiveled around, expecting to see Daphne alone coming to meet him. But she held Emily in her arms. The distraught look on Daphne's face sent a chill of alarm rushing through him.

He stood, turning to face her move fully. "Daphne, what's the matter?"

"Nathan, it's the baby. She's burning up."

Eighteen

Nathan drove back into the city with all the finesse of a Manhattan cabbie. He wanted to take Emily to the hospital where her regular pediatrician, Dr. Peterson, had visiting privileges. Daphne agreed, as it was the same hospital where Garrett practiced. Daphne sat in the backseat of the car with the baby, praying they didn't get into an accident before they made it to their destination.

Looking down at little Emily, Daphne wanted to weep. She was so listless that Daphne truly feared for her. She should have told Nathan earlier that she thought Emily might be coming down with something. They should have taken her to the doctor immediately. But in all honesty, she'd thought she'd been letting her worries about being pregnant color her judgment.

Finally Nathan pulled into a spot on the corner of the hospital building. They'd called Garrett on the way to the hospital. He'd promised to meet them in the pediatric emergency room. He stood waiting at the intake desk.

"How is she?" Garrett asked, walking toward them.

Garrett extended his arms and Nathan placed the baby in his hands. "She's got a fever, she wouldn't eat this afternoon, and she's been very quiet all day."

"Come on," Garrett said, holding the baby in one arm and unzipping her snowsuit with the other hand. He led them to an examining room that held two beds with standard hospital curtains cordoning off each area.

Emily's doctor waited for them inside. By then, Garrett had gotten Emily's snowsuit off and the two men began to examine her.

Daphne rested her head on Nathan's shoulder, while he answered the doctor's questions about what Emily had eaten, who she'd been exposed to, how she'd slept, and when the fever had started. Tears stung the back of Daphne's eyes, and it was an effort to remember to breathe.

Dr. Peterson turned to face them. "We're not finding anything. Emily's eyes, ears, and nose are all clear. But her eyes aren't tracking well, and there's a slight bulge in the fontanel. We'll need to take blood and urine and do a lumbar puncture and see what turns up."

"A lumbar puncture?" Nathan asked.

"A spinal tap. We drain some of the fluid from the spinal column to test the contents."

"Why is that necessary?"

"It's fairly standard procedure in cases like this," Dr. Peterson said.

"Don't try to soften it up for me. What do you think is wrong with her?"

Garrett cleared his throat. "At this point we suspect meningitis."

Daphne squeezed her eyes shut, feeling a wave of dizziness wash over her. She didn't know much about the illness, except that it could be fatal, especially in infants. She glanced up at Nathan. He appeared completely calm, completely in control. Yet she knew how much he loved Emily; she knew how much this had to be tearing him up inside. His arm tightened around her waist, stroking her side in a comforting manner.

"Then let's get on with it," Nathan said.

Daphne held herself together during most of the examination, but when she saw the size of the needle they intended to use on the baby, she started to tremble. "Oh, my God, Nathan. Poor Emily."

"We need quiet here," Dr. Peterson said. "Or you'll have to step outside."

"Garrett, take Daphne out of here. I'll hold the baby."

She didn't want to leave, but she couldn't seem to get herself together, either. She didn't suppose she would help any by staying. When she felt Garrett's hand on her arm, she went with him.

Outside the room, she leaned against the wall alongside the door. "I am such a coward." She looked up at Garrett for sympathy.

"No, you're not. You'd be surprised how many parents can't take it. When Elise was giving birth to Alyssa, they gave her an epidural for the pain. Now, I was doing an emergency room rotation at the time and I'd seen more blood and gore than you can possibly imagine. But when I saw them put that needle in Elise's back I passed right out on the floor."

Daphne couldn't help giggling, thinking of six-foot-six Garrett crashing to the floor. "You must have shook the room."

"Probably. I wouldn't know as I was out cold at the time. A fact Elise has never let me forget. But I don't think it's cowardly. It only means you love her."

Daphne bit her lip. She did love Emily, as much as she would her own daughter. "Is she going to be okay?"

"You know I can't give you any guarantees. Medicine isn't like that. But I have seen Emily Elizabeth in action. She's a scrappy little girl, and she's in the best hands in the field. So don't borrow trouble."

"I won't." She tried to force a smile to her face and failed miserably.

Garrett slipped his arm around her shoulders, urging her forward. "Let's go get some coffee."

"Can you do something else for me? Can you run a test for me—a pregnancy test?"

"Sure, Daphne." He scrutinized her face for a moment. "Are you feeling all right?"

"I'm fine. I just want to know."

Garrett nodded. "I'll take you down to the lab."

Less than ten minutes later she had her answer. Garrett had left her in one of the chairs ringing the lab area while he had the test processed. She sat with her elbows on her knees, her face in her hands, so she didn't notice his presence until he sat beside her. She gazed up and noticed the huge grin on his face.

"Congratulations, Dee. The rabbit bit the dust."

She blinked. "What?"

"Forgive me for dating myself. The test was positive. You're pregnant."

"I knew what you meant. I'm just a little stunned, that's all." And overjoyed and scared all at the same time.

"I take it you guys didn't plan this."

She shook her head. "No, and promise me you won't say anything to Nathan about it."

"Why not, sweetheart?" He squeezed her knee sympathetically. "I know for a fact Nathan will be happy about this."

"He needs to concentrate on Emily now. We both do. There will be plenty of time for me to tell him when she's well."

"All right." He held out his hand to her. "We'd better get back."

The doctor had just finished by the time they got back to the room. Nathan held Emily in his arms, rocking her. Daphne went to him and he pulled her into his embrace. She laid her cheek against his chest.

He stroked his hand over her back. "Are you okay?"

"I'm fine. What are they going to do?"

"They'll admit her and start her on antibiotics right away. We'll know more in a couple of days when the cultures come back."

"A couple of days?" How were they supposed to wait all that time before they found out anything? As with everything else in life, the pain of not knowing was ten times worse than any certainty you could dream up.

Nathan squeezed her side. "If the antibiotics work she should start to get better within twenty-four hours."

"Nathan, we need to get the IV started," Garrett said.

Daphne watched as Nathan kissed the baby's cheek and allowed Garrett to take her. Then Nathan pulled Daphne into his arms, pressing her cheek against his chest. He didn't fool her one bit. She knew he sought to shield her from watching what they were doing to Emily.

She pulled away from him and turned toward Emily. She took Nathan's hand, giving his fingers a squeeze. "I'm fine, Nathan, really."

"Then let's go upstairs. They're going to bring Emily up to the pediatric ward in a few minutes."

The pediatric ward was virtually empty, so they ended up with a private room for Emily. Nathan refused to leave Emily and Daphne refused to leave Nathan, so she and Nathan ended up sleeping on a hospital bed Garrett had brought into the room. Or Daphne dozed, while Nathan paced the floor or stared out the window or hovered over the baby's bed, which resembled a big metal crib. Daphne didn't want to sleep; she wanted to stay up with Nathan, to give him back some of the support he'd given her. But the baby growing in her body exerted itself, demanding that she rest.

She woke with a start at about four in the morning. Elise and Jenny were in the room with her, but not Nathan.

"What are you two doing here?" Daphne sat up, smoothing her hair back from her face. "Where's Nathan?"

Both women came over to her and embraced her. Elise sat beside her on the bed. "We couldn't stay away, and since Garrett has some pull around here, we didn't have to."

Jenny sat on her other side. "We raided your apartments and brought you some things—toothbrushes, clothes. We figured neither of you would be too concerned with personal hygiene."

Daphne looked from one woman to the other. "Thank you." She blinked, trying to banish the last of her drowsiness. "Where's Nathan?"

"He said he was going to the men's room."

Daphne scanned Jenny's face. That's what he'd said, but Jenny's expression told her she hadn't believed him. Why should she have? There was a bathroom right here in the room.

Daphne slid off the bed. "I'd better go find him."

She checked the entire ward, the cafeteria, everywhere she could think to look for him. She found him in the last place she'd expect him to go—the tiny hospital chapel at one end of the third floor.

He sat in the middle of the second bench, his arms folded on top of the bench in front of him, his forehead resting on his hands. She hated to see him like this, completely humbled, completely alone. She walked the short distance to him and sat beside him. He didn't acknowledge her in any way.

She didn't know what to say, how to reach him. As stoic as he'd been while the crisis was upon them, she'd known that inside he'd been devastated by Emily's illness. And she knew that if they lost Emily, she would lose him. He wouldn't survive it; he wouldn't be the same man he was before.

Leaning forward, she laid her arm across his shoulder and her cheek on his arm. "It's going to be okay," she whispered.

He lifted his head and looked at her. In his eyes she saw reflected all the pain she knew resided in his heart. "I can't lose her, Daphne. I can't. She's the only thing I've ever done right."

Coming from anyone else, that comment would have struck her as the height of selfishness. But she knew he possessed a deep core of fatalism. He believed that what happened to Emily now served as punishment for whatever sins he imagined blotted his soul.

She wanted to tell him about the baby growing inside her, but she couldn't. It would seem too much like she was offering him her own child as a substitute for Emily. One child could never replace another.

Instead, she cupped his face in her hands, forcing him to look at her. "Don't make me smack you, Nathan. That is a lot of nonsense and we both know it. I know you're worried about Emily. I'm worried, too. But you can't give up now. Emily needs you and so do I."

He turned his head and kissed the palm of her hand. "Do you need me, Daphne? I've waited so long to hear you say those words."

She'd told him she loved him, and it hadn't moved him so strongly. She scanned his face, wondering why he valued the words *I need you* more than *I love you*. "Why?"

"I never wanted to be a man like my father, one who was completely inconsequential to the people who were supposed to love him."

She laughed and hugged him to her. "You, inconsequential? Never. That would be like saying the San Francisco earthquake was just a few bumps. You came back into my life and shook it all up. And I'm so very glad you did."

She leaned up and pressed her mouth to his, kissing him

with all the love and tenderness she felt, all the hope she had that everything would turn out all right.

When she pulled away from him, he touched his thumb to the corner of her mouth. "Let's go back and see Emily."

When they got back to the room, Garrett had joined Elise and Jenny in Emily's room. Daphne went to the baby's crib. She slipped one of her hands through the bars to run her fingers over the baby's soft hair. "How is she?" she asked Garrett.

"Still the same." Garrett patted her shoulder. "I wouldn't expect to see any change yet. All we can do is wait."

Garrett turned to Nathan. "Have you thought of calling Emily's mother?"

Daphne felt Nathan stiffen beside her. "No, I haven't."

"Maybe you should."

Nathan sighed. "Maybe you're right."

He left the room a few moments later. But he didn't come back right away. She'd almost gone to look for him, when he returned to the room. He looked shell-shocked, but she didn't question him when he came to stand beside her. She assumed he hadn't gotten the response from Monica he'd wanted. He'd tell her when he was ready.

After a while, the others went home, leaving Nathan and Daphne alone with the baby. They changed into the sweats and T-shirts the women had brought them. When Daphne emerged from the small bathroom, Nathan took her hand and led her to the bed.

He kissed her cheek. "You look really wrung out. I want you to rest."

She snorted. She felt like something the birds had picked over and left for dead. But he didn't look any better than she did. "Only if you rest with me."

They lay down on the bed spoon fashion, facing Emily. She couldn't wait any longer. "What did Monica say?"

"She didn't say anything. I got her father's housekeeper on the phone."

"Why wouldn't Monica talk to you herself?"

"She died about a month ago."

Daphne blinked. She leaned back and tilted her head so she could see Nathan's face. His expression gave away nothing of what he felt. "How?"

"She wouldn't tell me. I have a feeling it wasn't an accident."

Daphne sighed, and rested her head on her folded hands. Her gaze settled on Emily. Poor little girl. Daphne realized she'd been harboring the hope that somehow Nathan and Monica would work out their differences and Monica would become a part of Emily's life. Now, Emily would never know her mother.

"Go to sleep, sweetheart," Nathan whispered in her ear.

She closed her eyes, but it was a long time before either of them slept.

By the following night, Emily had improved considerably. Her fever was down, and she'd eaten most of her dinner. By the following day, she was much more alert, and fascinated by the IV still attached to her little arm.

Daphne tickled her little tummy to distract her. If the baby started to bother the IV, they'd have to tie her arms down to keep her from pulling it out. "Feeling better, are we?" The baby gurgled and worked her little legs.

Nathan came into the room then, followed by his grandmother, his sister, and Yasmin. "Look who I found wandering the halls."

Daphne hugged each of the women. They crowded around Emily's crib, staring down at the baby. "She looks much better," Nathan's grandmother announced, nodding. "How much longer does she have to stay?"

"Another few days."

They all turned, hearing an unexpected male voice. Dr. Peterson came in. "How is our girl doing today?" He walked over to the bed and pulled Emily's chart from its holder at the base of the crib.

Daphne watched the doctor as he scanned the pages, noting that his eyes strayed in Nina's direction a couple of times.

"I see hazel eyes run in the family," he said, replacing the chart. He walked over to the head of the crib and smiled down at Emily. "Grandma, grandchildren and now great-grand."

"Emily has brown eyes," Nathan countered.

"Not anymore. They've lightened a great deal since I saw her for her last checkup. They're not quite hazel now, but they probably will be."

Daphne gazed down into Emily's eyes. She would have sworn Emily's eyes were brown, too. How could she not have noticed how much greener her eyes had become? Probably because she saw Emily almost every day, she hadn't noticed the gradual shift in color.

Daphne glanced up at Nathan, wondering at the strange expression on his face. His gaze met hers, and she'd swear his eyes looked a little misty. That didn't make much sense, but a moment later, he excused himself and left the room.

She followed him, but she didn't have to go far before she found him. He was leaning against the wall outside Emily's door. His legs were crossed at the ankles. One of his arms was crossed over his body, the other hand shaded his face. She laid her hand on his shoulder. "Nathan, what's wrong?" she asked.

He lifted his head. "Nothing's wrong, Daphne. In fact, everything's right."

Her brows knitted together. "Are you feeling okay?"

Nathan sighed, running his hand up and down her arm. "Maybe I should have told you this from the beginning."

"Told me what?"

"A few days after the day she and I were supposed to get married, Monica sent me a letter. In it she told me she wasn't sure who Emily's father was. Emily was born two weeks before Monica's due date, so that threw off her assumptions about who'd fathered the baby. Or at least that's what she wrote in her letter."

"So, Emily could have been my brother's child."

"No. She slept with Michael, hoping to convince him that the child she already carried was his. But she realized Michael was too wrapped up in Jenny to really care about anything else. She claimed there was someone else who might have been Emily's father. She didn't tell me who.

"At first, I thought it was a ploy to extort some money out of me after she didn't show up for the wedding. But when she never asked for anything, it got me wondering.

"But she'd told me Emily was mine, Daphne, and I fell in love with my daughter. I wasn't giving her up. I wouldn't have cared who her biological father turned out to be."

No wonder he hadn't been willing to fight for Emily in court; if they'd done a paternity test, he'd have had no legal standing to keep her. Even if Monica hadn't challenged his custody, the courts certainly would have. With no blood tie and his track record in the tabloids, he'd have stood little chance of keeping her.

"Is that when you came to me?"

He nodded. "Looking back, it didn't really change anything—my being with you. Monica could have tracked me down in two seconds flat if she'd wanted to. But with you I felt . . ."

"Safe?" she volunteered when he trailed off.

"Yeah." He ruffled her bangs. "I know what a badass you can be when somebody riles you."

She poked him in the chest with her index finger. "And don't you forget it."

He caught her hand and pulled her toward him. He wrapped his arms around her waist and buried his face against her neck. "She's mine, Daphne, she's really mine."

Daphne hugged him back, and in her mind she added, *She's ours.*

One week later, Daphne lay on Nathan's bed, playing with the baby. In a couple of hours she would have to give Emily her final dose of medication, but Emily was already back to being her normal busy, happy self. At the moment, Emily was chewing on the head of the Bert doll, the counterpart to the Ernie she'd bitten to death.

Nathan came into the room, went to the closet, and slipped on a pair of shoes.

"Where are you going?" she asked him.

"Out for a little while. I'll tell you about it when I get back."

Nathan rested one hand on the mattress next to her. She leaned up to accept his kiss. "I have something to tell you, too. Don't be gone too long."

"I won't." He kissed the baby, then smoothed his hand over her hair. "You two stay out of trouble while I'm gone."

Daphne just laughed. As soon as Nathan was out the door, she picked up the phone and dialed. While she waited for him to answer, she wondered if she were doing the right thing or making more trouble for Nathan and herself.

* * *

Nathan drove out to Long Island to the cemetery where the housekeeper told him Monica was buried. It was the only information the woman would give him, other than that Monica had died. He didn't know exactly what he expected to find, but he'd felt he had to come. He owed her that much, at least to say good-bye.

He parked the car where the gatekeeper instructed him. The grave itself wasn't hard to find. A large, ornate headstone marked the spot where she was buried. On it was inscribed her name, the dates of birth and death, and underneath it the words, *Loving Daughter, Devoted Mother.*

What a travesty. As far as he knew, Monica had never loved anyone but herself and had never been devoted to anything beside her own pleasures. Suddenly, he felt worse instead of better for having come.

He bent and placed the flowers he'd brought next to the headstone. "Good-bye, Monica," he said, unable to think of anything else to say. He stood, intending to leave, but sensing the presence of another person, he turned in the opposite direction. An elderly man stood before him, holding his hat in his nut-brown hands.

"Can I help you?" Nathan asked.

"No, but maybe I can help you. I'm Marcus Trent, Monica's father."

Nathan had suspected as much. He shook the hand the man extended toward him. "I'm sorry about your daughter."

He nodded. "I know, son. Otherwise you wouldn't be here. She had cancer, you know. Ovarian."

"No, she never told me."

"They found the tumor when she went to the doctor to find out if she was pregnant. The doctor told her she should terminate the pregnancy. Heaven help me, I told her the same thing. I told her she should concentrate on getting well. But she wouldn't listen to anyone."

Nathan nodded. If she had listened, he wouldn't have Emily. But if she were ill, why hadn't she told him? If she knew she was dying, why wouldn't she have wanted to see her own child? Nathan just shook his head. "Why sacrifice so much to bring a child into the world then abandon it?"

"Monica was a change-of-life baby for her mother and me. Margaret had already been showing signs of Alzheimer's even before she became pregnant with Monica, but I didn't notice it. I worked long hours and when I came home, well, I wasn't as attentive as I should have been.

"And when I did realize how much my wife had deteriorated, I hired a nurse to care for her at home." He paused, twisting his hat in both hands. "Have you ever known anyone with Alzheimer's?"

Nathan shook his head.

"It's heartbreaking. Half the time she didn't know who she was, let alone who any of the rest of us were. By the time she died, she needed more constant supervision than her six-year-old daughter. I didn't know it at the time, but Monica had been terrified of her mother."

"What has that got to do with Emily?"

"Don't you see, son? She never would have subjected her daughter to the same experience. She'd refused any sort of treatment while she was pregnant, fearing she'd hurt the baby. And afterward, it was too late. Didn't you notice how fast she'd lost weight after she gave birth?"

No, he'd been too busy being angry with her for being negligent in taking care of Emily. "Why didn't she tell me?"

"That I can't answer. Maybe because she thought you'd feel sorry for her. The last thing she wanted was anyone's pity, not even mine. All she wanted was to make sure someone would take care of Emily. That's why she insisted you marry her. She wanted to see how far you'd go to protect Emily, but I doubt she ever intended to go through with the marriage. My Monica was no angel, but she did love her daughter."

Nathan closed his eyes and dragged in a breath. In her own way, Monica had loved Emily more than he'd ever imagined. Her actions were misguided, but he couldn't fault her intentions. He only wish he'd known. Maybe then he could have spent his time trying to convince her of the error in her logic rather than hating her.

Feeling the older man's hand on his shoulder, he opened his eyes and looked at him. "How is my granddaughter?"

He'd told the housekeeper that Emily was ill, but hadn't given any more details. "She's doing much better. Thank you."

"When can I come see her?"

"How about Sunday afternoon for lunch?"

The old man nodded. "Sounds fine." He patted Nathan's arm again. "Thank you."

Nodding, Nathan started to leave, then turned back. "How did you know I'd be here?"

"Your wife called me and asked me to meet you here."

Daphne, damn her. She knew him better than he knew himself. He headed back to the car and drove home. As he expected, she was waiting for him when he opened the door. She sat on the stairs that led up to her apartment.

"How did it go?" she asked him. "Did you get the answers you wanted?"

He slipped out of his coat and hung in on the coatrack. "I got some answers. I'm not sure they were the ones I wanted."

He told her about Monica's illness and her exit from Emily's life because of it. "I should have confronted her," he added. "I should have made her tell me what was going on with her. Instead, I gave in to the juvenile need to hide out. I robbed both Emily and Monica of a chance to know each other for whatever time they had together."

He walked through the open apartment door, into his bedroom, and started to shrug out of his clothes. He didn't realize Daphne had followed him until she spoke.

"How can you possibly know that anything would have changed if you'd confronted Monica? I didn't know her, but she strikes me as having been a strong-willed woman. She probably would have done exactly as she wanted, no matter what you'd said."

Nathan sat on the bed, turning his head toward her. She stood leaning against the door frame, her arms folded in front of her. "We'll never know that now, will we?"

"No."

Nathan lay back on the bed and looked up at the ceiling. "I'll tell you one thing. I have had enough drama to last me for a long time. I don't want to hear anything about births, deaths, illnesses of any kind. I want us to settle down and have a nice quiet life raising Emily."

He turned his head to look at her. She'd clamped her teeth on her lower lip and a troubled look haunted her eyes.

"Baby, what's the matter?"

"Nathan, I'm pregnant."

He blinked and sat up. "What did you just say?"

"I said, I'm pregnant. We're going to have a baby."

As if in a daze, he got up and walked to her. He touched his palm to her flat abdomen. "How long have you known?"

"When you sent me out of the room the day we brought Emily into the hospital I had Garrett do the test."

"That was days ago. Why didn't you tell me?"

"I thought we both needed to concentrate on getting Emily well again."

He cupped her face in his hands and kissed her cheeks,

her eyelids and finally her mouth. "You do know that you're going to have to marry me and make an honest man out of me."

"Is that what you want?"

"That's what I've wanted almost since I moved in here." He went to his dresser and returned carrying something in his hand. "I bought this for you when I went to L.A. I hadn't found the right time to ask you."

He handed her a small, square jewelry box. She bit her lip, looking from him to the box. She lifted the lid to reveal an exquisite round-cut diamond. The stone was four carats, easily.

"Oh, my God," Daphne said in a voice full of awe. "I can't wear this." She extended the box to him.

"Why not?"

"Think of the women I work with. It would be like shoving their poverty in their faces."

He laughed and hugged her to him. "That's what you're worried about? That you'll offend your clients' sensibilities?" He kissed the tip of her nose.

"What did you think I meant? That I wouldn't marry you? I love you, Nathan. I let you walk out of my life once. I don't intend to make that mistake again."

She cupped his face in her hands and kissed him with all the love, all the passion she felt. When she pulled away from him, he took the box from her.

"How about you keep this one for special occasions, and I buy you something more sensible for every day?" Without waiting for her answer, he slid the ring on her finger.

The ring fit perfectly. Daphne slid her arms around his neck. "Only if I pick it out. You don't know the meaning of he word *sensible*."

"Maybe not, but you'll have plenty of time to teach me."

And from the next room, Emily wailed. "Da da da."

It was the most wonderful sound either of them had ever heard.

Epilogue

One month later

"Would you please relax? She's coming."

Nathan paused in his pacing around the perimeter of Jenny's father's kitchen and turned toward Jenny. He saw the amused look in her eye and glowered at her. "What is so funny?"

"You. Aren't you the man who once told me he'd be satisfied if the woman he loved simply loved him back? I believe you said, 'to hell with all the other trappings.' That was you, wasn't it?"

He'd said that what seemed like a lifetime ago, before he'd had any inkling that Daphne would come back into his life. "Yeah, me and my big mouth. What did I know?"

"And now here you are, obsessing because your bride is fifteen minutes late."

"And speaking of late, where is that husband of yours? Does he have the rings?"

"He's helping my father roust some squatters off the front lawn."

"Squatters?"

"I'm sure you haven't noticed this, but we've been over-run with reporters trying to get a scoop on your wedding. The first of them arrived a couple of hours ago. They've been collecting out there ever since then, like something out of *The Birds*. So Daddy borrowed a couple of shotguns. He claimed he was trying to scatter the birds out of the trees like Tom Skerritt in *Steel Magnolias*. The only thing that went scattering was the press, back into their vans."

He and Daphne had taken up Jenny's father's invitation to use his house for the wedding, as they'd thought its remote Connecticut location would afford them some privacy. They should have known better. "We should have done what you and Mike did and elope."

"And have two families mad at you for not having a proper ceremony? My mother still hasn't forgiven me."

"Would you please go see what's keeping her so long?"

"Sure thing, Nathan. Try to stay out of trouble while I'm gone." She slapped him on the backside, sending white-hot pain shooting through him. "I'm going to get you for that, Scanlon," he vowed.

She stuck out her tongue at him. "Promises, promises."

As she turned to leave the room, Michael entered. He caught Jenny in a sensual embrace and brought his lips down on hers for a lingering kiss. "How's my baby?" he asked.

Jenny patted her stomach. "Just fine."

Nathan watched the two of them in growing disgust. "Mike, will you please stop mauling your wife so she can find out what's keeping Daphne."

"I'm going, I'm going," Jenny said.

Michael, usually the soul of asceticism, practically bounced over to him, punched him on the shoulder playfully and said, "You've really got to lighten up, man."

"There, how's that?"

Daphne turned around to face the mirror. Elise had just finished fastening the string of tiny buttons closing

Daphne's wedding gown. Daphne shifted a little, but it did nothing to relieve the tightness in the dress around her midsection. "I feel like a water balloon that's about to burst. I have some nerve wearing white. Everyone is going to notice I'm expecting Nathan's child."

"You look beautiful, Dee," Elise said. "All white symbolizes is that it's a first marriage. Now, if your veil falls off, that's another story."

Daphne laughed and hugged her sister. Leave it to Elise to know the proper way of things. "And remember, Alyssa . . ." Daphne glanced over her shoulder at her young niece. "This is not the way to do it. Wedding first, babies second."

Alyssa gave her a disgusted look and pushed out of the chair she'd been sitting in. "I think I used to like you better when you didn't like men. You're starting to sound like my mother." She clomped out of the room, just as Jenny came in.

"There are worse things that could happen to me, I guess."

"Worse things than what?" Jenny asked.

"Starting to sound like Momma hen over here."

"Well, I hate to sound like a nag, too, but if you don't get downstairs soon, my father's going to have to retile the kitchen floor."

Daphne took a deep breath, giving one last check to the pins holding her veil in place. "I'm ready."

Daphne's father stood at the base of the stairs waiting to escort her down the aisle. The women helped her down the stairs, then left the two of them alone. "Are you nervous, sweetheart?" he asked her.

She managed a weak smile. "A little."

"It's not too late to back out now."

Her father had never said one word to her either way about Nathan's reappearance in her life. "Is that what you think I should do?"

"No, honey. Nathan's a good man, and he loves you. But you have to do what you think is right."

"Then I say, let's walk down the aisle."

They walked to the double doors that opened into the music room, where Jenny, Elise, and Alyssa waited. One by one they preceded her down the aisle, followed by two of Nathan's little cousins who served as flower girl and ring bearer.

While Daphne waited for the traditional flourish of "Here Comes the Bride" to sound, she glanced over at her father. "Who's going to take care of you now? I've been so negligent these past few weeks."

"It might surprise you to know I'm quite capable of taking care of myself. Now let's get in there before that young man of yours comes out here to get you."

She nodded and took his arm. When they reached the front of the church, Jasper lifted her veil and kissed her cheek. "Be happy, Daphne," he whispered, fluffing her veil in place.

"I will, Dad."

She looked up into Nathan's eyes as her father placed her hand in his. She hadn't seen him in a full week, as she'd been here taking care of the arrangements for the wedding. She hadn't realized how much she'd missed him until now, with him standing in front of her.

"Hi, stranger," she said.

He made a show of looking her up and down. "Nice dress. Is it new?"

On the most sober, momentous day of her life, in front of one hundred assorted guests, Daphne Thorne began to laugh. She threw her arms around Nathan's neck and hugged him. "You're crazy," she whispered.

He hugged her, too, running his hands over her back. "Yup. Crazy about you." He cupped his hands around her shoulders. "Are you ready to marry me?"

She pulled back enough to look at him. "Yes, Nathan. Yes, I'm ready." They drew apart and turned to face the priest.

"It's about time, you two," he scolded, sotto voce. "For a moment, I thought you were starting without me."

When the ceremony was over, Daphne and Nathan stood outside the music room in an informal receiving line. Nathan's grandmother was one of the first to come through the doors. She carried Emily in her arms. The baby was busy singing her familiar chorus of "Da da da." Nathan reached for his daughter. "Come to Daddy, sweetheart."

But Emily had other ideas. She grabbed hold of Daphne's sleeve and wouldn't let go. "Da da da," she repeated.

Daphne welcomed the baby into her arms, settling her against one hip. Emily seemed fascinated by her outfit, looking from the elaborate beading of her dress to the headpiece that held her veil in place.

"Mijito," Nathan's grandmother said, an amused grin on her face. "It appears 'Da da da,' doesn't stand for 'Da da Daddy,' but rather 'Da da Daphne.'"

Nathan looked so put out by the situation that Daphne had to press her lips together to keep from laughing. That is until Emily gave her veil a tug and pulled it right off her head.

Daphne glanced down at the baby, who had begun to munch on the netting. She tickled her little tummy. "Tattletale," she accused.

Nathan took the veil from the baby's grasp. Having nothing better to do with it, he draped it over the head of one of his little cousins passing by. The little girl grinned up at him and danced away.

"Thanks a lot," Daphne protested, elbowing him in the ribs. "I'll probably never get that back." She turned to see who was next in line, only to find Bradley standing in front of her.

"I guess I'm supposed to offer you congratulations."

Daphne sighed. "That's what most people are doing, yes." She stiffened as he leaned toward her to kiss her cheek.

"The best of everything to you, Daphne," he said.

She stared at him a moment, shaking her head, unable to gauge his sincerity. But when he gave Nathan the most perfunctory of handshakes, almost looking embarrassed at having done so, all she could do was laugh.

Nathan shoved his hands in his pockets and gave a mock shudder. He leaned over and whispered in her ear. "I can't like that guy, Daphne. I just can't like him."

Sherry came up to her next, embracing both Daphne and the baby. "I'm so happy for you," she said, beaming. She hugged Nathan, and in a stage whisper said, "See if you can talk her into giving us a raise."

Daphne watched as Bradley and Sherry walked away. Sherry said something to him, and he tilted back his head and laughed. She'd never seen Bradley so much as crack a genuine smile before. "Sherry seems to be good for him."

"Let's hope. I'd hate to have to pay another visit to your office."

Daphne slanted a look up at him. "You're not allowed anywhere near my office." But she appreciated his protectiveness, both toward her and for anyone he thought others might take advantage of. She laced her fingers with his. "You're a good man, Nathan Ward."

He grinned. "What I am is a hungry man. When do we get to eat?"

"You're thinking about food now?"

He put his arm around her, gathering her to his side. "Food first." He leaned down and nibbled her ear. "You second."

Daphne bit her lip and lowered her head as heat flooded her cheeks.

"Can't you two wait a little while for that?" Daphne looked up to find her brother and Jenny standing in front of them. "It's bad enough I've had to watch Garrett paw Elise all these years. Now you." Michael punched Nathan on the shoulder. "It's disgusting."

"Need I remind you," Nathan said, returning the favor, "that you are the youngest in the family? This overprotective brother routine has got to go."

Still arguing, the two men walked off in the direction of the backyard, where the reception was being held.

Daphne looked at Jenny and the two women burst out laughing. "Men," Jenny said. "You can't live with them . . ."

". . . you can't bury them in the backyard without the neighbors getting suspicious," Daphne finished.

Jenny sighed. "Thank goodness."

"Yeah."

Arm in arm, the two women went to find their husbands.

Later that night, Daphne stood at the window of their hotel room, staring out the window. Nathan had been in the bathroom, doing God-knew-what for the past half-hour. She closed her eyes and inhaled deeply as she felt his arms close around her from behind. His hands settled over the small rise in her belly. He smelled of soap and aftershave and a natural scent all his own. "What took you so long?" she asked.

"I wanted to make myself pretty for you."

Laughing, she turned in his arms so that she faced him. He still wore his shirt and trousers, though his shirt was open at the collar and his sleeves were rolled up. She placed a soft kiss at the base of his throat. "Why do you still have on all these clothes?" Her fingers went to the buttons of his shirt, undoing them quickly. She pushed his shirt from his shoulders, letting it fall to the floor.

When she reached for the waistband of his pants, he covered her hands with his own. She looked up at him questioningly. "Don't tell me you're planning to make love to me with your pants on."

"No, but there's something I have to tell you first."

"Oh?"

"A while back, Mike and I sort of had this bet going."

"Really? What kind of bet?"

"That you'd throw me out of your apartment before he got Jenny pregnant."

Daphne folded her arms across her chest. "This is what you guys spend your time doing? Making pointless bets about serious issues that affect the rest of our lives?"

Grinning, Nathan shrugged. "I guess you could put it that way."

"What were you supposed to do if you lost?"

"Well, originally the loser was supposed to tattoo the winner's name on his butt, but we decided that was stupid."

Daphne rolled her eyes. *"That* was the stupid part?"

He took her hand and led her over to the bed. "Then we decided to tattoo our wife's name. But Garrett came up with the idea of using something that symbolized each of you."

"Considering you are tattooed, I assume you lost."

"No, Daphne, we both won. We both got what we wanted. Jenny's pregnant."

"I know."

"And your brother now has a great big red rose on his posterior, since that's Jenny's middle name. And I've got this." He lowered his pants to let her inspect it.

"It's, um, lovely, but what exactly is it?"

"It's a crown of laurel leaves. When Daphne ran from Apollo her father took pity on her and turned her into a laurel tree.

"And Apollo took the branch of the tree as his emblem, awarding crowns of laurels to the victors of athletic competitions.

"So both literally and figuratively, I'll spend the rest of my life resting on my laurels."

He sat next to her on the bed and shed his trousers. When he straightened, she rubbed her hand over his chest. "I wouldn't mind if you wanted to get back to your career."

He cupped her shoulders in his palms. "No, baby, that's not what I want." He lowered her to the bedspread and laid down beside her. "I'd rather spend my time helping you raise Emily and this other little rugrat growing inside you."

He brushed aside the fabric of her short, white nightgown to run his hand over her bare abdomen. "And besides, with the success of 'Always,' Mike and I have been considering another collaboration. I'll let someone else worry about recording it."

"As long as that's what you want."

"That's what I want."

Daphne closed her eyes as Nathan lowered his mouth to hers for a tender kiss. A flood of emotion washed through her: happiness that they were finally a family, contentment that whatever came, they'd face the future together.

He lifted his head and smiled down at her. "You know something? I really have led a charmed life. Everything I've ever wanted has always fallen into my lap sooner or later. Everything except you. You're the only thing I ever had to really work at getting."

She leaned over and nipped his shoulder. "And now that you've got me, what are you going to do with me?"

He winked at her. "Give me about fifty years. I'll figure it out eventually."

Dear Readers,

While researching a career for my heroine, I came across an organization that does fantastic work, as they say at their Web site, "helping low-income women make tailored transitions into the workforce." Dress for Success is a nonprofit organization that provides interview clothes for poor women across the U.S. and in several foreign countries worldwide.

I spent a day working at Dress for Success, and I can't tell you how fulfilling it was to see women walk in, apprehensive, unsure of what to expect, and walk out with renewed self-confidence and smiles on their faces. And I have to admit that I borrowed the idea for the Professional Women's Group that Daphne runs straight from the organization.

I hope you will support the wonderful women of Dress for Success in their effort by making a donation. You don't have to send cash—one of your old suits will do (larger sizes are especially in demand). When you clean out your closet this spring, please see if there's a suit that's still in good condition and suitable for an interview, have it cleaned and send it to Dress for Success. You can access their Web site at www.dressforsuccess.org to find the location nearest you.

I couldn't end this letter without saying a special thank you to all the readers who've written to me to tell me how much you've enjoyed my books. Your encouragement, advice, good humor, and good wishes mean so much to me. Please keep writing to me.

And for those of you who keep asking—a sequel to *Spellbound* is in the works. This time the hero (hard-boiled homicide detective Adam Wexler) is from New York and the heroine (Jarad's best friend, actress Samantha Hathaway) is from L.A. But caution, folks: sparks fly from the first moment these two meet.

All the best,
Deirdre Savoy

Readers can contact her at:

Deirdre Savoy
P.O. Box
Baychester Station
Bronx, NY 10469

or by e-mail at
DeeSavoy@aol.com

ABOUT THE AUTHOR

Native New Yorker Deirdre Savoy spent her summers on the shores of Martha's Vineyard. The island proved to be the perfect setting for her first novel, SPELLBOUND, published by BET/Arabesque Books in 1999. SPELLBOUND received rave reviews and earned her the distinction of the first Rising Star Author of *Romance in Color*; she was voted Best New Author of 1999 by both readers and reviewers at the Web site. Deirdre's second book, ALWAYS, published by BET/Arabesque Books in October 2000, was selected as a Top Pick by *Romantic Times* magazine. Her third book, ONCE AND AGAIN, a sequel to ALWAYS, was released in May 2001.

A graduate of the Bernard M. Baruch College of the City University of New York, she has worked as a secretary, a legal proofreader, and an advertising copy writer and news editor of a popular Caribbean-American magazine. She currently teaches a Literacy through Science curriculum for grades K-2 at a school near her home. Deirdre is a member of Romance Writers of America and the African-American Online Author's Guild. She lives in Bronx, New York with her husband and two children. She enjoys reading, dancing, calligraphy, and "wicked" crossword puzzles.